WHAT THE CRITICS SAY
ABOUT L. RON HUBBARD'S
BUCKSKIN BRIGADES

"... Mr. Hubbard has reversed a time-honored formula and has given a thriller to which, at the end of every chapter or so, another paleface bites the dust.... [has] an enthusiasm, even a freshness and sparkle, decidedly rare in this type of romance."

NEW YORK TIMES

"... a crack adventure yarn ... exciting ... historically accurate in its exposure.... *Buckskin Brigades* presents a new struggle and a new scene in fiction."

DURHAM HERALD

"... a thriller with a new locale ... an adventure yarn with a distinct new setting in fiction ... historically true ... exciting reading."

RALEIGH OBSERVER

"It brings a bit of belated justice for the Indians."

SAN DIEGO UNION

"Against a true historical background ... moves an exciting tale of scalping parties and forest warfare, duly seasoned with romance ... Good reading for lovers of western and Indian lore."

ATLANTA CONSTITUTION

BUCKSKIN BRIGADES

The words MISSION EARTH, the MISSION EARTH LOGO and WRITERS
OF THE FUTURE are registered trademarks owned by L. Ron Hubbard
Library. BATTLEFIELD EARTH is a registered trademark owned by
Author Services, Inc., and is used with its permission.

ISBN 1-59212-012-1

10 9 8 7 6 5 4 3 2 1   2005

Library of Congress Control Number: 2005925146

CONTENTS

	INTRODUCTION	ix
	PREFACE	1
Chapter 1	THE ECHOES OF A SHOT	3
Chapter 2	TWO SMOKES FOR TROUBLE	11
Chapter 3	THE REQUEST	25
Chapter 4	YELLOW HAIR RECEIVES ORDERS	31
Chapter 5	ARRIVAL OF THE BRIGADES	49
Chapter 6	STRANGE MEN AND STRANGE MANNERS	53
Chapter 7	McGLINCY IS INSPIRED	67
Chapter 8	THE BUTTER TUB	73
Chapter 9	THE WINTER PASSES	81
Chapter 10	THE AMBUSH	87
Chapter 11	THE NOR'WESTERS SUBMIT	93
Chapter 12	YELLOW HAIR DECLARES WAR	101
Chapter 13	THE GHOST-HEAD	107
Chapter 14	UNDER FIRE	115
Chapter 15	TO TRIAL AND THE GALLOWS	121
Chapter 16	GRAPEVINE	131
Chapter 17	YORK FACTORY	137
Chapter 18	THE FRIENDLY ELEMENTS	143
Chapter 19	McGLINCY DEPARTS	157
Chapter 20	THE CHIPMUNK	167

Chapter 21	REUNION	171
Chapter 22	YELLOW HAIR PERSUADED	179
Chapter 23	THE DANGEROUS TREK	183
Chapter 24	THE RECEPTION	189
Chapter 25	WHO IS YELLOW HAIR?	197
Chapter 26	HIS LORDSHIP SEES	207
Chapter 27	TIDINGS OF WAR	213
Chapter 28	DUEL WITHOUT CODE	219
Chapter 29	A USE FOR THE RENEGADE	231
Chapter 30	YELLOW HAIR SEES	237
Chapter 31	BRIGADES WESTWARD	243
Chapter 32	DEATH TO THE BLACKFEET!	251
Chapter 33	LET THERE BE WAR	259
Chapter 34	THE WHITE RUNNER	263
Chapter 35	WOLVES	267
Chapter 36	CHARGE	273
Chapter 37	HYAI, PIKUNIS!	281
Chapter 38	TRIUMPH	287
Chapter 39	THE GRAND COUP	293
	APPENDIX	297
	GLOSSARY	303
	ABOUT THE AUTHOR	311

INTRODUCTION

It was a land of legends.

Men heard fantastic tales about its violent waters and towering mountains, about gigantic monsters and beavers seven feet tall and gold nuggets as big as your fist.

The land was huge. It stretched from the Great Lakes to the Pacific Ocean, from what are now the states of Oregon and Montana all the way north to the Arctic Circle. A man could be baked alive on its wide open plains or he could freeze to death on glacial rivers so huge and powerful that they carved mountains out of the rocks.

It was the great Northwest, the stage that L. Ron Hubbard chose for *Buckskin Brigades*.

The novel opens in 1806, when the American republic was only thirty years old, younger than most of its citizens. The young nation could claim only fifteen states at that time, and the Mississippi River was the boundary of its western frontier.

Texas and the great battle of the Alamo were still three decades away. The "West" as we have come to know it, with its cowboys, its stagecoaches and cattle drives, were yet to be born. But the Northwest was booming.

Since the beginning of the seventeenth century, the Northwest had been a rich source of furs—fox, lynx, mink, otter, and beaver. The English controlled most of it through the Hudson's Bay Company (H.B.C), on the southernmost rim of that great bay. Chartered in 1670, the H.B.C. was declared "the true and absolute Lordes and proprietors" of the great Northwest.

The only serious challenge to its authority came from a group of brawling, defiant individualists called the North West Company, which was formed in 1775. Known as "Nor'Westers," they were equally as willing to fight each other as they were the members of the H.B.C.

Unlike the H.B.C., the Nor'Westers journeyed from their headquarters in Montreal and from the northwest shore of Lake Superior into the wilderness to trap their own furs, build their own fortified trading posts and barter with the Indians they encountered.

To defend its rich empire, the H.B.C. sent out "brigades" to build forts, take over the wilderness territories, and fend off the Nor'Westers.

While this conflict expanded into what is now the Rocky Mountains, American President Thomas Jefferson was preparing to send an expedition into the same area. It was called the Corps of Discovery but history would know it more by its leaders, Lewis and Clark.

Before the expedition could leave, the United States bought the Louisiana Territory, 900,000 square miles for 15 million dollars. No one, however, consulted the actual owners—the Indian nations who lived there.

Meanwhile, the expedition gathered the rest of their thirty-man team and the supplies they would need —their largest single expenditure was to be $669.50 for presents for the Indians—cooking utensils, mirrors, shirts, handkerchiefs, needles, rings and peace medals that had a likeness of Jefferson on one side and two hands clasped in friendship on the other.

They left St. Louis, Missouri, on May 14, 1804. They journeyed north up the Mississippi and then west up the Missouri River. It took a year and a half for Lewis and Clark to reach the Pacific Ocean via the mouth of the Colombia River. The expedition arrived without incident. It paused, rested, and then began its fateful return.

On July 3, 1806, just after entering what is now Montana, the expedition divided into two parties. Clark turned south. Lewis continued east to explore the headwaters of the Marias River.

On July 26, 1806, Lewis encountered his first Blackfeet Indians, and thus begins L. Ron Hubbard's *Buckskin Brigades*.

It is the story of Michael Kirk, a very blond white man who was raised by the Blackfeet, called by the name "Yellow Hair." The viewpoint is a synthesis of the worlds of Michael Kirk and Yellow Hair, of the white man and the Indian, of 1806 and today. At times, the reader will feel he is crouched by a fire, listening to the story being told by those who were there, or those who heard about it, in the way that all good stories should really be told.

On the Indians' side of the ledger, this story is meticulously accurate. No detail was omitted, even down to such esoteric parts of Indian ritual as the fact that when pipes are passed in a lodge, they are never passed across the open door but must retrace their step until they reach the other side of that portal.

The fate that finally befell the Indians is not told in *Buckskin Brigades*. The story that is told is one of pride, of courage, of a great people and a great nation—the Blackfeet—before the immorality, the diseases and the drugs of the white man took their toll.

L. Ron Hubbard knew the Blackfeet well. He grew up in Montana and had been made a blood-brother. He listened to their stories, sang with them around the fire and shared in their dances and rituals.

When he wrote *Buckskin Brigades* he was living in the heart of the country he was describing, the fur-trading Northwest. But this novel represented more than just a personal familiarity. It was an opportunity to capture a portion of American history and tell it the way it really happened.

To assist the reader, a glossary has been added which includes not only terms colloquial to the nineteenth-century Northwest but also several other words and terms that were in use during the period covered in the book.

Maps have also been created so the reader can better follow the adventure.

But the best news is the story itself.

The discovery of the original manuscript in the author's literary archives allowed the publisher to include details of the full story as it was originally written by the author, without any of the alterations that had appeared in earlier versions.

For all the avid readers and collectors of L. Ron Hubbard's works and those of you who are discovering his fiction for the first time, we are proud to present to you this new edition of his masterful history of the Northwest.

—Bridge Publications

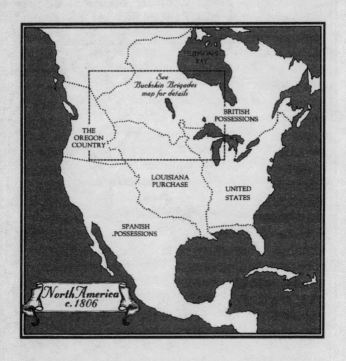

HUDSON'S
BAY

*See
Buckskin Brigades
map for details*

BRITISH
POSSESSIONS

THE
OREGON
COUNTRY

LOUISIANA
PURCHASE

UNITED
STATES

SPANISH
.POSSESSIONS

*North America
c. 1806*

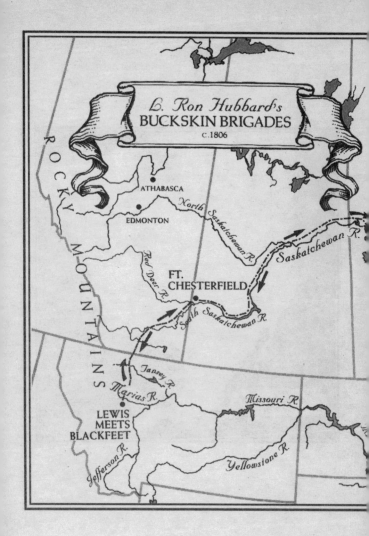

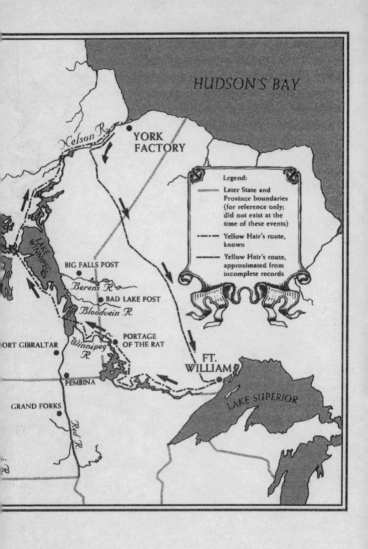

HUDSON'S BAY

YORK
FACTORY

Nelson R.

Legend:

———— Later State and
Province boundaries
(for reference only;
did not exist at the
time of these events)

—·—·— Yellow Hair's route,
known

———— Yellow Hair's route,
approximated from
incomplete records

BIG FALLS POST

Berens R.

BAD LAKE POST

Bloodvein R.

LAKE WINNIPEG

PORTAGE
OF THE RAT

FORT GIBRALTAR

Winnipeg R.

FT.
WILLIAM

PEMBINA

LAKE SUPERIOR

GRAND FORKS

Red R.

BUCKSKIN BRIGADES

L. RON HUBBARD

GALAXY PRESS, L.L.C.
HOLLYWOOD

PREFACE

Another novelist in another place has said that only a very brave man would attempt to write a preface to his work.

It is my contention that only a very brave man would have attempted this novel at all.

My surprise will be very great indeed if no man's indignation prompts him to score this book as a thorough lie. If this does not happen I shall be very hurt and feel that this book has not been read.

Flattery, however, has too long been practiced on this subject by my worthy, hard-working brothers, the Beadle penny-a-liners. From them the prevailing tone of this type of book has been, "And another redskin bit the dust."

It required a peculiar kind of courage to condemn one's own race, a worse kind of cowardice to malign men dead these hundred years.

But I stand with my right hand on a stack of affidavits. I face a library full of facts. And in this book I have tried to set forth the fur traders, not as they are thought to have been, but *as they were*.

I have overdrawn no picture with my Mc-Glincy—now yours. Look, if you will, to the greatest authorities of those times and you cannot but corroborate my statements.

But my interest bas been, primarily, with the Blackfeet. When I was two and a half years old I am told that I danced one of their dances to the throb of their drums. I have forgotten. But I cannot forget everything I have found to their credit and in this book I have tried to present them, not as they are, but as they were at the height of their power—the mightiest body of fighters on the plains; the truest of gentlemen.

If I have erred in presenting them, I am not conscious of that error. I have only tried to show what it was that the voracious trader wiped out.

L. RON HUBBARD

CHAPTER 1

THE ECHOES OF A SHOT

They never saw each other, they were utterly dissimilar and neither ever heard the other's right name.

And yet upon their lives and upon this almost-meeting hangs the bitter and bloody saga of the West.

One of them was Captain Meriwether Lewis, the great explorer, former secretary to the late President Thomas Jefferson and Governor of the Louisiana Territory.

The other was Michael Kirk, who is better known among his adopted people, the Blackfeet, as Yellow Hair, scout and warrior, whose exploits rolled on every tongue from the Shining Mountains to Quebec.

They almost met on the banks of the Marias River, according to the journal of the Lewis and Clark Expedition, under the heading of July 27th, 1806. The entry has been overlooked because it was on this very date that Captain Meriwether Lewis shot a Blackfoot chief.

It is generally agreed by his friends that Captain Lewis acted in his own best interests. This proves to be very true when it is remembered that, although Captain Lewis indulged his misplaced sense of justice to his own satisfaction, the shot he fired found its echoes in the dying screams of white traders without number and the

3

wails of Blackfoot women mourning their own dead.

It is significant that famous Hell-Gate in the Rockies was not named because the river there was turbulent. It was so called because at Hell-Gate white men, spurred by greed for profits in furs, entered the forbidden hunting lands of the Blackfeet.

Patriotically, the people of the Territory have condemned the British trader, saying that the Nor'Westers harangued the Blackfeet into making continual war upon the Americans.

Nothing could be farther from the truth in spite of the fact's general acceptance. The British trader was too interested in his own scalp and too altogether powerless to hold any such sway over a tribe such as the Pikunis.

No, the truth can be found on the banks of the Marias River whose mute bluffs stared down upon the wanton scene.

Not the British trader, but Captain Meriwether Lewis was to blame. With insufficient cause he provoked the wrath of the mightiest tribes on the Great Plains.

Yellow Hair was nearby, innocent of any knowledge of the affair when it happened. But Yellow Hair was to bear the brunt of that sad meeting, and the entire course of his life was to be changed by a man he was never destined to see. He was to suffer the effects of a bullet he had not even heard or felt.

To be just and fair and to further qualify the startling beginning of Michael Kirk's renown, it is necessary to borrow a few lines from one of the most memorable documents of the West, the Journal of the Expedition of Lewis and Clark:

Saturday, July 26, 1806. . . . At the distance of three miles we ascended the hills close to the riverside

(Marias), while Drewyer pursued the valley of the river on the opposite side. But scarcely had Captain Lewis reached the high plain, when he saw about a mile on his left a collection of about thirty horses. He immediately halted, and by the aid of his spyglass discovered that one half of the horses were saddled, and that on the eminence above the horses several Indians were looking down toward the river, probably at Drewyer. This was a most unwelcome sight. Their probable numbers rendered any contest with them of doubtful issue; to attempt to escape would only invite pursuit, and our horses were so bad that we would most certainly be overtaken; besides which, Drewyer could not be aware that the Indians were near, and if we ran he would most certainly be sacrificed. We therefore determined to make the best of our situation, and advanced towards them in a friendly manner. The flag which we had brought in case of such an accident was therefore displayed, and we continued our march slowly toward them.

Their whole attention was so engaged by Drewyer that they did not immediately discover us. As soon as they did see us they appeared to be much alarmed and ran about in confusion, and some of them came down the hill and drove their horses within gunshot of the eminence, to which they then returned as if to wait our arrival. When we came within a quarter of a mile, one of the Indians mounted and rode full speed to receive us; but when, within a hundred paces of us, he halted—and Captain Lewis, who had alighted to receive him, held out his hand and beckoned for him to approach—he only looked at us for some time, and then, without saying a word, returned to his companions with as much haste as he had advanced. The whole party now descended the hill and rode toward us. . . . Captain Lewis now told his men that he believed that these were Minnetarees of Fort de Prairie. . . .

When the two parties came within a hundred yards of each other all the Indians except one halted; Captain Lewis therefore ordered his two men to halt while he advanced; and after shaking hands with the Indian, went on and did the same with all the others in the rear. . . .

Captain Lewis now asked them by signs if they were Minnetarees of the north and was sorry to learn that his suspicion was too true. He then inquired if there was any chief among them. They pointed out three; but though he did not believe them, yet it was thought best to please, and he therefore gave to one a flag, to another a medal, and to a third a handkerchief. They appeared to be well satisfied with these presents, and now recovered from the agitation into which our first interview had thrown them, for they were generally more alarmed than ourselves at the meeting.

In our turn, however, we became equally satisfied on discovering that they were not joined by any more of their companions, for we consider ourselves quite a match for eight Indians, particularly as these have but two guns, the rest being armed with only eye-dogs and bows and arrows.

As it was growing late, Captain Lewis proposed that they should camp together near the river; for he was glad to see them and had a great deal to say to them.

They assented; and being soon joined by Drewyer, we proceeded towards the river, and after descending a very steep bluff, two hundred and fifty feet high, encamped in a small bottom. Here the Indians formed a large semicircular tent of dressed buffalo skins, in which the two parties assembled, and by means of Drewyer the evening was spent in conversation with the Indians.

They informed us that they were part of a large band which at present lay encamped on the main branch of the Marias River, near the foot of the Rocky Mountains, and at a distance of a day and a half's journey from this place. Another large band were hunting buffalo from the Broken Mountains, from which they would proceed in a few days to the north of the Marias River. *With the first of these there was a white man* . . . .

Captain Lewis in turn informed them that he had come from the great river which leads toward the rising Sun; that he had been as far as the great lake where the Sun sets; that he had seen many nations, the greater part of whom were at war with each other, but by his mediation were restored to peace . . . that he had come in search of the Minnetarees in the hope of inducing them to live at peace with their neighbors. . . .

They said they were anxious of being at peace with their neighbors, the Tushepaws, but those people had lately killed a number of their relations, as they proved by showing several of the party who had their hair cut as a sign of mourning. . . .

Finding them fond of the pipe, Captain Lewis, who was desirous of keeping a constant watch during the night, smoked with them until a late hour, and as soon as they were all asleep he awoke R. Fields, ordering him to arouse us all in case any Indian left camp. . . .

Sunday, 27th of July, the Indians got up and crowded around the fire near which J. Fields, who was then on watch, had carelessly left his rifle near the head of his brother who was still asleep. One of the Indians slipped up behind him and, unperceived, took his brother's and his own rifle, while at the same time two others seized those of Drewyer and Captain Lewis.

As soon as Fields turned round he saw the Indian running off with the rifles, and instantly calling his brother, they pursued him fifty or sixty yards, and just as they overtook him, in the scuffle for the rifles, R. Fields stabbed him through the heart with his knife; the Indian ran about fifteen steps and fell dead.

They now ran back with the rifles to the camp. The moment the fellow had touched his gun, Drewyer, who was awake, jumped up and wrested her from him. The noise awoke Captain Lewis, who instantly started up from the ground and reached to seize his gun, but finding her gone, drew a pistol from his belt and, turning about, saw the Indian running off with her.

He followed him and ordered him to lay her down, which he was doing just as the two Fields came up and were taking aim to shoot him, when Captain Lewis ordered them not to fire as the Indian did not appear to intend any mischief. He dropped the gun and was going slowly off as Drewyer came out and asked permission to kill him, but this Captain Lewis forbid as he had not yet attempted to shoot us.

But finding now that the Indians were attempting to drive off horses, he ordered three of them to follow up the main party who were driving horses up the river and fire instantly upon them; while he, without taking time to run for his shot pouch, pursued the fellow who had stolen his gun and another Indian who were trying to drive away the horses on the left of the camp.

He pressed them so closely that they left twelve of

their horses but continued to drive off one of our own. At the distance of three hundred paces they entered a steep niche in the river bluffs, when Captain Lewis, being too much winded to pursue them any farther, called out, as he did several times before, that unless they gave up the horse he would shoot them.

As he raised his gun, one of the Indians jumped behind a rock and spoke to the other, who stopped at the distance of thirty paces, when Captain Lewis shot him in the belly. He fell on his knees and right elbow, but raising himself a little, fired, and then crawled behind a rock. . . . Captain Lewis, who was bareheaded, felt the wind of the ball very distinctly. . . and . . . retired slowly toward the camp. . . .

We, however, were rather gainers by this contest, for we took four of the Indian horses and lost only one of our own. Besides which we found in the camp four shields, two bows with quivers and one of their guns, which we took with us, and also the flag which we had presented to them, but left the medal round the neck of the dead man, in order that they might be informed who we were.

The rest of the baggage, except some buffalo meat, we left; and as there was no time to be lost, we mounted our horses . . . and pushed as fast as possible . . . to the south. . . .

In itself, the affair was small enough, had not Captain Lewis made two great errors. He thought these people were Minnetarees when, actually, they were Blackfeet. And he had underestimated the necessity for civilized conduct amid those people he termed barbarians. In the years to come, that shot would be cursed and its echoes would take the form of red, running rivers.

But, at the moment, Yellow Hair, known also as Michael Kirk, knew nothing of either Captain Lewis or the United States of America.

CHAPTER 2

TWO SMOKES FOR TROUBLE

To Yellow Hair, farther down the stream, about six miles away, it was not the 27th of July, 1806, and the country about him was not part of the Louisiana Purchase. The date, to Yellow Hair, was merely a late midday in the Thunder Moon and the wide, vibrant country about him was indisputably the southern portion of the Pikuni country, owned, policed and governed by the Three Tribes. As usual, he was impatient. Tushepaws had dared raid a Pikuni camp and the interlopers were to be intercepted by the war party which Yellow Hair and White Fox were supposed to join, but which, unknown to either of them, was being entertained through the courtesy of interlopers worse than the Tushepaws—the United States of America.

Restlessly Yellow Hair stamped up and down the river bank, scanning the green and red bluffs, pausing occasionally to snap a word or two at the imperturbable White Fox who crouched immovably beside a small, smokeless fire, slowly broiling strips of tender buffalo meat.

"Why don't they come?" demanded Yellow Hair. "They know where we are."

"They will probably come in due time," said White Fox without moving his gray head. "Of course you can never be certain, but they said they would come and we must wait."

"You told me that yesterday. Find something new to tell me today. Stop ogling that meat and take a glance at this sky. Disgusting! Motionless. Not even a cloud moving. Not a leaf! Not a puff of dust to be seen. And look at those herds. Look at those herds! They act as though they had never seen a hunter."

"Patience," said White Fox, annoyed but little.

"Patience!" barked Yellow Hair. "What use have I for patience? Those Tushepaws came and killed our people. They have no eyes and cannot read our boundaries. They have no ears and cannot hear our laws. They have their own hunting ground and yet they come rolling into ours like so many ill-mannered bears and murder us."

"Save it for the Tushepaws," said White Fox, calmly turning the willows on which the strips were impaled.

"I'll save it for the Tushepaws," roared Yellow Hair with ferocity. "If we let this invasion pass without an attempt at punishment, they'll come again and expect us to welcome them as brothers. Hyai, the Pikunis will be the laughing target of the Plains. And that Low Horns! What does he know about raiding? He and those seven old fools have probably stopped to hunt rabbits. That's the game for them. Rabbits. Big, fierce rabbits with long teeth."

"Maybe sweating would cure it," said White Fox, mildly, seeming to address the meat instead of Yellow Hair.

"What?"

"Love," murmured White Fox thoughtfully.

"What about love? I was talking about the Tushepaws and I've certainly no love for those wolverines."

White Fox had the ghost of a grin floating about his slightly cynical lips. But he kept the joke to himself and slowly turned the buffalo strips, carefully tucking up the sleeves of his hunting shirt.

Yellow Hair paced down the bank like a panther, turned and came up to the fire again, raking the bluffs with optical broadsides.

"Hyai, what I'll do to those Tushepaws," said Yellow Hair.

"Others of us will be there," commented White Fox. "At least, we might be there."

Yellow Hair snatched up the elkskin case which contained his rifle, untied the thongs, withdrew the lengthy weapon and carefully looked to the priming. Satisfied, he restored it, and then with a decisive jerk, lifted his saddle by one stirrup and tossed it over his shoulder.

"You can wait all day if you like," said Yellow Hair. "You can wait tomorrow and the next day. When it gets to be Falling Leaf Moon, I'll come back and ask you if they've come."

White Fox turned the strips again and glanced sideways at Yellow Hair. The youth evidently meant what he said. And White Fox knew what lay behind this anxiety to be gone.

A girl with shapely face, stormy eyes and soft hands, a girl who could ride like a warrior, was the cause. Bright Star, daughter of Running Elk, had quite ruined Yellow Hair's reason. If he were ever to find favor in Running Elk's estimation, he would have to roll up a good war record and acquire many horses.

"Little fellow," said White Fox deliberately. "You look very brave in your white buckskin. But will the Tushepaws think so?"

Yellow Hair's voice cracked like lightning. "Are you trying to insult me? You think I'm a coward? Well, then! Alone I—"

"Alone you stay with me," said White Fox, quietly. "You have forgotten that you were allowed to come only to carry my Thunder Medicine Pipe, my robes and my shield. If you were a real warrior, now, and if you had a grand coup or two in your pretty beaver cap, you could go. But—"

Angrily, Yellow Hair slammed his saddle to the ground. Walking like a mountain cat he came back to the fire and loomed over White Fox. As Yellow Hair was very tall, judged even by Pikuni standards, and he was in the best of condition, it was easy to see that he could have eaten up White Fox in two gulps.

White Fox casually turned the meat, his old weathered hands very steady.

Suddenly Yellow Hair's blue eyes softened. His big mouth spread in a good-humored grin and he slapped White Fox so hard upon the back that he almost knocked him into the fire.

Laughing, Yellow Hair sat on his heels and deftly raked a strip of meat off the willow grate.

"Love," said Yellow Hair, "might do a lot for a man's bravery, but it never did much for his reason. I think about Bright Star and then I think how Running Elk demands that I show what kind of man I am and . . . well. . . ."

"Another piece of meat?" said White Fox. "It's roasted through now."

"Ah, but what I'll do to those Tushepaws," said Yellow Hair. "Hyai, how I'll wade through them! They will think a prairie fire has hit them. And I'll take their horses—"

"Some others of us will also be there," said White Fox, mildly.

Yellow Hair laughed in high good humor and took another strip. "The way I feel today, I could whip the whole Tushepaw nation all by myself—Look, White Fox. Smoke!"

They leaped up and went higher on the bluff.

Far to the west across the dun-colored hills and the green prairies, a column of darkness stuck like an eagle plume out of the river bottom. It was abruptly cut off and then again released.

"Two smokes," said White Fox. "There's trouble."

"Perhaps they've met them already," said Yellow Hair, very worried at being left out of it.

They brought in their horses and saddled. They jammed their possessions into their war sacks and mounted.

Peeling his rifle as he went, White Fox led the swift way toward the smoke plume.

Frightened antelope fled at their approach. A herd of chunky brown buffalo stampeded. Small prairie dogs popped out of their holes to inquire in impudent whistles what the matter was.

Yellow Hair flayed his gray war pony into greater effort and very soon they drew near to the high bluff of the Marias River.

But instead of a fight they were confronted with a group of dejected Pikunis who stood listlessly before a tall lodge.

Propped up by a folded robe, Running Elk tried to lie

dejection — lowness of
15 spirits.

still in his agony. Covered by another robe was the slowly stiffening body of Wolf Plume.

In amazement Yellow Hair bounced off his horse, looking everywhere for a sign of enemy dead. He would have spoken had not White Fox silenced him with a commanding sign.

The war party which had left the Pikuni village so jubilantly had undergone a horrible change.

Divested of their war bonnets, their shields and their horses, they were bewildered at the disaster that had overtaken them from such an unexpected quarter. Their keen, intelligent faces were still stamped with disbelief that this thing had happened.

Low Horns, a powerful member of the Kit-Fox Society, was now senior warrior of the group.

"It is useless to pursue them," said Low Horns. "We have no weapons."

"I still have mine," said Yellow Hair. "White Fox and I—" They signed him again to silence.

"They are very powerful people," said Low Horns, shaking his head. He straightened to his tall height and turned to face White Fox.

"Today but one," said Low Horns, "we were coming down the river to meet you and search out the Tushe-paw party. We saw a white man walking down along the bank and we stopped to watch.

"A moment later we understood that we were in a trap. While this white man by the river had distracted us, other white men tried to come up on us from the rear. When we understood that they did not mean to go away, we thought to make a fight and die at least honorably in spite of their many guns.

"But the leader," continued Low Horns, making a

sign with two spread fingers before his mouth, attempted to take us another way. He was the same liar, the same Kitchi-Mokan, who appeared with so many of his people two years ago among the Mandans.

"All night long he talked to us, as we have heard he talked to the Mandans. He talked of how we must not go to war with anyone, just like he told the Mandans. You will remember that when the Mandans believed this Kitchi-Mokan spoke true, they forgot their sentinels and, in spite of what this Kitchi-Mokan had promised them about the Sioux, were attacked and made to suffer great losses at Sioux hands.

"Then we knew who he was and that he spoke false as he did toward the rising Sun two winters past. He told us again and again that we should all be friends, and to be polite, we let him talk away most of our sleep.

"But he had already said that he had another party of whites soon to join him and he made certain that we would be ready for their killing when the other party arrived. Thus, he posted sentinels to make sure that we did not try to leave and showed that he had other plans for us than friendship, as he did not have the politeness to trust us as we had trusted him.

"In the night, Running Elk and I became very worried, knowing that we might be killed. As we had only two rifles and little ammunition, and as our horses were too far away along the river, we could not fight in case of attack, and yet, if we fled, we would be shot down as soon as the sentinel gave warning.

"Then, the only thing for us to do, we did. To keep from being shot, we must take their guns. This we tried, never thinking that death would be the penalty.

"Wolf Plume snatched a rifle and raced away with it

17

just at dawn. But the sentinel quickly overtook him and although Wolf Plume made no effort to shoot him, which he could easily have done, the sentinel plunged a knife into Wolf Plume's heart.

"Then we all ran away and tried to get our horses as quickly as possible. Running Elk and I went up the river, but this leader, he of the forked tongue, ran after us, shouting. At last I thought I understood what this Kitchi-Mokan was saying and I shouted to Running Elk, 'He tells us to stop!'

"We stopped and too late we realized that he only wanted to have us as standing targets. I yelled a warning to Running Elk and dived behind a rock, but before Running Elk could move, this Kitchi-Mokan, although his order was obeyed, shot Running Elk.

"They stole four of our horses, took all our baggage as we had known they would do, and left us here with our dead.

"I have finished."

White Fox lifted the robe and looked sorrowfully at Wolf Plume, whose smooth bronze chest was jagged with its knife wound.

Yellow Hair knelt beside Running Elk and tried to take the old man's hand. Instinctively, Running Elk drew away.

"Your brothers, the whites, have done this," said Running Elk, voice jerky with pain.

"*My* brothers," gaped Yellow Hair. "You are delirious. White Fox, get some water."

White Fox did not move and the boy realized with a jolt that the others were looking at him with hard eyes. He swept the circle about him with his glance and then

came uncertainly to his feet, fingers unconsciously
searching out the knife in his belt.

The silence continued for a long while and then, at
last, Yellow Hair cracked.

"Stop it! What's the matter with you? Is there something wrong that I have done? Have I spoken out of
turn?"

Swiftly he searched their impassive faces for the answer to his question and failed to find it. Low Horns,
Hundred-Horses, Double-Coup, Singing Bear and Lost-
in-Mountains all wore the same expression. He had seen
it before when they had gathered to pass judgment in
the Grand Council. Their big, weather-stained faces
were unreadable and their brown eyes were narrow. The
wind moved the white fringes of their hunting shirts.
Otherwise they might have been clay medicine figures.

They were not actually threatening him. It was more
deadly than that. They were just looking at him, apprais-
ing him, taking in his tall straight body, his white, sensi-
tive face, the alarm in his usually reckless blue eyes.

Yellow Hair glanced down at his white skin leggings,
his shirt and his belt as though there might be something
wrong with them, but they were all in perfect order.

The echoes of the shot from Captain Meriwether
Lewis' rifle had not died between these high bluffs.
Soundless, but roaring, it was increasing and would con-
tinue to increase for years, decades, even centuries.

And the first one slapped by the echo stood gripping
the handle of his skinning knife, facing the elders of the
tribe.

Yellow Hair took hold of himself. In bold, even sar-
castic tones, he said, "Because you have been surprised

and beaten, you are looking upon the youngest here as a likely target for wrath. You are old warriors, mighty and honored, and your war bonnets stop the wind with their plumes and coups. But your heads grow as stiff as your joints. Why are we standing here like women? Why do we let this lying Kitchi-Mokan escape unharmed after he has slain one of us and wounded another? It is because you are afraid. You tell me you have no horses and cannot follow. You tell me they have taken your weapons. You say they are great warriors so that your own cowardice will not loom so large. Why did you not kill them if you suspected their treachery?"

"Peace," cautioned White Fox.

"Peace! You'll have no peace now. When you return to our lodges, do you think Wolf Plume's sisters will give you peace? Ah, but you are too old. Your bravery is beyond question. They will not give you women's clothes to wear. Not you. Low Horns, head of the Kit-Foxes—Hyai, I would hate to be you!"

"Silence, whelp!" snapped Low Horns.

"Ah, to be sure. Silence! But do not look to me to carry your blame. The story you could tell would be simple. You bring me out on my first war party and I bring you bad luck. Oh yes, I could take the blame, but I won't. I am going to follow up that party of Kitchi-Mokans and challenge this Fork-Tongue to personal combat. You—all of you—stay here and wail like the old women you are."

"Stop!" ordered White Fox. "Warriors, you forget that he is young. Do not punish him. He does not know what he is saying."

"I know what I am saying," said Yellow Hair. "Oh,

yes, I am young. You can stand there and stare at me if you wish. . . . Stop it!"

Low Horns recovered himself a little. He nervously glanced up at the butte to see if his scout had signaled any news about the Kitchi-Mokans. When he looked back, he said, "So long have I seen this youth in our lodges that I had become used to the whiteness of his face, the light color of his hair."

"Low Horns," said White Fox, quietly, "your memory has turned bad. Have you forgotten Many-Guns, Yellow Hair's father? It is many winters since he first came to us with this boy and only a few less winters when he died. Have you forgotten that Many-Guns was a Kitchi-Mokan? I see that you have.

"Remember, Low Horns, when you were younger this Many-Guns helped us against our enemies, the Snakes. Remember how his fine shooting turned back a Snake charge and saved us all?

"Remember, Low Horns, how this Many-Guns grew to be a great warrior with us? How he led a large party far, far south into the territory of the Almost-Whites across the deserts? Look, Low Horns, the rifle this boy carries is that one last carried by Many-Guns. Look at his face, Low Horns, and you will see the face of his father.

"It is true that this boy is not of our blood. It is true that he is often impatient and reckless and mischievous. But he is no less a Pikuni."

Low Horns looked uncomfortable. He searched the faces of his four warriors as though trying to shift the blame upon them.

"Yellow Hair," said Low Horns in a throaty voice, "I

did not mean anything by this. If I have injured you, I am sorry. But it came as a shock to me that you were white, and I think it came as a shock to all of us. So long have you been in our lodges we had forgotten, and also, I am ashamed, we forgot the debt we owe your father. We cannot permit you to follow this white Fork-Tongue because he would certainly set his men upon you and have you killed as they killed Wolf Plume. Forget this, Yellow Hair, as though it had not happened. Hyai," he added, feeling better, "do you think we are as cruel and cunning as these Kitchi-Mokans? Quickly, build us a new fire with your pistol lock. Running Elk must have broth and medicine."

Yellow Hair's spirits did not immediately rise. He lit the fire and nursed the small blaze until it was large enough to take care of itself. After that he wandered down the river to a quiet eddy and bent over to wash the single black stripe of joy from his head.

But before he stirred the quiet water he saw his reflection looking back at him and he knelt to examine it.

In the past he had fitfully wondered about the color of his scalp and the lightness of his skin, but he had never actually given it any intensive thought. He had been only a few winters old when his father had died and he remembered very little about it except the depressed sadness of the village at the time. He connected the shiver, which he always experienced when he saw a fully covered sleeper, with the death of his father, but that was all.

And now as he knelt beside the river, studying his blue eyes, it came to him as a shock that he was not really a Pikuni at all. True, he was a member of the All

Friends Society and aspired to the Society of the Horns, but even that did not make him a Pikuni.

His lip curled a little and the reflection sneered back: "Kitchi-Mokan!"

He spat and the image was shattered by the ripples of the startled pool.

CHAPTER 3

THE REQUEST

Running Elk died late that night.

Everyone knew that he would die, as the slug had torn him horribly. But he knowingly hastened his death by talking.

With only the flicker of sparse flames lighting up the interior of the lodge and showing where most of the warriors slept, Yellow Hair did not notice at once that Running Elk was beckoning to him.

Yellow Hair was on guard. Lost-in-Mountains had reported that the Kitchi-Mokans had gone swiftly out of the country but both White Fox and Low Horns had agreed that a guard was necessary.

Finally Running Elk spoke.

Yellow Hair turned and saw the moving hand and crept over to the edge of the willow wand bed.

"I did not mean to draw away today," whispered Running Elk.

"I have forgotten it."

"That is well. In a little time, Yellow Hair, I will find the place the Great Spirit has reserved for me in the Sand Hills."

"It will be a mighty place, Running Elk."

"I will know the stories of our people who have not

come back to tell them, but, Yellow Hair, I will never be able to tell Bright Star."

Down in the cottonwoods an owl hooted dismally. It knew that a great man would die.

A wolf's quavering howl sounded far off on the darkened plains.

"Hear?" said Running Elk. "He knows too. Yellow Hair, I have been a foolish old man. I have been too vain. I have held my head too high to see the path before my feet, and now that I trip, it is too late. We are a day and a half's journey from my people, and I understand that I have been wrong. Someday, Yellow Hair, you will be a great man in the tribe. The Pikunis will need you to guide them. You are swift and strong, Yellow Hair. You are brave. The Pikunis will need all their brave men.

"When I was young, standing outside my father's lodge to watch the girls pass by, only one white man had touched our country. That was long, long ago. He came to us on the big river to the north and he asked us to follow him down to trade in our beaver pelts. He said the white men were many and powerful and had many things to trade us. Guns, blankets, cooking pots. . . .

"But my elders refused to go saying that many people starved on the way down to the white trading village, that the Pikunis must remain on their plains where they had horses and much meat. They cared nothing for travel on the rivers and they did not believe that there were many whites and they could not understand what whites wanted with the pelts of the sacred beaver.

"Then came another white man and he built a trading fort on the big river to the north. Soon after, two more white men came and drove the first one away with guns.

Finally more and more white men had arrived until there are many, many posts to the north and toward the rising Sun.

"They have given us guns, cooking pots, blankets and knives in return for small animals we easily catch along the streams. We have taken advantage of their foolishness and we have not tried to discover why they should value these furs so highly that they murder each other to get them.

"At last, Yellow Hair, I have begun to think that there may be hundreds of these whites. Many-Guns, your warrior father, told me so. He even said that there was another great Lake to the rising Sun as well as to the setting Sun and that along this great lake were thousands of whites. He told me that those men were cruel, often unjust and not to be trusted even though they were members of his own tribe.

"He told me that these whites would come gradually into our nation, that they would take our lands as they had taken other lands which did not belong to them.

"He said that the white men did not respect the boundaries of our land, that he refused to believe we had boundaries—when you know yourself, Yellow Hair, that we, the Three Tribes, occupy, own and govern immense territory.

"But I grow lengthy and I have not long to talk. I have a strange feeling tonight. My sight is clear like a fire which flares up just before it goes out. When I close my eyes I can see our people driven westward. I can see them starving. I am troubled.

"Yellow Hair, do not be offended at my brothers. You are brave and strong, but you are also kind and can forgive. You have needed us for years. You will be the needed one in time to come. Train yourself for war, learn the ways of these whites, help us keep them out of our nation. You can see what they do to us, what they have done to me. Once these people defeat us, we are no more. This Kitchi-Mokan who talked so much and told so many lies is only one of many. I know now what your father meant. These white people will tell us anything and then break their promises as I could snap an arrow.

"When you return to camp, Yellow Hair, the way will not be an easy one for you. I was wrong to deny you Bright Star. But one must be careful. You know that, Yellow Hair. See what has happened to Lost-in-Mountains. He allowed a brave to take his eldest daughter and now we know that that brave is neither a good fighter nor a good provider. And yet you have seen how that brave has demanded his rights, how he has taken all the other daughters of Lost-in-Mountains. And even if this brave is killed, Yellow Hair, the man's brother who will then own the women and goods is even worse. Although it happens rarely, one has to be careful.

"You will forgive me, Yellow Hair. Now it will be difficult for you to take Bright Star as your wife. She is fine and beautiful. She is brave and resourceful and even though her moods are stormy she would make a good woman for you. And you need a good woman, Yellow Hair. Too long you and White Fox have lived in a lodge together without women. You must have clothes and new robes and better food.

"Even if Bright Star refuses you, do not despair. My son Fleetfoot will know you speak the truth when you tell him what I have said.

"Stay with us, Yellow Hair. Take Bright Star my

daughter and be happy in a great lodge. Take my horses and my robes. They are yours. Let the sun shine in your heart.

"I am an old man, Yellow Hair. It is right that I die still a warrior. Do not let them mourn for me.

"I have finished."

Yellow Hair gently shook White Fox's shoulder and whispered in the gloom, "He is dead."

CHAPTER 4

YELLOW HAIR
RECEIVES ORDERS

The two trails which had almost met diverged, never again to even closely approach.

Captain Meriwether Lewis, having accomplished the purposes of his expedition, returned to the United States with his voluminous reports. He received acclaim. He was awarded the post of governor over a territory which reached from the Mississippi to the Pacific—an immense land which had been "sold" by a power six thousand miles across land and the Atlantic to another land which immediately accepted "sovereign" rights to "colonize and exploit."

The actual owners, not important enough to be consulted, were for the moment left alone.

Michael Kirk—Yellow Hair—went back to the Pikuni seat of government, not in triumph, but in sorrow, not to renown but to a sorry problem which must be met and faced.

Yellow Hair hated that return.

With a few of their mounts rounded up for them, the warriors straggled slowly homeward.

What was left of Running Elk was lashed across a saddle and covered with a robe. Wolf Plume, shrouded

31

in the same manner, with only his stiff hands showing beneath the dangling stirrup, was led back to his people.

They traveled constantly. They had no heart to stop and sleep. Marking their course by the stars across the undulating dark plains they came, at sunrise, within sight of the town.

The long, regular lines of lodges gleamed whitely in the half-light like so many snow-capped peaks detached and set down upon the plains in orderly fashion. Beside them bubbled the main branch of the Marias River, silky smooth, and about them and behind them reared the shaggy and green-forested crags of the Rockies. The horse herds were grazing quietly. Thin mists of smoke rose up from early fires.

The party stopped in dejected silence, gazing sorrowfully upon the scene. They had pressed forward until now when they found their hearts unwilling.

When they had left, the lodges had poured forth gay crowds to wish them luck. The keeper of the sacred Beaver Roll had gone galloping down the streets shouting out their names and glorifying them.

When they had left, the sun had been daunted by the dazzling whiteness of their hunting shirts and the blazing color of their plumed war bonnets.

And now, to creep back at dawn, defeated, carrying their dead, shorn of their shields and weapons . . . it was bitter but it had to be done.

A scout on a knoll had sighted them. Standing upright the sentry furiously waved a robe.

The signal was picked up on the plain below. Suddenly-awakened men sprinted for the horse herds. Others swung up on their buffalo ponies which had been tied beside their lodges.

Eager for news, not stopping to read the altogether too plain message of that swinging robe, people poured forth.

Yellow Hair eased back beside White Fox, well in the rear.

"We should not be here," said Yellow Hair. "We were not with the party."

"Not anxious to meet Bright Star?" replied White Fox. "You were eager enough for the kill. It is a sorry warrior who cannot take defeat and victory alike."

"I don't mean that. I wasn't with the party, but Bright Star will think I was. She will be angry with them and I don't want her to associate Running Elk's death with me."

"You are wise," said White Fox. "Cut down this coulee before they come up. You still have time."

"No. I'm staying. I just don't like it, that's all."

"One glance is worth a year of explanation," shrugged White Fox.

Bear Claws, keeper of the sacred Beaver Roll, came up to them first. The smile faded out of his eyes and he searched their faces anxiously. Then, when he glanced at the two burdened horses, he knew that Wolf Plume and Running Elk were dead.

In stony silence, Bear Claws turned his mount and looked down at the vanguard of the crowd.

Yellow Hair squirmed in his saddle and the creak of the tight leather was as loud as a pistol shot.

Bright Star, mounted on a fleet pony, came next. Her head was thrown back and her silky black hair danced behind her in the wind. She drew up and looked at them. She saw the horses covered with the robes and looked again at the group.

For an instant her lovely face showed pain and then she too turned her mount to face the others.

When she had looked at him, Yellow Hair had read the anxious questions in her eyes. Where was he when this happened? Why was her father dead while other members of her party lived?

It lasted too long for Yellow Hair. The gay shouts of the coming people died in their throats and then nothing but the whisper of the river could be heard.

In silence they rode down into the village.

In silence they placed Running Elk in his lodge and Wolf Plume with his people.

In silence they sent their mounts into the horse herd.

They were waiting.

Then it came.

The sound of wailing came from Wolf Plume's lodge as his women gave themselves over to grief. Similar cries came from the lodge of Running Elk.

Bright Star's voice was not added to the misery. Bright Star stood outside her lodge, her face buried in the mane of Running Elk's favorite pony.

Yellow Hair wanted to go to her, but that was forbidden him. Instead he sought refuge in White Fox's big lodge. He peeled out of his hunting shirt, unbuckled his belt and stripped off the hip-tall, gay fringed leggings.

Magpie, a small Tushepaw youth who had been taken into the lodge after a raid the year before and who remained there in comfort but as a sort of servant, was very glad to see Yellow Hair home. But he did not dare say anything about it. Not now. He opened a bundle of clothing and laid out white, untrimmed clothes, made of the smoothest elkskin. White clothes for sorrow.

Yellow Hair gathered a robe about his shoulders and

with Magpie trotting after him, headed for the river to wash away the stains of travel.

Yellow Hair bathed in silence and came up on the bank. He combed his sun-colored, shoulder-long hair with his fingers and then rubbed himself dry. He took the clothes from Magpie and dressed.

They returned to the lodge and Yellow Hair caught up his buffalo bow and sent Magpie scurrying to the horse herd for a fresh mount.

White Fox had come into the lodge. He sat against a comfortable, springy willow backrest, stuffing Indian tobacco into his red-bowled pipe.

"Tomorrow things may be better," said White Fox. "Maybe they won't be. But they might be. Straighten up."

Yellow Hair gave him a sidewise glance.

"You've had no sleep," said White Fox. "You need it."

"Sleep with that ringing in my ears?" snapped Yellow Hair. "For every wail there I have an ache here." He touched his breast and looked hard at the painted inner-lining of the lodge as though he could see through it and outside. "I am a fool, White Fox."

"Later on you will have many responsibilities. There is no need to borrow them now. You offered to follow and kill that Kitchi-Mokan. Low Horns forbade it and I would not let you. You are not to blame. I will tell them so at the Grand Council when it assembles to discuss this."

"Talk will do nothing. There has been too much talk. When I should have been speeding on the hot trail of that murderous Kitchi-Mokan, I was talking. And now there is talk of more talk."

"You are hurt. You will forget it."

"You did not see the way she looked through me."

"I should have known it was love. My young brave, if you had already been the son-in-law of Running Elk, you could claim his vengeance as your own. But you are not even of his clan."

"You didn't see the way she looked at me."

"I did see it. Women have short memories, Yellow Hair."

"Bright Star," said Yellow Hair with heat, "is not just another woman."

"Of course not. You love her."

Magpie thrust his worried face into the entrance and told Yellow Hair his horse was waiting.

"Running away?" said White Fox.

"I'm going out and kill an antelope."

"Peace offering?"

"Decency."

"Stop worrying," pleaded White Fox. "I will tell them at the Grand Council that you were thirty arrow flights away when it happened."

"More talk," said Yellow Hair. "I won't be there. What use have I for excuses? Why should I go and weary my tongue explaining. If you want me I'll be somewhere within a day's ride, but don't try to get me to come to the Grand Council. I won't!"

Statement to the contrary, he was there, four days later when it was held.

Each day he had killed tender game and each evening he had left it just outside Running Elk's tent, scratching on the flap to let them know it was there.

He had carefully stayed out of sight, trusting that a little time would let Bright Star think. She would realize that she had no provider in her lodge as her two brothers were even younger than she. She would understand that Yellow Hair was giving her a chance to recover.

But on the night of the Grand Council, Yellow Hair knew that he had been wrong.

The Council was held in the big ceremonial lodge of the Kit-Foxes, of which Low Horns was the leader. The night was chilly and the plains were damp with recent rain. The wind came whispering down out of the northwest, moist and sweet.

The Council had already assembled. The pipe was being offered to the Earth Mother and the Above Ones and had already started on its journey with the sun's rotation.

At the eleventh hour, Yellow Hair left White Fox's lodge to cross over toward the Council.

Bright Star was standing in the dark outside the doorway, a small shaft of firelight catching in her eyes and long lashes as she looked in.

Yellow Hair touched her shoulder. She spun about to face him.

"It is you," said Bright Star. "Do you wait upon an accident to approach me?"

"If I read less in your face I would have come before."

"It was fortunate you spared yourself the trouble, Kitchi-Mokan."

"That is not quite fair."

"But it is true. My heart tells me that it is true. Oh, I would not think of calling you a coward. Not in so many words. But there is a call of blood to blood and when the leader of the killers went away, you did not follow. Why?"

"I was forbidden to follow."

She disregarded the edge in his voice and gave way to her feelings. "Yellow Hair doing as he was told? Hyai, do not expect me to believe that. Ah, these fine stories you tell me. Yellow Hair bows to no man. Yellow Hair, as mighty as a big white bear, obeys no orders. His destiny is war and defeat to our enemies. Ah, yes, you have said these things. Time after time I listened to your empty boasting and now, when Running Elk lies dead, when he is mute within the Sand Hills, you come mewling to me about what your orders were.

"Somewhere that traitorous Kitchi-Mokan lives. He must die! But I cannot look to another Kitchi-Mokan for vengeance. Once already you let that other one ride away without any effort to follow. You would again. He is of your blood. . . ."

"You are full of words," said Yellow Hair. "You care nothing for the truth. If I am a Kitchi-Mokan—"

"You cannot deny that!"

"I can deny it!"

"Hyai, but you are brave when it comes to shouting down a weak woman! Go into that Council and shout them down if you have the courage. You are crawling with fear. You were afraid to come to me and ask for your pardon. You cannot have it now. You think you can coax me to become your sits-beside-him woman! I would rather marry a mountain goat and spend my life on the crags eating grass."

"No man in this town would dare say those things."

"I am not a man and I thank the Above Ones for it. If you do not like what I say, strike me. You are not afraid to do that."

"You cannot bait *me!*" cried Yellow Hair, his voice

rising with fury, shaking until his fringe quivered. "I do not have to stand here and stomach your lies!"

"No! But you would rather stand here than go inside and face the Council. Shout at them. Ah, but you shake with terror at the thought of it."

He stabbed out and hurled her away from the lodge flap. He ducked and went in. His mouth was compressed with rage as he skirted the inner-lining and sank into the seat left for him.

Ordinarily, one so young and so lacking in trophies of prowess would not have been admitted to the lordly and select group. But as he had been with the war party and as he would be called upon, he was needed.

The pipe was on his right, coming toward him. Bear Claws beside him took the redstone bowl and puffed ceremonially upon it. Across the circle sat White Fox, a fleecy buffalo cap upon his handsome head. The black horns which jutted out made him look Satanic. He was watching the pipe, afraid that Bear Claws would not pass it to Yellow Hair.

But Bear Claws, after only an instant's hesitation, followed through. White Fox relaxed as Yellow Hair took his drag at the long stem. They still accepted Yellow Hair as a Pikuni. And though there had been no real danger that they would not, the situation and the state of their nerves were extreme.

Presently Low Horns arose and told his story exactly as he had told it on the scene. When he had finished and had said so, White Fox stood up and added his own whereabouts to it. When he had told them he had finished, Lost-in-Mountains rose and gave them a few things the Kitchi-Mokan leader had told the party on the night before the murder.

"He was full of words," said Lost-in-Mountains, making a fork out of his two fingers and stabbing away from his mouth. "He told us that our land belonged to someone he called a Great White Father, who had bought it from another Great White Father of whom we had never heard either.

"It was very puzzling. We had not been to war. No Kitchi-Mokans had come to attack us and drive us away. And yet he said this Great White Father owned our land.

"He said, this Fork-Tongue, evidently thinking we were little children—an attitude no grown man ever liked—that we should come down to the long river and trade with his posts down there. He said we were to bring our beaver pelts toward the rising sun, not into the north as we have been doing because, he said, that north people were not Kitchi-Mokans and that north country belonged to another Great White Father.

"We were amazed that these Great White Fathers should be so numerous and it was very confusing. But this is probably because a man who lies with little skill forgets his stories almost before they are told.

"Low Horns and I have been talking about this and we have asked White Fox who has been to many far lands and we at last remembered some of the things the white and honored Many-Guns told us long ago.

"There are at least two of these Great White Fathers and they send out their white and very lawless sons to tell monstrous lies to the rightful owners of this country. There is possibly another one who spoke a very queer language and who deserted some of his people in our country to the north after a fight with the Great White

Father of the people who now trade with us on the big river in the north.

"Of course, this Fork-Tongue told some small things which were true. We all know, by report from other nations near us, that he went all the way to the Lake-in-which-the-Sun-Sets, evidently spying out the numbers of warriors of each nation preparatory to a general attack by the sons of his own particular Great White Father. Men, as we know, who cry the loudest for peace are those who are only trying to cover up their own wishes for war.

"This, then, have I to offer to this Grand Council. I do so with all respect.

"The Kitchi-Mokan Great White Father already covets our country. The Great White Father of the people in the north only covets our trade—as they have done for twenty double hands of winters according to legend.

"We can safely pursue our trade for the weapons and metal we need with the Great White Father in the north. We must resist the treacherous advance of the Great White Father in the east, as he clearly cares for nothing but our lands and has already shown us the blackness of his mouth through his scout.

"I therefore recommend to this Grand Council that we resist all Kitchi-Mokans coming from the south and east and continue our trade in the north for guns and ammunition with which to do the resisting. This is our only course if we wish to save our country.

"I have spoken."

Lost-in-Mountains sat down. Bear Claws rose and asked some questions and then sat down. White Fox was asked to rise and tell what the late Many-Guns had said about the Great White Father in the east.

"Under the law of the Kitchi-Mokans," said White Fox, "Many-Guns had done much wrong. Many-Guns had been high in the government of the Kitchi-Mokans, but because another man thought he knew more about government than Many-Guns, our white and honored friend was challenged to a contest with pistols.

"Although everything was legally correct under white law, with witnesses and such, when Many-Guns shot and killed his enemy, he found himself in grave trouble at the hands of the friends of this enemy. Through trickery—evidently afraid to step into the open with their fight although they outnumbered our friend—they took from him his lodge, his horses and a thing they call 'money.'

"Many-Guns suffered, then, the death of his sits-beside-him woman and, in search of peace and forgetfulness, he journeyed far with his very small white son until he was taken in and cared for by our people.

"You know the exploits of Many-Guns. You know his honesty and his bravery. You know that his standards and codes were almost as high as our own. I give you this as a sample of the justice in the country of the whites.

"I have finished."

Bear Claws rose and asked a few questions and then said, "If this is the way these Kitchi-Mokans govern their country, we want nothing of it. I vote to accept the reasoning of Lost-in-Mountains and his outlined policy."

The votes were cast and the judgment was accepted as a law of policy to be strictly followed for the benefit of the tribe.

Bear Claws then brought forth another point.

"Members of the Council, it is now in order to call for a trial."

Yellow Hair glanced up. White Fox held his breath.

"Low Horns has told us that this Fork-Tongue has some queer, meaningless name which makes no sense. It is therefore difficult to remember. But we know how this man looks."

White Fox relaxed.

"This man," said Bear Claws, "is not quite so tall as we are, nor so well built. He has a long neck. His hair is fuzzy and short, coming down in front of his ears in a peculiar fashion and hanging over his collar behind, but only a very little way. He has a big nose which, though narrow, is long and oddly straight. He has flat cheeks and a little, thin mouth. His brows are black while his hair is light and his eyes are set close together. He is very nervous and fidgety and he talks disconnectedly. His ears are floppy.

"This man's description should be kept with us. This must be because he has violated our code of war by talking peace and then killing with trickery, which is not war, but murder.

"As a murderer he should be treated like any other murderer and I vote that he be executed on sight when met again by any or all of the Pikunis under any conditions whatever, therefore passing upon him the sentence which would be passed upon us by any of us for a similar deed."

The vote was taken.

In accordance with the judiciary's ruling, all warriors everywhere would be so informed.

So far Yellow Hair had not said a word. He had

barely listened, so deep was he in thought about the rift between Bright Star and himself.

But he caught this last and he jerked at Bear Claws' sleeve for permission. Receiving it, he bounced to his feet as though shot from a bow.

"Members of the Council. You have passed the death sentence upon this Kitchi-Mokan, which is fitting and well deserved. I revere your learned judgment and your authority.

"But to state a policy of action and then pass a sentence upon a man who is not even in our possession is not enough. If these Kitchi-Mokans intend to snatch our lands away from us and drive us into the barren and foodless mountains, something besides talk is in order.

"I know that I overreach myself by talking this way. But has it occurred to any member of this Council that not one of us can understand a word of the Kitchi-Mokan tongue? Will it not be necessary to understand the queer customs of this undisciplined tribe in order to meet success in repelling them?

"This Fork-Tongue, according to word received from the Beside-the-Big-River people, this Fork-Tongue has effected juncture with his larger war party and the whole has withdrawn far to the east. I understand from White Fox that there are many, many Kitchi-Mokan warriors. Perhaps hundreds. Their country is hard to reach.

"But instead of letting them come to us, why is it not possible for one or two of us to go to them? Let us tell this Great White Father of all Great White Fathers that we do not intend to sit like little children and old women and let him snatch up this country. And while on that same mission, we could demand and receive custody of this Fork-Tongue for his crime. Low as

Kitchi-Mokans might be, they certainly could not refuse the common courtesy shown by even the strongest tribes.

"I suggest that I leave immediately for this country. Through a queer trick of Old Man I have a white face and light hair. I can get through to this Great White Father and tell him that if he does not behave the Pikunis will assemble their three strong arms and wipe him from the Earth.

"I have finished."

He sat down abruptly.

The pipe passed in a complete circle while the group deliberated.

Then White Fox, with his face narrow and slightly annoyed, stood up.

"Members of the Council. You will forgive Yellow Hair. We all know that he cannot wait for man or buffalo and that his dreams are bigger than his head. For all that he is brave and handsome and strong. A young woman of our acquaintance rowed with him just now outside this council lodge and she is probably listening this very minute. Let her know that we honor her young man too much to allow him to commit suicide by approaching the treacherous whites. We forbade him to follow this Kitchi-Mokan killer and robbed him of his fancied glory in that quarter, but neither can we allow him to hurl his strong young body into the claws of the white wolves.

"I have spoken."

But it was not as easily passed over as that. Low Horns and Bear Claws favored the move. So did Singing Bear and Hundred-Horses and Lost-in-Mountains and Double-Coup. So did the leader of the White-Breasts

Clan. So did the head of the Lone-Fighters.

They discussed it singly at great length and then they reached a verdict.

Bear Claws rose.

"Members of the Grand Council. A youth of great promise has offered his services. They were refused before and we cannot refuse them now lest we bring dishonor to his name and to the name of Many-Guns, his father, much revered.

"I vote that we pursue a course of quiet preparation and constant alertness. I vote that we prepare ourselves in every way to meet these people who now say they own this nation on the plains.

"And to further these ends, I vote that this youth Yellow Hair be allowed to follow his own suggestion and only obey our methods of following it.

"I vote, as we have agreed, that Yellow Hair approach the fort on the river in the north. There he will pretend willingness to help the whites who are slaves of the Great White Father in the north. As both these Great White Fathers, I am told, speak the same tongue, it will be necessary for Yellow Hair to learn it and to school himself in the customs of the Kitchi-Mokans. By pretending friendship for these slaves of the north, Yellow Hair can help us trade for guns and he can help us later when it comes to a fight with the Kitchi-Mokans.

"I have spoken."

The vote was taken and it was so agreed and it was in this manner that Yellow Hair was thrown, as White Fox said, to the white wolves.

But any warrior there would have dared more and so it was not asking too much of the youth.

Yellow Hair gave the despairing White Fox a jubilant

grin and stalked out of the tent.

Bright Star was waiting in the shadow of a lodge. She did not speak. She stood with wide, dark eyes, very afraid for him.

Yellow Hair passed her grandly with a smile.

CHAPTER 5

ARRIVAL OF THE
BRIGADES

It was a six-day trip north with the tribe.

White Fox and Yellow Hair made it in four and a half, changing horses often and pushing ahead just as fast as Yellow Hair wanted to go.

White Fox was pessimistic about it. No good had ever come to the Pikunis from white hands that he had ever seen and he despaired of even recovering Yellow Hair's body.

White Fox had good reason for misgivings. The factor at Fort Chesterfield had an uncontrollable temper and was altogether too quick with a pistol. About the fort hung hired bullies and lawless voyageurs, most of them having fled from white justice and eager to play the overlord to any hapless Indian who fell under their sway.

Ruled by despots, each and every Nor'West company man was something of a despot in his own small sphere.

That quick-tempered Yellow Hair would take offense at these men was inevitable. Cleanly bred and cleanly raised, Yellow Hair was not likely to appreciate the refinements of fur trading and, thought White Fox, a knife in the back would be his lot.

Terrible things had happened before at these trading

posts—perplexing things a clear-thinking Pikuni could not understand.

Tribal chiefs in all the nations had long ago decreed that spirits must not be given to their people. Disobeying authority which was unquestionable, the factors in these forts rolled out the liquor in barrels.

As there are weaker souls in every civilization and every race or division of race, so were there weaker warriors who could not resist spirits when it was so freely given.

The two men came to the top of the hill above Fort Chesterfield and looked down upon the Saskatchewan's wandering length.

The stockaded fort was teeming with men who were evidently much excited as they walked quickly without going anywhere. The gates were open and voyageurs patrolled the river banks, looking southeast with expectancy.

"Maybe this isn't a good time for you to go down there," said White Fox, hopefully. "Maybe they are at war."

"You can see for yourself it looks like the start of a feast. No need to plead. What's to be done must be done, White Fox."

"I wasn't pleading."

"Hyai, but that place looks interesting. I wish I had come here before. Why didn't you let me?"

"Because—because it is better that you stay away. Every time our people come here to trade, you know what happens. That fat white man down there in the greasy shirt gives out whisky and somebody gets drunk in spite of everything the rest of us can do. And then the drunken one gets mad and kills his wife or his child. . . .

Hyuh, but that's a sorry place, that fort. Would that these numerous white fathers all get the red sickness."

"Look there!" pointed Yellow Hair joyously.

White Fox peered distrustfully down at the eastern bend of the river.

Around it swept a flotilla of canoes, paddles flashing in even rhythm, white foam curling around their bows. Kneeling in the frail bottoms were rows of men who wore bright silk headbands and who sang loudly as they came.

The canoe in the lead caught Yellow Hair's eye. It had a sort of tent spread amidships and under it sat the most resplendent being Yellow Hair had ever seen.

The fellow lolled at his ease while his boatmen toiled. There was a sort of tyrannical majesty about him, much heightened by the effect of his red coat, his gold lace and his cocked hat.

In one hand this personage gripped the hilt of a short sword which glittered wonderfully. In the other he grasped the neck of a whisky bottle. At his feet was a box of such bottles, now half empty, in which stood quarts in stoic rows, ready for the execution.

The personage's face was large and red and floppy at the jowls. His nose was massive, soft and blue. His eyes were jiggly, but this did not detract in the least from his bearing and kingly appearance.

From a jackstaff floated a bright and resplendent flag, the Union Jack, which occasionally tangled the head and arms of a voyageur beneath it, but who went grimly on at his toil and who sang very loudly except when the cloth got in his wide black mouth.

Altogether it was a wonderful sight, full of martial blare and monarchial color.

Alexander McGlincy, known as "Major" because he had once held a captaincy in some obscure militia, a partner in the mighty Nor'West company, was arriving on business.

And when Alexander McGlincy arrived, he arrived.

"Maybe," said White Fox, uneasily, "you had better come back with me."

Yellow Hair did not hear him. He was dazzled. "That's a great white chief," said Yellow Hair.

"He's drunk," protested White Fox. "And when those fools get drunk, anything can happen. Please, Yellow Hair, stay with me and come home. We can tell the Council that we thought it better not to let you stay."

"I'll go down and give him my respects," said Yellow Hair.

"He'll probably give you a bullet to take home," mourned White Fox.

"I have my orders. When I talk to that chief I'll make him eat out of my hand."

"He'll bite it off, most likely."

"Hyai, we'll see about that," said Yellow Hair. "If he tries anything with me . . . But I'm wasting time. Go home and tell them I have arrived. And tell Bright Star that I send my love and will presently send her a red coat with trimmings before the end of this Red Moon."

"Goodbye," said White Fox with an effort.

"Goodbye," said Yellow Hair. And raising his hand, he rode down toward the fort.

CHAPTER 6

STRANGE MEN AND
STRANGE MANNERS

Alexander McGlincy landed and history was instantly made at Fort Chesterfield.

Alexander McGlincy deigned to bow to Brock Luberly, the factor, and the procession filed with stately pomp through the stockade gates. Three steps behind McGlincy came the half-empty case. Three steps behind that came a full one.

A cannon over the gate boomed, tipping McGlincy's hat with its concussion.

The voyageurs cheered. The Union Jack flapped on the flagstaff. An Indian dog howled. Brock Luberly stood on the steps before the trading door, opened said door, bowed, and Alexander McGlincy, creaking, clinking and belching, entered.

Inside the room a French-Canadian voyageur leaped to his feet and upset his chair; but McGlincy was too great a man to take offense at the fact that a man would think of sitting down with a Nor'West partner outside.

All the while McGlincy had been gripping the neck of his whisky bottle. Now, with the air of an explorer taking over an ocean or two with the dub of a sword, McGlincy set the bottle on the table and, using it as a pivot, turned and backed carefully into a crude chair.

Everyone else remained standing and staring, ready to hop the instant the partner so much as twitched his eye.

McGlincy took a comforting drag at the bottle to compensate himself for his expended energy. He pushed his hat back into place, hiccupped heavily and remarked, "Well, damme, I'm here!"

Brock Luberly nodded in anxious agreement. The voyageurs nodded.

One head in the room failed to move and McGlincy stabbed a black glance in that direction.

The man was sitting down!

McGlincy raised himself forward, concentrated hard, straightened out the image and then relaxed.

It was all right. The seated man was Father Marc Lettau, the post priest, and while not all priests could be allowed to remain seated during such an event, Father Marc was not like all priests. Wise men let Father Marc do pretty much as he pleased.

The courtesy accorded the cloth in this case was not necessarily born of reverence. Father Marc had been built for quite another profession. He weighed about two hundred and forty pounds and was six feet one and one-half inches tall. None of it was fat. It was all muscle and brawn and it bulged quite a little beneath his coarse brown frock.

Father Marc had a big face, a big mouth which grinned and merry, small eyes which lighted their best in a wrestling match.

"How is Fort William?" said Father Marc.

"William? William?" growled McGlincy "How is Fort William? Terrible. Bone dry."

"Fort William dry?" said Father Marc.

"Ay, dry as August. Didn't I just come from there?"

Father Marc grinned. Brock Luberly went into spasms of laughter, slapping his thighs, bending double, straightening and whooping until his face got purple with effort.

McGlincy also laughed when he observed the effect. In fact he repeated it several times and finally poor Luberly had not a bit of wind or energy left.

McGlincy changed the subject. "Damme, but that was a party we had! Duncan didn't come around for three days after. Fights! Lor' what fights! Seven Indians killed the first night after we issued out the rum."

He enlarged upon it for some time until Father Marc asked for other news.

Instantly McGlincy became a man of weighty affairs, bowed with the woes and worries of the fur trade. He mentioned that the Fort William party only happened once a year and a man needed it with all these other troubles. Even great men, said McGlincy, needed to let loose once in a while.

Father Marc then inquired after the Hudson's Bay Company men and the effect was similar to that produced by a fuse and match in a powder keg.

McGlincy pounded the bottle so hard on the table that it sounded like shot volleys. He sputtered and choked. He scowled and seemed very upset.

"The courts," puffed McGlincy, "have said that this 'raiding' has got to stop. Rot the courts! What do a lot of wig-weighted fools know about the fur business? Lads, don't take no notice of the courts. We're in Indian Country, they're in Montreal and what they don't know won't hurt 'em a mite.

"Damn the fools that think we can sit like tenpins and

let H.B.C. snap the trade and the Indians right out from under us."

"The charter—" began Father Marc.

"Damn their charter!" exploded McGlincy. "It ain't legal, that charter. Who says they got a right to this whole country, eh? Who says it?"

Brisk heads quickly denied that anyone there said it.

"Fools! What's a charter got to do with it? Furs is the thing and we're here to get furs and God blind me we'll get 'em. Beaver's up. Forty pounds a pack. Forty pounds, my bullies! And the courts says we can't keep fighting the H.B.C. Well, I says we can keep fighting and I guess that settles it!"

Luberly croaked, "That settles it!"

Father Marc grinned.

McGlincy leaned forward and looked cunning. "Afore the end of the month the H.B.C. will be skimming down the Saskatchewan. The northern brigades will be gunwales deep with pelts. Well," he grated with a heavy wink at one and all, "them pelts is the rightful property of the Nor'Westers because they be coming through our areas.

"We've done it before and we'll do it again. Campbell's north right now with an army of bullies. And you know what he's doing? Oh, you don't know. Well, I'll tell you. H.B.C.'s Peter Fidler is up at Isle à la Crosse up the Athabasca with just eighteen men. Campbell's got orders to keep that damned Fidler hemmed in so the Indians can't reach him with furs. How's that?"

Luberly fawned in admiration.

McGlincy crouched ahead a little more. His scowl took on a cunning squint. "When that damned boy Labau tried to desert from us to H.B.C., you know what happened to him? Schultz was sent after him and stabbed him to death. Well, to make it look right we had to dismiss Schultz—but he wasn't no loser by it. The courts didn't dare touch him and they don't dare say a word except to whisper to us we better stop 'raiding.' We ain't got a thing to fear. Anything can happen out here. But we don't want this to get too bad. From now on we're going to use strategy.

"I just got word our friend Haldane—who's pretty near as important a partner with us as I am—smashed into H.B.C.'s post on Bad Lake just this May. Their man Corrigal didn't think a guard was important and one night in marched Haldane. We got a hundred and eighty packs of furs out of that. At forty pounds a pack.

"If Haldane can do it, I can. But I ain't that crude. I got to think this out and then Motley and his pretty boys come down . . . ." He broke off in a chuckle and took a long drag out of the bottle.

"At Big Falls near Lake Winnipeg, the H.B.C.s thought they'd build a nice little fort. You know what happened? Ho, ho, it was funny! Good old Alex McDonnell came up, waited until all of Crear's men was out fishing but two and then broke into the warehouse and when Crear demanded his rights, McDonnell told him they was owed on a debt to us.

"But Crear didn't believe it so McDonnell's men had to pound some sense into his head with rifle butts. And when a fool named Plowman jumped into stop it, McDonnell gave him a dagger in the heart.

"We got furs and provisions too out of that. Oh, that McDonnell is a sly one, he is, but crude! He ain't got the brains I have. You just wait until the H.B.C.'s brigades come swinging down this river and I'll show you how it's done. The fools won't know the lid's off and we'll take them easy."

The bottle was empty and Luberly leaped to get another which he speedily opened. Not often did a Nor'West partner talk like this to his men. It warmed Luberly's heart—if he had one.

Luberly was starved for news. He had been cooped up in Fort Chesterfield through a long and chilly winter with only a handful of bullies and voyageurs to abuse—a pastime which eventually drags. Thickly built, with a shaggy beard hiding most of his face, Luberly could put up a terrifying fight. He was habitually dressed in a hunting shirt which shone blackly with overlayers of grease.

He placed the open bottle before McGlincy and then stepped back, thoughtfully wiping his nose on his sleeve, trying to get up enough nerve to ask McGlincy a question.

But the opportunity for it never came.

A man thrust his head into the room and sang out, "There's a young hunter out here that wants to see the Major."

Luberly stiffened and stamped toward the door. "Tell him Mr. McGlincy is busy and what the hell does he mean . . ."

"Now, now," grunted McGlincy. "Maybe it's a runner with some news for me. I think I can take the time to see him."

Luberly said imperiously to the messenger, "Show him in! Don't stand there gaping!"

In a moment the door slid wide open. Silently, Yellow Hair strode into the room.

He gave his surroundings a quick glance which, for all

its speed, marked every object in the place, sorted out the various entrances, appraised the goods on the counter, measured the length of McGlincy's sword, appreciated Father Marc's possibilities as a wrestling opponent, noted two knives and a pistol in Luberly's belt, counted the full bottles in McGlincy's opened case, turned critical at the dirt which smeared the floor, and had seen that the guns in the rack against the wall were all primed.

In another glance, after he had come to a stop in the center of the floor, he had read straight through McGlincy, Father Marc, Luberly and a narrow-faced clerk. He knew that McGlincy had been boasting, that Luberly was fawning, and that Father Marc was disrespectfully amused.

He did not stop to think about the contrast he made there. His antelope-skin hunting shirt was perfectly clean. His white, hip-length leggings were without a single spot. His weapons gleamed with polishing.

There was nothing slumped about his posture, which made him much different from the rest. He looked like an antelope poised for instant motion in any direction, and yet he was perfectly at his ease.

He was careful, for once in his life, to observe formalities because he saw the reverence the red-jacketed one was accorded by the others.

"I come from my chiefs with greetings to the white chief," said Yellow Hair, fanning his words gracefully into signs in case no one there understood Pikuni.

McGlincy bridled. "What the hell's this? Talk English!"

Yellow Hair was startled. Throughout his nations if even an avowed enemy gained entrance to a lodge he was always suffered to speak without interruption or heckling until he was finished.

However, Yellow Hair repeated the signs in silence. This time, although it galled him to do it, he added the query sign by shaking his right hand jerkily back and forth, palm out, shoulder-high. Then he made an incomplete ring—a sun—out of his right thumb and forefinger, raised it in a sweep over his head and finally brought it down over his heart.

He had not only given the white chief greetings but he had hoped that the white chief was happy—had a sun shining in his heart.

He started to state his business in dignified, sweeping curves, but again McGlincy interrupted.

"If he can't talk," snapped McGlincy, "tell him to get out!"

The tone jarred Yellow Hair and the hostility bit into him. His blue eyes went dangerously slitted and he raked McGlincy with contempt. The man had no more manners than a Digger. White Chief? More likely a white slave.

Yellow Hair started to say what he thought—and he was never hesitant about doing so—but Father Marc, quick to see the change, interposed.

"He's trying to tell you hello, McGlincy," said Father Marc. "He's got some business and he's from the Blackfeet. You had better listen or we'll all be dead men."

"Well, rot him, why didn't he say so?" snarled McGlincy, angry at having his ignorance pointed out. "You think I can't read sign? Well, I was just putting him in his place, that's all. If he's some damned *bois brûlé*, he'd better learn some manners. You've got to handle these beggars right. Think I don't know how to handle a half-breed?"

Yellow Hair's memory stirred uneasily at this barrage of English. It seemed to him as though he knew the words, but could not quite grasp their meaning. However, the feeling was quickly sped. Yellow Hair was getting mad.

"Talk up," snapped Luberly. "What do you mean breaking in here and interrupting gentlemen? You'd better learn your manners, young fellow, or I'll teach 'em to you."

It was very fortunate a second time that Yellow Hair only received the tone and not the full import of the words. At that moment the absent White Fox, had he seen Yellow Hair's face, would not have given a chewed-up rabbit hide for Luberly's life.

Yellow Hair had two thoughts and he had to choose one of them. He was here on tribal business and he did not want to go back without having completed it. The other thought was that two of these three men were not even worth scalping. He could give them that which they richly deserved and take his chances on getting across the stockade and out of the fort.

Again it was Father Marc who tried to smooth matters.

"McGlincy," implored Father Marc. "It doesn't make any difference whether this man is a *bois brûlé* or a Chinese. He's from the Blackfeet and you can read in those clothes that he is no common savage. He's a Blackfoot and if you don't know the Blackfeet, I do. They're fine fellows, but they have their pride. Swallow some of your own before it's too late."

"Pride, has he?" said McGlincy, pounding the table with his bottle and leaning forward. "Pride, you say? We'll take that out of him. So these damned savages think they're too good for us, do they? So they're getting uppity, are they? It was about time I came up here. Lucky I knew about those brigades coming and had the time to spare. . . . Brigades, did I say? Brigades? Wait!"

The change in tone held Yellow Hair's hand. He was speculating just how much whisky would pour out if McGlincy's stomach was punctured and was quite ready to put the matter to test when McGlincy straightened up and smiled.

"Marc," said McGlincy, "find out about his business."

Father Marc started to sign query but Yellow Hair had had enough discourtesy. He decided that the Pikunis were better off to leave this fort strictly alone and he would tell them so. As the message he would carry was more important than immediate trouble, Yellow Hair turned and started toward the door, walking unhurriedly but with great dignity.

"Wait!" said McGlincy, imperiously.

Yellow Hair did not turn, did not care to understand. He would settle with this McGlincy later.

"Hey!" barked Luberly. "He says to wait and, damn you, you'll wait!"

Luberly's anxiety to play up to McGlincy was very unfortunate. Luberly leaped forward and snatched Yellow Hair's shoulder and spun him about.

Yellow Hair had already suffered far beyond his normal endurance. Besides that, his trained reflexes were quicker than his thoughts. To be touched by an enemy meant but one thing. That enemy wanted to count a grand coup before he killed you. If he failed to touch you harmlessly before he cut you down, he would count only an ordinary coup.

Luberly snatched again, evidently to jerk Yellow Hair toward McGlincy.

Yellow Hair bent suddenly. His deft hands shot out. He pivoted. Luberly left the floor with a terrifying uprush. Screaming, he was borne lightly aloft.

Yellow Hair threw him like a lance straight across the room, square at the biggest target there—McGlincy's scarlet coat.

Luberly's scream knifed off.

In a tangle of black and red, out of which came a racking hiccup, McGlincy and the factor collapsed amid the chair splinters.

The bottle gurgled a pool upon the floor. Father Marc started up and stayed halfway.

Yellow Hair shouted, "Hyai!" and whirled to sprint before guns blazed.

But the scream had given the warning. The crowd of voyageurs and bullies who had been listening at the door surged inward the instant it opened.

Yellow Hair's knife flashed upward and started down. Strong fingers grasped his wrist from behind. A bully smashed him on the head with a pistol butt and he went down in a swarm of fireflies.

Something enormous and brown had interposed itself between the crowd and the fallen scout. Bullies were hurled back. An instant later Yellow Hair started up, straight into the path of the recovered Luberly's knife.

Luberly, hit by a brown juggernaut, bowled back.

A tremendous weight promptly settled on Yellow Hair's chest and Yellow Hair's own pistol waved in a detached manner above his head.

Finger on the trigger, Father Marc quietly stated, "The first man that moves to kill him will get this."

Silence and dust settled gradually. Yellow Hair struggled with little avail because, as he soon perceived, the Mighty Monk was sitting solidly upon him.

As there seemed no immediate prospect of dying, Yellow Hair glanced upwards and saw McGlincy towering above him. The sight was very novel because McGlincy appeared to be upside down and when viewed in that fashion it was hard to see anything but his soft paunch.

"I'll have your life for this," promised McGlincy.

"And who would absolve you?" said Father Marc complacently. "I can't allow such things to happen in my presence. It's disrespectful of you. Have you no reverence for the cloth?"

"Let him up!" howled McGlincy. "I'll flog him until he hasn't got an inch of hide!"

"You'll do nothing of the kind," said Marc.

"Aw-r-r-r-r! To think a damned half-breed . . . Let him up and we'll beat him out of the fort!"

"And you can't do that either," stated Marc. "You don't know these Blackfeet. They're the best fighters on the plains. They'd be back here in a week. Do you want to get killed?"

"Then what the hell will we do with him?" shrieked McGlincy.

Luberly knew he could afford to postpone his revenge. He grinned slyly. "Lock him up."

"You'll place him in my custody," said Father Marc.

"All right! All right! Anything! But he's going to stay locked up until we can think of something better!" McGlincy stomped and growled and finally sat down in another chair and rescued his bottle. "Take the fool out of my sight."

Yellow Hair was not to be taken away so easily. It finally required the services of four bullies to drag him across the yard.

They heaved him into a narrow room and securely bolted the door.

Yellow Hair stared out of the grate, fury leaping like lightning inside of him.

Oh, what he'd do to these fools! How he'd make them suffer for this!

He'd send Bright Star a red hunting shirt all right, with a dirty brown scalp to match.

White slaves! Hyuh!

CHAPTER 7

McGLINCY IS INSPIRED

As there was only a little whisky spattered upon his coat, Alexander McGlincy showed no signs whatsoever of the encounter. Luberly was less fortunate as his jaw was rapidly swelling to the size of a shot pouch, but even this was not visible as it was impossible to penetrate the wilderness of his beard with the naked eye.

These men were too used to brawling to give the actual physical part of it a second thought. But they were intensely annoyed, nevertheless.

McGlincy growled until his jowls flapped. "The impertinence of him! Damned savage! Think of it. To come into *my* presence and start a fight with no provocation whatever. Treacherous as an Indian. But he didn't last long. Rot me, no. I showed him a thing or two about manners."

"I'll say you did," applauded Luberly.

"You saw how he shivered with fear when I stood up. Didn't make a move. Positively petrified, he was. Well, he can thank his stars he was among white men or he'd be dead by now."

Luberly coughed and looked around and uneasily ran his blackly stained sleeve across his face, sniffling cautiously. He saw that they were alone. Father Marc had evidently gone to see that the young savage was securely locked up.

"Sir," said Luberly, "I'm kind of worried about—well, you see, he's most likely a half-breed and he probably stands in good with the Blackfeet."

"What do I care about that?" snarled McGlincy.

An unaccountable thought flashed through Luberly's greasy head: McGlincy didn't have to care. When a reprisal came, McGlincy would be far away and Luberly would be left holding the sack—or rather, Yellow Hair. Luberly did not have enough intelligence to realize how completely he really hated this despot; he did not philosophically decide that a show of fawning adoration and flattery is sometimes employed to cover hate and distrust. He simply realized that McGlincy was not in the least worried about the fate of one Brock Luberly and certain assorted bullies and voyageurs.

"The young fool didn't come here for any good," said Luberly. "The Blackfeet are even worse than the rest of these Indians. You know what happened down at the forks last year?"

"What," snorted McGlincy, clearly showing that any information Luberly had could not possibly be of importance.

"Franklin was handing out liquor to these devils and one of them got pretty abusive."

McGlincy snorted again. "Nothing new about that."

"The heads of the tribe," pursued Luberly with caution, "had, as usual, told Franklin not to hand out spirits to their people."

"The people drink 'em, don't they? What did Franklin care about a flock of dirty niggers?"

"He didn't. But when this one brave got drunk he accused Franklin of having stolen his packs of furs, when any trader can tell you that it's policy to put out the whisky first and that this Indian certainly wasn't *robbed.*"

"Don't be so damned long-winded," groaned Mc-Glincy.

"Yes, sir. I was just saying—"

"Then say it!"

"Yes, sir. Anyway, Franklin gave this brave some laudanum in his whisky, like we have to do lots of times; but this time he gave quite a lot to put the buck to sleep quick and the buck turned up his toes and died—which of course served him right for raising so much trouble. And right away the Indians pow-wowed and decided it was murder. Can you imagine that?"

"Fools," sputtered McGlincy.

"So they surrounded the fort and demanded justice and Franklin had to shut his gates. But he fooled them. When he called them up within range under a truce flag he let 'em have it with a howitzer loaded with balls."

McGlincy chuckled in appreciation. "Pretty smart at that."

"Sure it was, but the bucks got madder than ever and threatened to burn the fort, but they couldn't because there were only about fifteen of them to begin with and Franklin had twenty men all armed, so it didn't come to anything after all."

McGlincy was quick to hide the fact that the story interested him in any way, as fitted his station and importance. He growled, "What's that got to do with this *bois brûlé?*"

"Well, if the Blackfeet find out, they won't stay their

hand very long to set him free."

"Well, damme, don't say you're afraid of a bunch of naked niggers?"

"The Blackfeet are bloodthirsty devils, sir. They wouldn't leave a post standing if they thought we'd hurt one of their own people, even if he *is* a half-breed."

McGlincy stared down his puffy blue nose in tipsy contempt.

"You think I hadn't thought of that?"

"Oh, yes, sir. Of course you had! But I was going to mention that the crowd that jumped Franklin wasn't Blackfeet."

"You leave the thinking to me," said McGlincy with a superior smile. He leaned forward and thumped the bottle on the table. "You think I didn't have all this thought out? Why do you suppose I let the young fool live? He deserved to be shot and yet I let him live."

As this seemed to imply McGlincy's benevolence, Luberly smiled in warm congratulation and appreciation.

McGlincy grinned, showing broken, yellow fangs. "McDonnell and Haldane and their bullies have pulled two good ones. But they were crude. Of course the courts in Montreal and England don't mean a thing out here, but you got to be careful just the same. What McDonnell and Haldane didn't have, I got."

Luberly looked bright.

"Brains," said McGlincy. "This fur trade is like a chess game, see? I got three canoes full of packs—at forty pounds a pack—and I show the H.B.C.s where they can get off and I pull it without a whisper against me any-place."

"How?"

"By scalping them, that's how," said McGlincy, leaning back and sagely tapping the side of his nose. And although this gesture passed for thoughtfulness to McGlincy, it was strangely enough the Indian sign which means "simple" or "an idiot." But McGlincy had no thought of double meaning. His mind was on beaver pelts, was always on beaver pelts and always had been until it seemed likely that his skull itself was fur-lined.

"When the brigades under Motley come swinging by here on their way to York Factory—before they get this far, you understand—the Indians ambush them and scalp them and run off with the pelts."

"But we couldn't make the Indians—"

"Luberly, you're a thick-headed fool. But then, that's not unusual. Damn you, can't you see it? *We* do the ambushing and the scalping."

"But good God, sir, the H.B.C.s wouldn't rest until we swung for something like that. They'd send brigades against us! They'd carry us off to England and the judges would string us on the gallows! Haldane and McDonnell did it in fair fight, but to ambush . . ." His outspokenness could only have been born out of the fact that he was even more afraid of hanging—a fate he had once before escaped in England—than he was of McGlincy.

"Now you see why I'm a great man," beamed McGlincy, again tapping his nose with his right index finger. "When the subject of laudanum came up, right away I had it. We slip this half-breed a drink with laudanum in it, we ambush the H.B.C.'s brigades, we hang the scalps on the half-breed's belt and make him believe he did it while he was drunk and then when the H.B.C.s put up a howl about it, we hand the half-breed over. We're clear, we've got the furs and we've hurt H.B.C.'s standing with the Indians."

The beautiful light of admiration shone upon Luberly's face. Stunned by McGlincy's brilliance, he could only sit and marvel at the greatness of the man. Overcome, Luberly could only wipe his nose on his sleeve and snuffle very loudly.

CHAPTER 8

THE BUTTER TUB

Father Marc Lettau, the Mighty Monk of the Nor'-Westers, had too much sense of humor for the proprieties of his profession. In fact, that was about all which could be said against him even by the men he had soundly whipped in wrestling bouts.

His peculiar quality was certainly an asset to his peace of mind, but not to his business—as a certain cardinal of France had once remarked, shortly after Marc Lettau's trial before an ecclesiastical court which happened to be trying Marc Lettau on a charge of irreverence. A long session of this court finally determined that Father Marc Lettau *had* been guilty of stating in an audible voice, upon seeing a particularly holy bishop thrown from a donkey, that "You'd think even an ass could recognize and appreciate Pierre's dignity."

The bishop of Quebec, when he had received word that Father Marc was being transferred to Canada—"in the hope that the mighty solitudes would quiet him"—had suffered through two sleepless nights before he discovered that Fort William needed a chaplain.

After that, happily forgotten, so it seemed, by his immediate superiors, Father Marc had shuttled from post to post throughout the Nor'Wester Empire, leaving majesty meant nothing special to him. But as he could whip three men at a time, whether they be bullies or partners, the Nor'Westers had long ago resolved to overlook the fact that they failed to impress him.

His sense of humor was sometimes directed toward Nor'West business practices, and partners writhed but managed to bear up. To Father Marc it was very funny that a handful of drunken white men should overlord a territory as large as the Russian Empire.

It was also very funny to Father Marc to think that a king who had been dead more than a hundred years had deeded over three-quarters of North America to half a dozen men who had never been closer to it than the Thames.

And when he combined these two thoughts—that the country was doubly owned over both the signatures of King Charles the Second and the founder of the Nor'Westers—and remembered that the land really belonged to the original inhabitants, the only thing which held back his laughter was his anxiety to be present at the final outcome.

Hudson's Bay Company brigades were fighting "American" trappers. Nor'Westers were fighting H.B.C. "American" trappers were fighting both. The Missouri Fur Company was fighting all three. The American Fur Company, the Rocky Mountain Fur Company and countless free trappers were squabbling individually and collectively with only one thing in common—their desire to monopolize the fur trade at the expense of the Indians.

And so Father Marc had a great deal of fuel for his humorous fires but for all that, time had dragged for him at Luberly's post.

With a craving to broaden his horizon for other humorous material at the expense of the Nor'Westers, Father Marc had long wished that he could speak the Blackfoot tongue. He yearned to know the nicknames the Indians used on the whites among other things and it was because of this that he turned the broadside of his attention on Yellow Hair.

It is necessary for even a priest to respect somebody besides his saints and again Yellow Hair was the target.

And as men have to be able to think before they can argue, and as Father Marc liked to argue, no one in the fort before Yellow Hair's coming had been able to put up much of a wit-battle with him.

Thus it was that Father Marc repaired to the *pot au beurre*, as the voyageur called his jail.

Yellow Hair was not faring very well in the "butter tub." After a week of it his moccasins were worn through from his pacing up and down in front of the door and his face was haggard because of the sleepless nights.

Never before had Yellow Hair been inside wooden walls. He was used to the big, roomy interiors of Pikuni lodges, the beautifully painted inner-linings, the easy willow backrests and the sufficiency of robes that went with even the poorest Pikuni households.

Wooden walls were something new and dangerous. A man could feel no security in them as he could only get out through one entrance. That this one entrance was barred and bolted made the place insupportable.

At night the place was so stuffy and hot that sleep was impossible. The stale air stuck in his throat and gagged him until he felt that his lungs would burst.

And, finally, the place was not clean. Drunken voyageurs had quite often been locked up here and drunken voyageurs are apt to leave their mark behind. Then, too, not even lice will stay with an inebriated *bateau* man and some of these had forgotten to get aboard when their owners had departed.

Whereas the place was no better and no worse than any other jail in the world, any jail is repulsive when a man enters one for the first time. But most men have known before entrance that there is, after all, such a thing as a jail. Yellow Hair had not had the least inkling of one's existence anywhere. He therefore had never been educated to believe that society as a whole has a perfect right to cage up any of its members for any period of time a casual judge may think up at the moment.

A lion or tiger suffers from the same ignorance. Upon first encountering a cage they can neither eat nor sleep, but as they are mere beasts, used, poor souls, to private lairs and a whole wilderness to roam in, no one gives the matter a second thought.

Rage had burned his eyes deep into his head. His mane of yellow hair was tangled and unkempt. His so lately spotless antelope skin was smudged and ripped.

Father Marc gazed upon this scene and sympathy immediately rose up within him.

He stood outside the door. Yellow Hair stood inside. They looked hard at each other for a space of minutes.

Father Marc lifted his hands and signed query, jerking his thumb toward Yellow Hair.

Something like hope flashed into Yellow Hair's eyes and he instantly signed back for water.

Marc fanned, "To drink?"

Yellow Hair emphatically slapped out, "No! To

bathe!" And he added emphasis by doubling up his fists and hammering down with his right past the knuckles of the left. "Very much!"

Father Marc was slightly puzzled as he turned away. He could not quite understand why a man wanted water with which to bathe. No Nor'Wester ever bathed and only one priest in the past hundred years had had a bath—and he had died from the effects of it.

But Father Marc decided that he could try to do something about it.

He went to McGlincy who was sprawling on his bed, bottle dangling from his fingers, eyes half closed.

"Alex," said Father Marc with surprising disrespect for such a great man, "I am worried about our young friend."

"Friend?" croaked McGlincy, trying to remember if he had any friends. He didn't think so.

"The Blackfoot half-breed or whatever he is," said Father Marc. "If his friends fail to see him in or about the fort—and I'm sure some of them will spy on the place for just that purpose—they are likely to come down and ask questions we are not prepared to answer."

"Uh," said McGlincy, recalling suddenly that he was to be in this fort himself for some little time.

"I am sure I could get his parole. Then he could move about . . ."

"Parole?" shouted McGlincy, sitting up straight. "What good is an Indian's word?"

Father Marc grinned. It had flashed across his mind that every man measures another's word by the yardstick of his own. But Marc had a favor to ask and he didn't mention the reason for his grin.

"I could see that he kept it, Alex."

"Huh! You think those damned savages might attack?"

"You never can tell, Alex."

"Huh!"

There ensued a long pause while McGlincy laboriously turned the machinery in his head and got fur out of the cogs.

McGlincy said, "Mornings he can walk along the river, but not out of range of two riflemen stationed on the walls. You will go with him. Afternoons and nights he will be locked up securely. See that you attend to the matter right away."

As it was now McGlincy's exclusive idea, Marc grinned again and withdrew.

It was still morning and Marc repaired to the butter tub instantly and unbolted it. With signs, as well as he could, he gave Yellow Hair the substance of his interview with the white chief.

At first Yellow Hair did not like the idea. He was impatient to be gone to his town in the south, but when he turned and saw the jail again, he immediately nodded.

The two riflemen were posted.

Side by side Father Marc and Yellow Hair walked down to the river.

Yellow Hair looked eagerly at the water and then back at the fort. It would be simple to swim the river. Two rifles would be no great hazard.

Father Marc was watching him. Yellow Hair looked carefully at Father Marc and saw no distrust in the fellow's eyes.

Clothes and all, Yellow Hair gave a sudden spring, hit the surface in a clean dive, swooped through the depths and came up close beside the bank.

The riflemen were startled but they caught the priest's signal not to shoot.

Contentedly, radiant with relief, Yellow Hair pulled off his clothes and dived in again to scrub himself with sand.

Thoughtfully Father Marc considered Yellow Hair's enjoyment and silently told himself that if a bath felt that good he would certainly have to try one some time.

CHAPTER 9

THE WINTER PASSES

The bullies of the fort marked the time with empty whisky cases which grew slowly and steadily outside McGlincy's door.

Yellow Hair marked the time in quite a different way, having no interest in McGlincy aside from an occasional speculation on his probable demise at an early date.

The plains turned to a dun color. The leaves fell dry as parchment from the cottonwoods along the banks and rattled on the ground when the wind blew down from the north.

The river at last froze over and the dark clouds laid down their white cargoes and one morning even the fort looked clean in its ermine mantle.

Yellow Hair had fared fairly well. Trouble treated him like a magnet and he could not escape—indeed he welcomed—two encounters with the French-Canadian voyageurs of the north. That he bested them was readily attested by the amount of skin missing from the nose of one and the blue-black rings about the eyes of another.

The only spectacular part of this encounter—and the only reason it is mentioned—was that the bullies were immediately placed in the jail, which was then too full to house Yellow Hair.

Just how this was managed only Father Marc could tell, but probably one of the reasons could be found in that pile of whisky cases.

Yellow Hair had conducted himself well on his parole for some time however before he was permitted to do any hunting in company with the men whose regular duties consisted of keeping the fort supplied with fresh meat and piling up the pemmican bags in the store-house.

And then, because these professional hunters were not skillful enough to be selective in their kills, hunting became a regular duty for Yellow Hair. With his gray he could single out a two-year-old buffalo cow unerringly. He never wasted an arrow because, after the Pikuni custom, he rode hard beside his game, close enough to reach out and touch the shaggy hump.

Yellow Hair knew nothing whatever about the H.B.C. brigades. Father Marc had not been a sharer in Mc-Glincy's plan and so he was blameless for Yellow Hair's fate.

The brigades of that year had been bright enough to portage far around all Nor'Wester forts, but there was always spring of the coming year and McGlincy laid his plans with gurgling complacence.

The only time during the whole winter that Yellow Hair caused any terror in the fort came when the Pikuni scouts raced ahead of their people to inform the fort that the Blackfeet were coming in to trade.

Luberly piled loaded rifles on his counter, thrust loaded pistols into his greasy belt and crammed shot into his howitzers until the muzzles were only two inches deep. He let the Blackfeet in two at a time to trade.

The French-Canadian-Algonquian interpreter relayed

the Pikuni question to Luberly time after time.

"Where is Yellow Hair?"

With a glance at the lean, hard warriors of the plains, Luberly would gulp and bluster and shout that Yellow Hair was gone on a long trip to another fort and would not be back for a long while.

It was not wholly true. Luberly's tense was wrong.

At the moment Yellow Hair was locked in a room with an armed voyageur on either side of him and a lethal-looking bully standing outside the window with orders to shoot if Yellow Hair showed his head.

Even so Yellow Hair saw White Fox and Bright Star. They did not come within the fort, but stayed in a small camp on the cleaner bank of the river.

No whisky was put out this time because Luberly knew that the high chiefs of the Pikunis were there outside, ready to enforce their request about spirits.

All in all it was so nerve-racking that McGlincy sobered up and showed himself and backed up Luberly's lie with a half hundred of his own.

And even Father Marc, though he found the situation very funny, was unwilling to sign the execution warrants of his friends by imparting the truth to Yellow Hair's people.

The crisis passed and once again Yellow Hair was let loose—on his parole for which Father Marc had pledged his own freedom.

Father Marc was making rapid progress in the Blackfoot tongue. When he had finally discovered that he was to forget certain letters—such as B, D, F, G, J, L, R and Z for which there are no equivalents in the Pikuni tongue or in any Algonquian dialect—he made remarkable progress.

The teaching amused Father Marc because, from the first, it had been one-sided.

Yellow Hair had probably spoken his last English at the age of six when his father had died, but that English had slumbered forgotten in the depths of his mind. It had not died and now to revive it was short work.

Yellow Hair, for all the restless energy that bubbled within him, had been trained as a Pikuni scout. He had a memory which could gather up half a hundred objects at a glance and then repeat them perfectly a month later. And when a man can look at a trail and notice the pattern of hoofprints, remember the weather of thirteen days past, recall the peculiarities of fifty different bands and reconstruct a history of the passage which would take two hours in the telling, a few things like words are not apt to be found difficult.

His greatest struggle was with writing. In savage despair at the meaninglessness of the a, b, c's he would invariably resort to his own pictographs. He saw no reason whatever to go to all the trouble of writing "sunrise three days ago" when all you had to do was make

and even the most ignorant white man could tell what you meant.

But after some nine months of alternating the excitement of the chase with the painful difficulties of language and letters, Yellow Hair gained his ends. He had come to the fort to learn the ways and the language of the whites and though he had rejected the ways in wholehearted disgust he had encompassed the letters.

And now with the Grass Moon growing near its conclusion and the Planting Moon almost at hand, Yellow Hair was ready to be gone.

But the ice in the river broke up in the warmth of a chinook wind and the South Saskatchewan opened with a roar and McGlincy's scouts came back with the news that Robert Motley of the Hudson's Bay Company had started back to York Factory, gunwales deep with furs.

CHAPTER 10

THE AMBUSH

Robert Motley set out with his cargo from the head-waters of the South Saskatchewan the instant travel became possible on the watery highroad.

There were reasons for haste. Through the winter, reports had reached his post concerning the savage raiding of the Nor'Westers. Hudson's Bay Company had, for much more than a century, held undisputed sway over three-quarters of America and it was not likely that the governors in England would fail in the counterattack against the upstart brigades that threatened the very existence of H.B.C.

King Charles II on a far off day in 1670 had decreed by charter in the most solemn tones that the Hudson's Bay Company had all sovereign powers of monarchy over almost two million square miles of continent with license to punish all trespassers at the Company's discretion.

The Nor'Westers would be punished.

Like most of the "Lords of the Outer Marches," Robert Motley held himself far above the democracy his position would seem to indicate that he assume. All winter he had been cooped up in a slab-sided fort with twenty clerks and voyageurs and he still remained aloof and forbidding. He felt the dignity of commanding a region whose boundaries were so far-flung (even though it was only a small part of the whole domain) that one man could spend a decade mapping it without half completing the task.

Lean, dour and hungry, Robert Motley sat in the stern of the clumsy Mackinaw barge listening to the grating of ice cakes against the hull and the creak of the monotonous oars.

He had seven men with him, one of them a young clerk from London. The rest were, for the most part, Orkneymen. One was a French-Canadian lately deserted from the Nor'Westers, for which feat he had been awarded "a wig (£1-5s) to keep him loyal".

The Orkneymen were sour northerners, much given to gloom—and no wonder. In their far-off land they had been faced with poverty and starvation until a bounty to the sum of £8 had lured them into the wilderness. Better than half of the men who had come to North America with them were now dead from Indian bullets, freezing, starvation, thirst, drowning, disease, murder and lesser accidents.

But they feared the brooding black eyes of Robert Motley more than they feared the wilderness, and so they rowed, watching their leader with intent eyes.

All the rest were dressed in buckskin in greater or lesser repair. Motley had managed to keep cloth clothes and even a white shirt intact. His black garments flapped about him in the chill wind, giving him the appearance of a skeleton risen, shroud and all, from a moldy tomb.

Motley was on the watch for any strange movement along the shore, but his eyes were not sharp enough. McGlincy's men were not moving. They were lying very still under the budding shrubs, just beyond a wide bend, rifles trained on the place where the barge would make its appearance.

The barge swung in toward the shore to avoid a series of snags that had jammed together in an eddy. Motley shoved on his steering oar. The Orkneymen heaved hard on the sweeps.

The starboard gunwale almost touched the overhanging branches.

The range was something less than thirty feet.

The volley crashed.

With a scream the clerk clapped his hands to his throat, blood gushing out through his fingers. He toppled backward into the river.

The oars caught against the collapsed bodies of three dead Orkneymen and dug deeply under the green surface.

Motley jumped erect and tried to steer back toward the channel but the dragging sweeps had already turned the boat straight into the cloud of powder smoke that now hung under the bank.

He gave a despairing glance at his packs of furs and heard the whistle of an arrow past his head.

"Overboard!" bawled Motley.

The four remaining men sprang with their leader over the side into the icy water. An arrow thumped, seeming to hold in the very surface, standing straight up, then plunged out of sight.

Motley struck out for the opposite bank, keeping under as much as possible, interposing ice cakes between himself and the dangerous south shore.

Chilled and cramped he dragged his length into a clump of willows on the other bank. He crawled on his stomach until he saw two of his men coming out. He helped them into cover.

Anxiously Motley surveyed the turgid stream for a sign of the two others. But they were gone—one with an arrow in his back and the second by drowning.

He took a long look at his barge. Unseen hands had pulled it up under cover. Only one man was in evidence and as he was more than a hundred yards away with his back toward Motley his identity could not be determined. The only characteristic Motley could pick out was the presence of an arrow quiver across the fellow's shoulders.

Motley waited to obtain no further information. Sharply commanding his two miserable Orkneymen to follow, he struck off at a fast walk toward the northeast.

Without a single weapon or a sack of pemmican, in cold weather, with only one pair of moccasins to a man, it is hard to understand how Motley survived his trip across the blustery plains.

Motley never had anything to say on the subject. After five days' marching he turned up, knocking imperiously on the gates of the Hudson's Bay fort at the South Saskatchewan fork.

Andy Nichols, the Hudson's Bay factor, asked no questions until he had given Motley food, waiting for Motley to volunteer the cause of his loss.

Motley told Andy Nichols about it with a great economy of words. He finished with, "Get fifteen men together and arm them. They are to be ready to march at dawn."

"But good God, Motley," objected Nichols, "you haven't the least idea of who did it and fifteen men are no match for a whole Indian tribe."

"I'll be the judge of that, Nichols. I saw one man dressed in buckskin. He had a quiver across his back."

"Some renegade white you think?"

"I know it," said Motley. "A renegade in the employ of the Nor'Westers. They'll give him up or I'll swing every mother's son of them from the English gallows. Take care of my two men and get those others ready. Remember, we march at dawn!"

CHAPTER 11

THE NOR'WESTERS SUBMIT

Shortly after the river ice broke, Yellow Hair was taken ill.

For more than a week his liberty had been much curtailed in spite of his continued success as a fort hunter. He had been kept under lock and his meals had been served by a sly-footed voyageur of malicious aspect. Yellow Hair had seen nothing of Father Marc for several days and though he suspected that the Mighty Monk would not be long in using his influence to raise the siege, he could not help worrying.

Walls had always annoyed him and a lock on the door was insupportable. To his clear mind the facts added up to injustice. He had given his parole long months before. The conditions had been very plain. If he behaved himself well, if he made no attempt to escape, if he hunted for the fort and returned punctually, and if he made no attempt to communicate with possible scouts from the Pikunis, he was to be allowed to do almost as he pleased.

But when a log-slab door was bolted upon him after continued evidence of his trustworthiness, Yellow Hair restlessly scented trouble.

His hate for the Nor'Westers had been with him so

long that it had become almost passive. He had adopted an attitude which did not too much disturb his peace of mind, regarding the factor and McGlincy with the same tolerance he would have used toward a pair of unclean animals.

The voyageurs were quite evidently slaves and as such they deserved neither thought nor attention. True, he had been very puzzled by this queer circumstance. It seemed the height of idiocy that thirty or more men, apparently sane and able-bodied, should submit so servilely to a drunken beast.

He realized that there was probably more to this than he could see on the surface. There must be another angle which lay in the country of the whites.

McGlincy had, during the winter, ordered two floggings. One man had been punished by his brigade leader. But the other had not suffered enough, to McGlincy's notion, and the great McGlincy himself had descended to the stake—military jacket, epaulets and all—and had proceeded to use the lash to such a great advantage that the voyageur had been ill and untended in the butter tub for more than a month.

Immediately after that Yellow Hair had carefully watched for revolt. But it did not come. The voyageurs thought nothing at all of it. They sang and drank and mounted guard on the runways as though nothing had happened.

Father Marc had not been able to throw satisfactory light upon this because he had had to deal with elements Yellow Hair had never felt or seen.

The Mighty Monk had explained with an expansive grin that in the country of the whites there were many, many jails in which men were kept. Some of these men had offended the Great White Father of the English, others had robbed people and murdered companions. Then two things had happened. The men had been willing to do anything to keep away from stone walls and the gallows. The H.B.C.s and the Nor'Westers both urgently needed personnel. And in addition to this it cost the Great White Father of the English a deal of money to feed men who neither worked nor fought.

Back in the country of the whites waited the noose and the barred door. Here in the Indian Country was freedom of a certain sort.

The voyageurs thankfully stayed loyal at one hundred pounds per year at best.

A few, of course, were lured away from the Canadian parishes by the sight of the money flung about by recruiting bullies; but these were too weak-minded in the first place to become strong-brained afterwards.

As Yellow Hair had been unable to understand the lure of cash, he was still very much in twilight about it.

In the face of all this weird reasoning, Yellow Hair, when he found himself sh`.t in without explanation, waited for the worst, which was not long in coming.

One morning, the *Pays d'en Haut* who brought his food looked more sly than ever. Yellow Hair turned from his place at the window, caught the feeling of effort behind the servant's calmness. An alarm bell jangled in Yellow Hair.

Waiting only until the door was shut, he approached his tray and looked critically at the slab of buffalo steak upon it. He had no reason to suspect the meat's condition and he was very hungry. Uneasily he began to eat.

These whites used something they called salt on their meat which gave it a sweetish taste. Yellow Hair had never been able to get wholly used to it.

He had never heard of poisoning food as that was limited to the South Americans and as he detected nothing different in the highly seasoned steak, he ate all of it.

The night before, an unprecedented thing had happened. Luberly had sent a bottle of trade whisky to him but Yellow Hair knew too much about whisky. It drove men mad. He had poured it out the window.

But he did not connect that with the steak.

At first he had a dull feeling in the region of his stomach. The meat felt heavy and then he did not feel anything at all.

The room started to blur. In sudden alarm, Yellow Hair stood up and snatched hold of the door with a hazy idea of calling the Mighty Monk.

No sound left his lips. He collapsed and the world turned black.

Unfortunately for him, Father Marc had never touched upon the subject of opium or its derivative, laudanum. Father Marc had never mentioned the British propensity for carefully distributing dope wherever they went—and his silence was odd because the insistence of the British upon their right to do this and their inconsistent sermons upon their attempts to better the world of mankind by conquest was so very funny that Father Marc had of course collected all the facts upon it.

But Yellow Hair, twenty-four hours later, awoke with a feverish face, a raw stomach and a great weakness without ever knowing what had happened to him.

He was all alone. No one had approached that door for a day and a night. He painfully lifted himself to the bed and sprawled upon it, unable to assemble enough strength to call out and demand the water he felt he must have or perish.

Stoically he suffered through another night, feeling only half alive and wholly wretched.

And then the sly voyageur came as though he knew all about it and gave him water and, later, a little food.

But Father Marc made no appearance. The sounds of the fort outside had not changed and obviously nothing of importance was happening.

Burning and freezing, Yellow Hair bore up through two more days.

And then Father Marc appeared, much startled at Yellow Hair's appearance, very solicitous after his health. But Father Marc had a very odd question on his lips.

"When did you get back?"

"I've been nowhere. I might ask the same of you."

"You can confide in me," said the Mighty Monk with terrible seriousness. "I know all about it and though I do not believe many of the things I have heard . . ."

Yellow Hair propped himself on his elbow. "Don't batter me with riddles. What are you talking about?"

"The Orkneyman we found floating down the stream two days ago. He had an arrow in his back."

"Orkneyman? You mean a servant of Hudson's Bay?"

"I do. But quiet yourself."

"No reason not to," said Yellow Hair sinking back into the bunk. "What do I care how many of these fool whites—Wait, you're looking at me oddly. You think my friends had something to do with that? Do you mean to accuse a Pikuni of shooting an enemy in the back? Ah now, Marc, mend your mind about it. Please do not confuse my people with your own."

"Perhaps you didn't know after all," mused the Mighty Monk. "Perhaps you *have* been here for the last week or more. . . . But, then, how do you account for a man in buckskin with a quiver across his back?"

"How do I account for it? Do I have to account for it at all? An arrow in the back of an Orkneyman, you say? A man in buckskin with a quiver? Well now, if I am expected to read your mind, you are trying to tell me that I have been gone from the fort, that I shot a white man in the back and that I returned."

"The Orkneyman was scalped."

"Too poor for even a coward's coupstick, these slave scalps."

"Perhaps. But the arrow was Blackfoot and Jacques Delage tells a strange tale about seeing a man at the head of an Indian war party higher up the Saskatchewan and Luberly tells of your coming in over the stockade wall last night much the worse for travel—and you certainly look as though you had been to much exertion."

"A man in buckskin could mean anyone. Why, there's no use to argue against such lies. The truth will soon be discovered."

The Mighty Monk had looked for the wild denial found in most guilty men, for the apprehension of facts before they were stated. He breathed in relief.

"But Luberly's word is never good," said Marc. "He says you had scalps in your belt and the voyageurs are buzzing with it." The Mighty Monk sighed, "I was afraid he was right when he said you had broken your parole."

That was more than Yellow Hair could stand. He swung his feet to the floor and his blue eyes glittered.

"He'll swallow that, the fool," said Yellow Hair.

"He'll chew it up and gulp it down. The lying beast says I have broken my word? The word of a Pikuni? Wait until. . . ."

The Mighty Monk thrust him back into the bunk. "You can't go on a one man raid, Yellow Hair. Not in the camp of the enemy. I'll take care of this."

"When I ask any man to fight my battles, I will be very old and weak, Marc. Let me go!"

The Mighty Monk, as his record shows, could whip any three men together in the Nor'Wester service and Yellow Hair was only equal to two Nor'Westers now in his weakened condition. The Mighty Monk held him down.

"That's what they want, you young devil! It would be sensible, wouldn't it, to walk into a pistol ball! Stay here until you're better. I'll make certain that the voyageurs know where you are and what's the matter with you. The killing of an H.B.C. Orkneyman is no crime to a Nor'Wester and even if you didn't do it, they'll probably offer you a medal on the strength of the rumor!"

Fume and squirm though he might, Yellow Hair was finally argued out of his intentions.

His captivity kept on for ten days without incident and then, one frosty dawn, he was jarred awake by the shout of a sentry on the walk.

"The English! A barge coming upstream!"

CHAPTER 12

YELLOW HAIR DECLARES WAR

Robert Motley only knew the facts, but those, to his prejudiced and bitter understanding, were quite enough reason to burn Fort Chesterfield and glut the river with dead Nor'Westers.

Aggravated beyond all caution by the aggressive raids of the rival brigades, goaded on by the memory of lost packs, backed by fifteen stalwart fighters, Motley would not have turned away if he had been faced with the entire English army.

He stood in the bow behind the loaded howitzer, as black and hunched as a carrion crow, his eyes sunk into his head like smoldering coal pits.

The keel grated on the beach and it lurched as the armed Orkneymen leaped to the bank. The bow was grounded securely and a gunner stood with smoking match ready to batter the log-slab palisades with solid shot.

Motley walked as though his knees had no joints. A pistol was gripped in his spidery hand.

A hundred paces short of the gate he stopped and roared, "McGlincy! Surrender, or I'll blow you to hell!"

There were two cannon over the fort gate but they were neither loaded nor manned. Such an operation would require at least a half hour. Startled *Pays d'en Haut* scattered along the runways and peered fearfully through the loopholes.

Orkneymen deployed and found cover and sniping stations.

Motley bawled, "Open the gates, you pork eaters!"

A halyard slapped against the flagstaff inside and creaked through a block. A bit of cloth cracked in the brisk wind.

Its color was white.

Scenting a trick, Motley glanced about to see that his men were in position.

Like a jack-in-the-box patterned after a particularly ugly Punch, McGlincy's head appeared over the palisades, cocked hat, ruffles and all.

"Damme, if it ain't the English," belched McGlincy.

"Ay, and what's more it's Motley!" shouted Luberly sighting through a loop.

"I demand your unconditional surrender, you blackguard!" bawled Motley.

"I'm coming down to talk," replied McGlincy, disappearing. "Riflemen, cover that fool out there."

A postern creaked on rusty hinges and McGlincy came forth with a tipsy grin. He had a bottle by the neck and when he had come up to Motley he sat down on a rock and perched the bottle on his knee like a scepter.

"Well, it *is* Motley," said McGlincy. "Good old Motley. Getting many furs downriver this spring?"

"You know how many," snapped Motley.

"Ah, now, I wouldn't say that. Of course, our spies do return with information, but—"

"I'm talking about the murder of my barge crew."

"Well now—hic—so that's where that blasted Orkneyman came from. Damme, Motley, but that was odd. I was standing on the beach and down the stream I see something coming that looked like a dead man and I sent out a canoe and you know what it was? An Orkneyman with an arrow in his back. Scalped, he was. And I says to Luberly, I says, 'them damn Indians ought to be taught . . .' "

"I've been upriver overland," said Motley in an awful, grating monotone. "I saw what the wolves had left of the poor devils."

"Was they scalped too?" inquired McGlincy, blinking. "Here, wet your pipes, Motley. Damned dry, this talking."

"Keep your filthy rotgut," snapped Motley, "and ladle it out to the Indians. You forced us to use—"

"Now, now, that happened thirty years ago or more. Now, tell me, Motley, who do you think pulled that trick on you?"

"You Nor'Westers pulled it."

"Ah me, but you're a man of stubborn convictions. You ought to be ashamed of yourself. Ain't we all honorable white men in a savage land? Hadn't we ought to protect ourselves? That's my policy, Motley, and that's why I picked him up for you. A young renegade head of a war party, he was. Tall, with a quiver across his back. He tried to run off our horses but I was too quick for him. I went galloping out and he drawed his knife and I—"

"Renegade? You mean a fellow in buckskin? Where is he?"

"I knocked him out and I says to myself, 'Damme, if

this don't account for that dead Orkneyman we found!
Just to show Motley and the H.B.C. we're gentlemen,
we'll wait until they comes along and if he's a man they
want—' "

"Where is he?"

"He used to be here at the fort, you know," said
McGlincy, "and he'd promised not to run away, but he
did, and—"

"How long ago was this?"

"About two weeks. Maybe three. He's got friends in
the Blackfeet and so when he tried to run off the horses,
I—"

Motley was beginning to quiver with anticipation.
"You've got him here now?"

"Safe and sound, all ready to hand over to you."

"Ay, God, but this is good. Good! He'll hang for this
at York Factory before summer is over. Bring him out."

"You had better come inside," said McGlincy.

"Not without my men."

"Why, that's all right. Bring them along and we'll have
a party, so we will. Hey, up there! Open the gates for
Mr. Motley!"

The gates creaked and the palisades yawned.

Motley, followed by his Orkneymen, marched inside.

McGlincy made a sign to Luberly. "I told you I was
right. Damned if we want a murdering savage in our
fort, Motley. Luberly, have the young wretch brought
down."

Luberly ran a greasy sleeve across his furry upper lip
and barked at two voyageurs.

The pair hurried across the yard and into the quarters.

Yellow Hair had been unable to see any of the movements of the men and he had not heard anything of the parley outside the gates. He quite naturally supposed that there was trouble with the English and that he would be needed in the fort's defense.

At this prospect of action, he almost grinned when the two voyageurs, with drawn pistols, unbolted his door.

He still did not sense that he was under guard when they walked with him across the trading room.

Confidently, he opened the door to the yard and stepped through.

The sight staggered him like a blow. At a glance he added up the equation before him.

Father Marc looking dismayed meant Yellow Hair was in trouble.

An open gate and the presence of the English inside meant that the English had no immediate quarrel with the Nor'Westers.

The sudden sweep of all eyes upon him confirmed his first idea.

The dead Orkneyman, Luberly's lies, Marc's questions, his illness and his late confinement, fitted like the metal parts of a cannon—which weapon was turned squarely upon him.

His reflexes were like steel springs.

He stopped abruptly one pace outside.

The slower-witted guards made one more step.

Yellow Hair stabbed out with his arms, swept them in front of him and banged their skulls together. With the same movement he hurtled backwards and inside the trading room, slamming the thick door shut.

The sound of its closing was echoed instantly with the bang of a rifle and the slap of a shot into timber.

Yellow Hair knocked the bolt into place. He whirled and secured the two other entrances.

He leaped over the trading counter and sent the armload of trade guns clattering off the shelves.

He banged in the head of a powder keg, spilled out a bag of balls, and before the men outside had understood his intention and had reached the door, he had already loaded his first flintlock.

Leveling it, he fired into the thick planking, taking a joint as his target.

Through the swirling white cloud of powder ripped the scream of a wounded Orkneyman.

Slapping another load home with a ramrod, Yellow Hair shouted, "Hyai! Yeeow! You fools come and get me! Open the door, McGlincy! Open it up! Batter it down! Come on, you bullies, here's your chance for glory! Come and get me, I can be got! Come on, you English, if you like to stomach lead! Hyai! Yeeow! My scalp is yellow! A fine scalp! Rip it off and wave it on your sticks! Take it and tell your women you've killed a Pikuni but don't tell them how many of you died! Come on, you whites, you brave bullies, you heroes! Break it in and get me! Knock it down! Hyai! Yeeow! Come on! I'm waiting!"

He stacked his loaded guns beside him on the floor. He pulled out bolts of red cloth and made a three-sided barricade. He taunted them and reviled them and sang his war song, ending each verse with the blood-freezing, head-splitting war whoop of the Pikunis.

And outside the door the brawny Orkneymen heaved forward on a cannon.

CHAPTER 13

THE GHOST-HEAD

Throughout the winter, the girl Bright Star had been suffering from the growing conviction that it was her action which had driven Yellow Hair to accept the mad plans of the Grand Council.

Time after time she had spoken of it to canny old White Fox and even though he assured her that Yellow Hair had been wholly under orders and had neither advanced nor seconded the scheme except to obey it, Bright Star, each time, uneasily remembered the fury into which she had goaded Yellow Hair.

He had avoided her in the town after that. The presents of fresh game had stopped. Apparently Yellow Hair had forgotten her entirely, taking it for granted that Long Bow would become her husband.

This was in no wise the case. Yellow Hair had known that any approach would only result in the lessening of his own aloof glory and he had understood that Long Bow, staying home, would suffer in her estimation. It was not part of Yellow Hair's hastily conceived plans to let Bright Star become anything less than his sits-beside-him woman.

But a man of Yellow Hair's active temperament does not long brood over the problems of love. Instead of thinking, he acts. His whole strategy of life is built about the basic belief that furious motion will overcome the most weighty intrigues.

It was action to go away to the fort of the Nor'-Westers. It was galling inaction to stay still and argue with a youth of considerable wealth. Yellow Hair's departure and the spectacular nature of his mission, encompassing as it did the welfare of the entire Pikuni people, gave him an opportunity for which all men of courage pray. He was sacrificing his own interests and perhaps even his life for the good of all—and there is nothing more glorious than that.

As though anxious to prove the excellence of his reasoning, Bright Star watched the approach of spring with increasing fear. In vain did the slender and sightly Long Bow parade out with beautiful clothing. In vain did Long Bow reform and take eagerly to the most risky pursuits.

Bright Star was convinced, when the rivers broke, that she had sent Yellow Hair to his death.

The chinook wiped snow from the plains like a chalk mark from a rock. The warm wind whooped and the rivers swelled and the prairie sod was borne away on the tumultuous breasts of thousands of temporary streams.

Buffalo trying to cross weak ice or swim the roaring rivers broke through, missed their landings and drowned, strewing the banks for miles with their brown carcasses.

Birds came with throaty songs.

Geese honked northward in flights like thunderclouds against the blue heavens. Wood pigeons settled in thousands of gigantic flocks and the drumming of their wings would deafen a man for an hour.

It was a restless time and Bright Star determined that Yellow Hair should long ago have returned.

One morning she found Magpie sauntering between the lodges. She looked intently at him for a moment and then beckoned. The boy came respectfully and saluted her.

"Magpie, there are horses in the herds belonging to Yellow Hair."

"Yes. But lately I have begun to think that they will soon be tribal property."

"Don't say things like that," said Bright Star, although she had been on the verge of saying them herself. "Would you bring in two of those ponies for me and saddle one?"

"You have a saddle?"

"I know that Yellow Hair had two. One was old, made of rough rawhide, too high behind and before. That one must still be in White Fox's lodge. Come, be a good boy. If you do this I'll make you a pair of moccasins so soft and light you'll be fleet as an antelope."

"If you mean to help Yellow Hair, I need no reward except to accompany you."

"You're very brave, Magpie."

"Anyone is brave when you smile."

"Hurry. It is already late. Bring them down to the willows beside the river. In a little time I will join you."

Magpie gravely saluted her again and sauntered onward. He was very young but in some ways very old. His small face betrayed no sign of the excitement which was bursting within him.

Calmly he went out and lied to the herd guards so well that they caught the horses for him. As Yellow Hair's boy-in-waiting, Magpie, although Tushepaw blood filled his veins, had a certain standing in the town which, of late, had measurably increased as people began to wonder about Yellow Hair's lengthy absence.

With a visage as calm as though graven from stone, he went back and, on the excuse that he had seen antelope nearby, fooled White Fox into giving him Yellow Hair's old saddle and a trade gun of ancient vintage.

Magpie saddled one horse and tied a bellyband around the other, fixed their thong bridles and led them down into the willows.

Presently Bright Star came to him. She had substituted leggings and shirt for her beaded elkskin dress and, at a hasty glance, appeared to be an extraordinarily handsome Pikuni warrior. She was slender and supple and the cool dignity of her face made her appear far wiser than her twenty summers.

Magpie lost heart a very little bit. He recalled terrible stories about the fort in the north and about all whites and he knew he certainly could not hope to do very much with the old trade gun.

"You are not going to tell anyone?"

"Last night," said Bright Star, "I had a dream. I could see Yellow Hair lying very ill in a square bed and a serpent upon his breast was about to strike him. I awoke in terror because I knew that it was sent to me as an omen. This morning I told Bear Claws. But women,"—she said it bitterly—"are not supposed to have sacred dreams and he told me it meant nothing. I told Long Bow and he said I had eaten something which did not agree with me. I told White Fox and he said that Yellow Hair could take care of himself. I told Lost-in-Mountains and he said that he, too, was uneasy but that travel had been impossible for weeks and Yellow Hair was supposed to wait for spring and that we should wait until the hot weather before we went north."

"Then—then, you mean to go all alone to the people in the north and ask them what has happened to Yellow Hair?"

"I must find out if he lives. We will approach the fort and watch from a hiding place. Somehow we will signal him or talk with him and, if he lives, beg him to come back to the village. He is probably angry with me, Magpie."

"He loves you."

"After I let Long Bow fight with him? Magpie, if you ever love a girl, remember that there is never such a thing as choosing between two. A maiden may madden you with another man but if she thinks she loves both, she loves neither. Come, Magpie, before somebody finds out that I have taken pemmican and clothing from my brother's lodge."

As Magpie was no more than fourteen, and as he felt untold responsibilities to his knight's lady, he would have allowed his tongue to be cut out before he would have communicated her plan to anyone.

And so they proceeded north with Magpie constantly scouting the country for hostile parties. They slept but little and always with one of them on guard and so well did they travel across the wet plains that they arrived at a spot near Fort Chesterfield in five days.

Their navigation had not been too good as Bright Star had only been to the fort once and Magpie never. But they knew they could strike the river north of the fort and then come down its bank.

This they did—to their sorrow.

Bright Star had come across five suns of prairie. She

had risked an encounter with Cree raiding parties which would result in a lifetime sentence of slavery for her. She was willing to face possible apprehension by the white traders—who considered any dark-eyed girl a portion of their loot in the Indian country. She was ready to face almost any dismal tidings.

But not Yellow Hair's death.

To Bright Star, who had happily avoided all contacts with the traders at close range, there was only one man in the world who had a scalp as bright as the sunlight. Any girl who had been raised among blonds of the north but who loved a man with dark hair would certainly have believed that he was the only dark-haired man in the world. And so it would be true on both counts.

Motley had tried to do her a favor but he knew nothing about her. In scouting upriver before landing at Fort Chesterfield he had found the place where his barge had been ambushed. With a few finer sensibilities, he had deplored the state of his dead and scalped companions who had been so cruelly mauled by wolves and he had dug a common grave for them. But Motley, as might be imagined, had been in something of a hurry to get at McGlincy's throat and he had not had time to dig very deep because water persisted in silting up the hole as fast as it was dug.

Nor had Motley collected all the bones, and with these as a marker, the wolves had industriously opened the grave again to finish the task of polishing up the skulls and tibias and metacarpals of the luckless Orkneymen.

And now, as Bright Star and Magpie came cautiously down the river bank, it was inevitable that they should sight the black and slimy grave.

A "ghost-head," to which the jawbone still clung, lay upright in the muck. This Orkneyman's yellow scalp had been removed, but not with any expertness, and as there is no food value in hair even to a wolf, a few blood-stained strands still clung forlornly to the otherwise bare white bones.

Magpie flung himself from his horse and hesitantly approached the thing. His eyes grew round in terror and, when he turned, shiny with tears.

Bright Star saw it. Stunned by shock, she steadied herself by gripping the saddle's high plate. Vitality went out of her and her head sank low upon her breast.

Sobbing, Magpie said, "He—he can't be dead! He can't be!"

Her quest was over. It was five days' travel back to her people. In five days the tribe would know. But they would expect her to carry on. Her father's brother would give her in marriage to Long Bow and now she could do nothing but obey.

Alive in body only, she turned her horse silently toward the south.

A sound of muttering thunder came from afar, but there were clouds of a dark and ugly aspect in the sky and thunder was to be expected.

Bright Star rode slowly onward, southward, to her home.

CHAPTER 14

UNDER FIRE

When the stubby howitzer was rolled into place the Orkneymen stepped back and Motley, with some ceremony, applied the spark to the touchhole.

White smoke blasted outward as the cannon leaped off the ground and rushed backward.

The trading room door was like a thick man hit in the middle by a war club. The center shot in, the hinges gave away. In a shower of splinters and wrenched nails, the door carried backward half the length of the room and leaned drunkenly against the counter.

Motley gave a hoarse command. The Orkneymen, snatching up rifles, pistols, knives and bludgeons, charged.

Yellow Hair's head was reeling with the concussion. The abrupt advent of daylight helped the smoke to blind him. But through the acrid and thick white fog he could see men coming.

He crouched over his parapet of red cloth and sighted down the long barrel of the first trade rifle. He squeezed the trigger and hastily shifted to the second in line. He fired that and rolled to the third. Down the sights he could see arms and legs and chests and he took his pick at random.

Not more than two Orkneymen could squeeze into

at a time. Yellow Hair piled them up over the
shold.

At Yellow Hair's sixth shot the attack collapsed. But
he did not wait for any parley about it. He blew out the
lengthy muzzles, rammed home wadding, powder and
shot and lined his weapons up again.

Motley howled orders for the reloading of the cannon. He was busy setting an example of grim efficiency
for his men and he, of course, had no time to take part
in the actual charging.

If Motley had ever had any doubts about McGlincy's
story they were now dispelled by the savageness of Yellow Hair's defense.

It is very difficult for a casual observer to understand
the theory of battle. Where war is concerned society has
denied all men the right to casualness and has
demanded instant and interested participation.

Quite probably, had Yellow Hair been fighting in the
service of the Hudson's Bay Company, Motley would
have seen to it personally that Yellow Hair be awarded
pounds, pence, wigs, decorations and positions of
authority.

But, unfortunately for Yellow Hair, he was only fighting in his own interests through a misconceived idea that
every man has a perfect right to stay alive. To do this he
had to counteract the employment of a cannon against
him by using all the rifles at his command. He had no
lust for killing whatever and indeed no interest in it. He
wanted very much to live to fight again and he had no
retreat except in the face of almost twoscore white men.

Motley, seeing his Orkneymen cut down—he knew
they were expensive as the H.B.C. agents had to give an
eight-pound bounty to every future member—and being

unable to instantly wreak his vengeance, vowed in roaring tones that Yellow Hair was all manner of beast, fiend, werewolf, savage, brute, barbarian, ruffian, adder, ghoul, butcher, monster, devil and ogre. Motley, by such means, spurred on his crew and made them believe it was a matter of world-wide importance on which hung the fate of H.B.C. to capture Yellow Hair.

Violence acts upon men as variously as whisky. It makes them happy, sad, brave or craven. Violence is, in fact, a much greater stimulus than spirits because it usually quickens reaction while whisky deadens it.

Violence made Major Alexander McGlincy more imperial than ever. He sat upon a runway, well out of gunshot from the trading door, bellowing unheard commands into the turmoil and pointing out strategic facts with the bottom of the bottle he clutched. It was enough for McGlincy to direct the affair. His position was so mighty that no man would ever dare question another motive than selfless zeal to conquer.

Violence reacted on Luberly in quite another way. Brought up halfway between the gallows and respectability he had always been servile toward both and was now crying the loudest for justice. He raced back and forth moving powder horns and kegs, shouting, brandishing a pistol and intent on being everywhere at once and in everybody's way. It might have been noticed that he too was careful not to approach the fatal door, but this must not be construed to mean hypocrisy on his part. He was showing McGlincy how interested he was in furthering Nor'Wester plans and making a most excellent show of helpful bravery.

The Orkneymen were working and sweating. They were angry and baffled but as they had only one small portion of the battle to accomplish—the attacking—their reaction needs no further illumination.

While not exactly happy about it, Yellow Hair was exultant. The Blackfoot trait of meeting death with a jeer was deeply instilled in him and his taunts were boisterous above the bark of rifles.

Yellow Hair would fire at a fleeting smoke shadow and yip, "Stand still! How can I hit you when you move? Come on, you bullies, line up for another attack. You can take me this time! I'm waiting, my heroes! Come on, come in, you're welcome to my lead. Have a slug! You there, stand still!"

And he would shoot a second rifle.

As a matter of fact, the odds against him were not so great as they immediately appeared. Outside there were only forty-one bullies, voyageurs, Orkneymen and leaders, only two cannon (excepting the howitzer in the barge), only a full round of rifles and pistols and something less than sixteen cutlasses.

The trading room's design was with him, of course. It was so built that it could be defended independently of the fort in case a group of Indians in the stockade treacherously objected to the theft of furs or the murder of a chief or some other foolish incidental. On the roof of this trading room was a place for a cannon which, in event of a hostile stockade full of braves, could be filled with a hundred or more bullets and discharged straight into the crowd of warriors, women and children who had, in foolish faith, come to trade.

And even now the trading room was remarkably preserved, having lost only one window, the door, part of the rear wall, a section of the counter and a scant third of the roof. It was hardly burning at all except immediately within the entrance and up the left wall where the powder kegs stood.

Yellow Hair had come through in fair shape. The cannon shots had been hard on his ears and he was gashed over his right eye and could not see through it. His face was black with smoke and his trigger hand was only slightly burned when one of the second-hand trade rifles had exploded at the wrong end.

And he still taunted them. He called for McGlincy and begged for a good target like his red coat or blue nose or some such obvious feature. He pleaded with unseen Luberly to sniffle and let him know where Luberly was. He called a half dozen voyageurs by name and promised them a fine party and a warming welcome if they would only call on him.

He thanked them for the fire they had set because the place had been so cold. He congratulated Luberly upon his excellent selection of rifles and his taste in powder.

Over and over he sang the praises of his sun-colored scalp and told them how proud their women would be if they took it home and hung it on the wall. He offered wagers on his shots, lost them, won them and kept a tally by adding to the heap over the threshold.

He had the advantage of them as they afterwards often said. While, they said, his marksmanship was poor and he screamed for mercy, they had no intention of killing him and would not have lost a man had not a powder keg exploded just after they had walked into the place. Their records dwell at some length on this feature of the fight and a suspicious nature would cravenly construe that they were trying to apologize for being so soundly whipped.

Even so it could not last forever.

Yellow Hair was blind. He could not breathe in the stifle of burning wood and he could no longer see any more of the doorway—because the rest of the wall was gone. Robbed of the wherewithal to spot targets, unable to reload with his injured hand, having emptied his last rifle, he took a pistol from his belt and stood up.

The grin on his face was a horrible thing to see. Skin blackened with powder smoke and reddened with blood, his white teeth, bared in a snarl of defiance, were the only recognizable feature of him.

He strode forward to the door. He was saving his one last shot for McGlincy and he was praying that the sunlight would let him see again.

For the last time the cannon roared and leaped. The roof smashed inward. A beam struck down and bowled Yellow Hair over like a tenpin.

He fell just outside the door, beyond the stacked bodies that lay there. To all appearances he was dead and to this he owed his life.

Satisfaction flooded Motley. He belted his own pistol and strode ahead to turn Yellow Hair over with his foot. When the boot toe had finished its prodding, Yellow Hair was on his back with outflung arms, blackened locks damply lying over the dust.

Motley hauled him aside by one foot and, belatedly, began to sort out his wounded from his dead.

CHAPTER 15

TO TRIAL AND THE GALLOWS

The Hudson's Bay Company had written off losses several times. They were used to it. They had been founded in the dim but glorious past to discover a Northwest Passage to the Orient. Only recently had their last expedition on that hopeless quest returned with word that no such passage existed. Accordingly, the governors opened up a fresh bottle of red ink and whittled a new quill pen and added up their lists of dead men and lost ships associated with the mythical passage to find and write off the round sum of a hundred thousand pounds—which, at a glance, is half a million dollars and quite a fortune.

Thus they were already inured to the agony of scribbling with red ink and the pounds, shillings and pence which Yellow Hair would eventually cost them in furs, rewards and indemnifications probably created very little stir—although the sum was sufficiently great to teach wiser men the futility of vengeance.

The debt was just starting when Robert Motley patched up his crew and prepared to leave.

It has already been noticed that Major Alexander McGlincy's worthy if somewhat sodden brain ran foggily inside a lining of beaver fur. It may well be added here that the valuable cogs of this wonderful machine looked very much like shillings. This is on the authority of a doctor who examined them after they were rather messily spilled and it is only necessary to recall the dealings with Motley to confirm the fact.

The trading room had quite naturally caught fire from the cannon as the range had been less than fifteen yards and the bark on the log slabbing had been eager to ignite.

Some unnamed heroes among the bullies (who needed very few threats and only one glimpse of McGlincy's pistol to activate them) had darted into the wreckage and had rolled out the keg of powder under the counter. Others had formed a line from the river to the stockade and had passed in skin buckets filled with water.

Now the fire was out but the damage was something to behold. Two thousand dollars worth of trade goods (according to Luberly's inventory, which is of course reliable) had been injured beyond repair.

Bullets into the bolts of trading cloth, water, fire, smoke, splinters, solid shot, grapeshot, one load of crowbars and powder stains had played havoc with the structure and everything in it. The gutted edifice would have to be ripped down on the instant and rebuilt as the Indians would probably come early to trade and there must be no sign of the fight.

Motley was not the strategist McGlincy was. Motley forgot he had had five men killed and three wounded, which left him a force of exactly seven. He forgot he was still inside the Nor'Wester fort and that one cannon, now loaded, was perched over the gate. He failed to realize that McGlincy had more than a score of men standing about with guns in their hands.

But McGlincy reminded him of this the instant Motley started to leave.

The major sat down on the high sill of the postern, blocking Motley's way. It was all done in great innocence and McGlincy appeared interested only in his bottle. But a young clerk was standing hard by with a quill, a pad and ink.

A bully casually sparked his flint and lit his pipe and sat down on the mount of the cannon above the gate.

"Well now, Motley," said McGlincy with the air of great wisdom—which is the easiest thing in the world for anyone to assume as it is only necessary to look serious, purse the lips and clear the throat imperatively.

"Out of my way," snapped Motley. "By God, I've had enough without further interference from you. Get up, you swine, and open those gates."

"Presently, presently. All the time in the world, Motley, now that we've helped you get your man. No rush. Damme, you look like you don't appreciate what we've done for you. There's gratitude, Luberly. We give him the renegade he's looking for, we let him burn us out, we offer him drink and wassail and he snaps at us like a cur dog."

"It's astounding!" gasped Luberly, swabbing emphatically at his hairy upper lip.

"We practically do his work for him and he orders us about. Blood and wounds, Motley, have you no breeding? No finer sensibilities? No gratitude?"

"I'm grateful enough. Out of my way, McGlincy!"

"Clerk," said McGlincy, looking wise again. "Since he's so lacking in decency, we'll have to give him the bill."

"Bill!" roared Motley. "I come in and do your dirty work and take this fool off your hands and you talk of a bill!"

McGlincy looked up at the pipe-smoking gunner above the gate and tapped his nose. He glanced around at his ring of bullies and voyageurs, inspected their guns critically and grinned.

"First," said McGlincy, carefully failing to note Motley's sudden alarm, "there is the matter of the trading post itself. As you have not injured the stockade nor the quarters nor the powder room, we'll let you off very light. Five hundred pounds, clerk. Put it at the top of the page."

"Five hundred pounds? You damned thief! It won't cost you ten pounds to rebuild it!"

McGlincy offered a drink to cool Motley's throat, but Motley could not have swallowed champagne, much less trade whisky.

"Five hundred pounds," said McGlincy, musing upon it and repeating it because it was such a lovely sum. "And now for the goods. Three loads were in there at six hundred pounds, making—what is it, clerk?"

"Eighteen hundred pounds, sir."

"Right. And now . . ."

Motley's voice was shrill with rage. His arms flapped as though he were a crow about to take flight. "You think that pigpen was a palace? You think you had diamonds for trade goods? Damn you, I'll . . ."

"And now," said McGlincy, swilling gently at his bottle as though this talk of pigs had reminded him of it. "Now, there's the matter of a slight bonus to my men for helping you."

The voyageurs cheered this news and thumped the

ground with their rifle butts. That was about their limit in using anything except a knife, but Motley failed to remember that and, looking about, saw how thorough was his trap.

"Ten pounds to a man. What's that, clerk?"

"Two hundred and ninety pounds, sir."

McGlincy took inspiration from a fresh bottle. He tapped his nose, belched and said, "And I think rental on the cannon should be placed at ten pounds and add to that a twenty-pound item to cover the lead and thirty pounds to pay for the powder. The last thing on the list is a five-pound fee for letting you use our beach. No, no, it isn't either. Rounding up this renegade should meet with some reward. Make that a hundred pounds, clerk."

"Yes, sir."

"And now give Mr. Motley the whole total and don't keep him in suspense."

"Two thousand, seven hundred and fifty-five pounds, sir."

Motley reeled and flapped his wings to stay upright. The clerk made out a blanket bill and gave it to him.

"I'm being easy on you," said McGlincy with a kindly, even fatherly smile. "I should have added five hundred pounds for myself to compensate for all the brainwork I did in directing the attack. But we'll let that go."

"You expect me to pay . . ." began Motley with a rising, hysterical intonation.

"Not in a lump. Just sign your name and we speed you on your way. Damme, it's a good thing I'm the most liberal man in the Indian country. You ought to thank me, Motley."

Shivering with anger Motley snapped the pen from the clerk's hand and slashed "Robert Motley as agent for Hudson's Bay Company" across the bottom of the sheet.

McGlincy waved a lofty hand and the gates swung back and Motley's battered crew limped down to their barge bearing their dead and wounded.

It had been discovered by an Orkneyman shortly before that the young renegade was alive and so Yellow Hair's unconscious body was lugged down to the water's edge, there to be tied and double tied before they slung him harshly into the boat.

Father Marc, not being a man of war, belonged to a church in which diplomacy and tactical efficiency were shaped into fine arts. He needed no crystal ball to tell him that he was *persona non grata* at Fort Chesterfield.

He was the only man there with the ability to reason this trick out and he was in no way held loyal by money and favor to the Nor'Westers. McGlincy would know sooner or later that one word from Father Marc would create a fury of investigation in England. Although undoubtedly clever, the scheme would fall apart with greater ease than those bolder raids of Haldane and McDonnell. Of course McGlincy had gained more in proportion to the risk and if everything remained quiet and if Yellow Hair was hanged by the neck until uncommonly dead, no more would be thought about it.

But Father Marc knew that he was a looming and muscular flaw in the whole affair. McGlincy knew that shillings could not shut his mouth and would begin to brood upon it as soon as the elation of the trimming had boiled down a bit.

Prompted by sympathy for the much-much-wronged Yellow Hair, and by a sturdy liking for his own life,

Father Marc immediately took strategic steps to stay alive.

He had disappeared shortly after the battle. He came forth now laden down with baggage. He had Yellow Hair's weapons and clothing and he had hastily packed his cassocks, adding his rosaries and lead medals as an afterthought.

He came lumbering down toward the Hudson's Bay barge, intent only upon placing his load therein.

A shout from the dismayed McGlincy stopped him.

Father Marc wheeled and called out, "I'll remember your orders, major. I'll see that they hang him, all right."

Slower-witted McGlincy could only gape and puff. He realized that if he ordered Father Marc to stay at the fort, the oddity of a Nor'Wester demanding a priest could not help but excite Motley's interest. If Motley for one moment suspected that this had all been a trick he would not rest until McGlincy swung.

A volley, a cannon shot—these flashed through McGlincy's mind. But he had already seen Motley escape unscathed from a melting volley and he could not risk it again as Motley's boat was ready to depart.

McGlincy did have one brilliant thought. "Mr. Motley! Hold for a minute! Don't you want the evidence?"

Motley, in the rush, had thought he had all the evidence needed to hang fifty such renegades, but on sober consideration he knew he could not make a wigged and robed court feel his own rage and certainty.

The clerk busily scribbled a few lines and half a dozen men, including McGlincy and Luberly, made their mark. Luberly whispered something in McGlincy's ear and then, in company with one of Motley's men, went to search Yellow Hair's room.

McGlincy knew what they would find. He had put them there himself.

The Orkneyman returned with four scalps—three blond and one black and all of them dark with dried blood.

Motley partially forgot the other bill when he beheld these trophies and, when he read the affidavit, he almost smiled.

Scalps would sway any court. The trader and the rivermen frowned upon scalps. They preferred the ears because, as often happened, the corpses wore earrings which made a fine show. But a scalp was something else again, neither so compact nor valuable as a nicely tanned ear.

The affidavit stated that these, the undersigned, had missed this renegade several days before the killing occurred; and he had been returned to the fort by Major Alexander McGlincy, Esq. (his signature was an X and the name had been written by the clerk) in a travel-worn condition; and that this renegade had been drunk and had shown the scalps as proof.

Motley kicked at the singed and slashed body in the bottom of the barge and in the hoarse tones which, for Motley, meant great glee, said, "This'll swing the fiend. No court in the world could deny his guilt. It was worth it!"

With his death assured on the gallows in spite of anything the priest could say, Yellow Hair was borne down the Saskatchewan toward Hudson's Bay.

McGlincy watched the barge slip out of sight. He was very satisfied. He had taken, in furs, one hundred and ninety-five packs at forty pounds a pack. In an I.O.U. he had another sizable sum. In all it amounted to ten thousand, five hundred and fifty-five pounds, or something like fifty thousand dollars.

And all clear profit, too.

Yellow Hair was the only man who would pay more than he could afford as no man can rightly stand to lose his life no matter the stakes, the honor, the reputation or the more common pay in coin.

Yes, everybody was pleased except Father Marc and the "renegade."

CHAPTER 16

GRAPEVINE

In cutting, trimming, drying, smoking and sacking the chronicle of Yellow Hair for posterity's digestion, it is necessary, at the risk of being repetitious, to hastily glance at the events that had hurled him toward York Factory on the mouth of the Nelson River in Hudson's Bay.

Before he had actively contacted his own people, whites, he had been a Pikuni warrior of great promise in spite of his restless and impatient temperament. Coolness in war would have come later if any hostile warrior or tribe had ever succeeded in beating him—which, it is fair to say, was not probable.

He had gained his first impression of his own people under the most trying conditions after Captain Lewis (in self-defense, of course) had caused one Pikuni to be stabbed and had expertly and cleverly brought down another with a rifle.

But with naive reasoning that must be greatly regretted, he supposed that whites, like Indians, had their good people and bad people and were, after all, human with natural human frailties.

When he had received discourteous conduct from the Nor'Westers, he was even then remarkably tolerant

L. RON HUBBARD

about it. But when they treacherously misused his parole
and cast aspersions on his word, he had begun to suspect
that the frontier of the whites was not all it was painted
to be.

At no time did he have to strain his imagination to
see these points. He had recourse to his own eyesight
and hearing. He did not have to stretch his opinions and
twist his facts. They were right there before him.

The gallant rider of the plains, he realized with a start,
was a knight and gentleman. And the whites who had
come out to these far-flung posts, who had bludgeoned
their way into a wilderness which they had neither
rented nor bought nor asked permission to use, were
not, after first glance, brothers to the "red man" as
everyone in the tribes had at first naturally supposed.

Because he had honor, cleanliness and a strict code,
the plains rider—whose skin was only a sixteenth of a
shade deeper than the faces of the frontier interlopers—naturally measured matters up according to his
own standards.

King Arthur was too good himself to see the vice in
the knights about him. The Indian—at the very first—
thought whites who came to them with mealy-mouthed
promises were as honorable as themselves. It took some
little time and a great deal of activity on the part of the
white vanguard to change that high opinion.

The trader and hunter, in his turn, following out the
pattern of thought expressed in a passage about
McGlincy, used his own measure of honor for the Indian
that he used for his own companions.

And thus we find Alexander Henry, that great
Nor'Wester captain, who was at the moment in Pembina, farther south, mocking every single instance of

Indian gallantry which came under his lofty and lordly notice. His opinions have, unfortunately, spread far and have lodged in the minds of people who should know less about Henry's opinion of the Indians than Henry himself.

This is mentioned because Alexander Henry, the stalwart leader of the Nor'Westers, produced a record. Unlike most traders, he could write and, when he was bored, he bored his readers as well and as constantly as possible. His "Ethnography of Fort Vermilion" was for many years the bible of Indian lore. The alcoholic remains of his findings still invade texts everywhere, while Henry himself sleeps forgotten in a remarkably pickled condition somewhere in North America.

A bestial drunkard, a sot without decency or compunction, Henry passed enduring judgment upon the late American Indian. A trick of writing too well known for much enlargement here is to make most of your characters so dull your comedian appears uproariously funny. By contrast even murder can be made noble. Henry was an unclean, lustful brute, but to make himself a hero in the Indian country, he carefully painted the Indian as worse than himself.

Only great research will reveal the true perspective of a people too hacked-down, thinned-out, mauled and maligned to leave a written record.

And in the face of all this, is there little wonder that Yellow Hair lost faith?

And in view of the way in which he was shipped like so much worthless rabbit fur to York Factory, is it any wonder that he suddenly conceived a deep and enduring hatred for his own race?

He was trained to be a gentleman and an Indian, and

somehow he could never bring himself to stomach the ways of the trader.

Judged by this perspective, it is hoped that Yellow Hair's subsequent actions and the reputation he has undeservedly left in trading annals will be carefully weighed accordingly. This is no attempt whatever to whitewash him and hold him up as a saint. God knows he was not. It is only the harsh record of actuality.

It is indicative of the trader's anxiety to believe the Indian worse than himself to notice how quickly the tale of Yellow Hair's "murderous debauch" spread through the country. From the Rockies to Quebec, from Hudson's Bay to St. Louis, men related the story, added their bit to it with wide, serious eyes, believed everything they heard about it, and importantly saw to it that the story rolled onward.

Every man on the North American continent connected with the fur business or the less-delicate business of stealing Indian land, knew the story by midsummer in various degrees of awfulness.

They not only knew what Yellow Hair looked like, they knew what he ate (wolf blood, some said), what he wore (nothing), how many wives he had (fourteen they said in Kentucky, but Canada held it down to eight), how he did his killing (knives in the back, from ambush, at night, without warning), and how many men he had killed in his career (somewhere between 231 and the actual number at the fort, five).

There was no little glory in knowing this story. And to gain that glory, as they always have, men made up what they did not know as long as they were sure they wouldn't be called a liar. And Yellow Hair's "heinous crimes" were already too well known to bar anything.

FREE

Send in this card and with any order you will receive a FREE POSTER while supplies last. No order required for this special offer! Mail in your card today!
❏ Please send me a FREE poster!
❏ Please send me information about other books by L. Ron Hubbard.

ORDERS SHIPPED WITHIN 24 HRS OF RECEIPT

___ *L. Ron Hubbard Presents Writers of the Future* volumes: (paperbacks)

❏ vol I $7.99	❏ vol II $7.99	❏ vol III $7.99
❏ vol IV $7.99	❏ vol V $7.99	❏ vol VI $7.99
❏ vol VII $7.99	❏ vol VIII $7.99	❏ vol IX $7.99
❏ vol X $7.99	❏ vol XI $7.99	❏ vol XII $7.99
❏ vol XIII $7.99	❏ vol XIV $7.99	❏ vol XV $7.99
❏ vol XVI $7.99	❏ vol XVII $7.99	❏ vol XVIII $7.99
❏ vol XIX $7.99	❏ vol XX $7.99	

___ *L. Ron Hubbard Presents the Best of Writers of the Future:*
(trade paperback) $14.95   _____

OTHER BOOKS BY L. RON HUBBARD

___ *Master Storyteller: An Illustrated Tour of the Fiction of L. Ron Hubbard*
hardcover coffee table book $49.95
___ *The Kingslayer* audiobook CD $25.00 ___ cassette $20.00 ___
___ *To the Stars* hardcover $24.95 ___ music $19.00 ___ audio $25.00 ___

Mission Earth® series (10 volumes paperback) $7.99 ea_____

___ vol 1 *The Invaders Plan*	___ vol 6 *Death Quest*
___ vol 2 *Black Genesis*	___ vol 7 *Voyage of Vengeance*
___ vol 3 *The Enemy Within*	___ vol 8 *Disaster*
___ vol 4 *An Alien Affair*	___ vol 9 *Villainy Victorious*
___ vol 5 *Fortune of Fear*	___ vol 10 *The Doomed Planet*

All ten volumes	$79.90	_____
Mission Earth hardcover	$22.95 each	_____
Mission Earth audio	$18.00 each	_____
specify volumes:_____		
All ten volumes hardcover	$229.50	_____
All ten volumes audio	$180.00	_____

___ *Battlefield Earth®* paperback $7.99___ hardcover $29.95___ audio $29.95___
___ *Final Blackout* paperback $6.99_____ Audio $15.95 _____
___ *Fear* paperback $7.99_____ Audio $15.95 _____

SHIPPING RATES US: $2.00 for one book. Add an additional **TAX*:**   _____
$.50 per book when ordering more than one.

SHIPPING RATES CANADA: $3.50 for one book. Add an **SHIPPING:** _____
additional $2.00 per book when ordering more than one. **TOTAL:**   _____

CHECK AS APPLICABLE:
❏ Check/Money Order enclosed. (Please use an envelope.)
❏ American Express ❏ Visa ❏ MasterCard ❏ Discover
★ California residents add 8.25% sales tax.

Card#:_____

Exp. Date:_____Signature:_____

Credit Card Billing Address Zip Code:_____

NAME:_____

ADDRESS:_____

CITY:_____ STATE:_____ ZIP:_____

PHONE#:_____ EMAIL:_____

Call toll free: 1-877-8GALAXY or visit www.galaxypress.com

BUSINESS REPLY MAIL
FIRST-CLASS MAIL   PERMIT NO. 75738   LOS ANGELES, CA

POSTAGE WILL BE PAID BY ADDRESSEE

GALAXY PRESS
7051 HOLLYWOOD BLVD
HOLLYWOOD CA 90028-9771

Thus, with safety assured in their reputations and with only glory to gain by addition, the mathematics of the story went toward infinity like a progressive equation in calculus.

The average mean of these lies added up to the "indisputable" facts that Yellow Hair was a half-breed; that he had scarlet paint on his face and wore his scalp tied with twisted matches which he set on fire as he went into battle to give himself an awful aspect; that he rode a stallion twenty-five hands high which knew how to kill with its hoofs; that he had assembled a band numbering about eighty; that he made incessant raids on the fur posts, butchering women and children with great glee, taking particular joy in dissecting babies (there were two white women and one child in the Indian country at this time); that he hung up traders and threw tomahawks at them to cut them into small pieces before death; that he had attacked one *bateau* and had kept the men alive through six days of torture with fire; that he always torched a post and laughed to see the poor white devils burn to death and partook of their roasted flesh afterwards; that single-handed he had kept an entire post at bay and had annihilated every man in it by himself to make good his escape; that, finally, the British army had succeeded in capturing him after an eight-day battle.

The object of these "facts" was certainly in no condition to deny them. Without medical attention (Father Marc's attempts had been forbidden) and without decent food, lying for the better part of the time on the soaking and sloppy footboards of Mackinaw barges, he was relentlessly transported to York Factory on Hudson's Bay. There he was dumped into an outhouse and denied clothing or blankets. Glowering guards were posted over him with orders to shoot to kill if he so much as spoke a single word.

Vengefully the governor and his staffs of statesmanship decided how they could get their money's worth out of, as they called him, "that inhuman fiend."

CHAPTER 17

YORK FACTORY

Father Marc Lettau remained on Hudson's Bay until early fall trying in vain to bring about a fair trial for Yellow Hair. But at last it became known to him that his presence at York Factory was embarrassing to the H.B.C. and that great relief would ensue upon his departure.

He realized that he was hindering Yellow Hair rather than helping because he was not allowed to see or communicate with him in any way.

The injustice of this was heightened by the geography which existed at the time and, indeed, continues to exist.

York Factory was very small when one came to contemplate the wilderness behind, above and below it. The place consisted of a big, severe house that was lead-roofed and had limestone walls. This red-painted edifice was the heart of the place. Above were mounted five cannon which commanded the bay and the woods. About it were grouped four bastions containing the powder, provision, garrison and trading facilities. Surrounding all this was a sturdy and high palisade. Around that was a deep trench and outside of the trench was another high wall.

This, considering the immensity of the Old Northwest, was very small space in which to forbid two men to see each other. The whole factory had the deadly aspect of a penitentiary as it only had two gates that were well guarded and studded with big spikes.

Just why this place was so opposingly built will forever remain a mystery because, in the two wars with France and during other raids, York Factory gained a very sorry record of swift surrender. In spite of the five cannon on the roof and the twelve cannon on the bastions, the double palisades, the trench, the signal code of beacons on the treacherous river mouth and all the rest of that elaborate paraphernalia of defense, York Factory opened its arms to any attacker like a true soldier's sweetheart.

It was something like eight hundred miles from the fort where Yellow Hair had committed the crime of defending himself. It was about a thousand miles north of the Nor'Westers' stronghold at Fort William on Lake Superior and, outside of the occasional contact with Henley House and some other immediate posts, it was as isolated as an agitator in exile.

Out from it ran two great highways—both very wet. One was Hudson's Bay and the Hudson Strait whence came the ships from England. The other was the Nelson River which took the fur brigades westward, southward and all over the map of Canada.

Thus it was that Father Marc was very lonely and quite as isolated in the fort as the fort itself.

He petitioned the governor for one last interview and was granted it in the officers' messroom.

The place had a huge iron hearth and beds built into

the wall. It was not a very cheerful place and the governor, who sat at an oval table, only heightened the atmosphere of chill.

Father Marc kept his feet. He saluted the governor with some carefully chosen Latin—which he knew the austere gentleman did not understand—and proceeded swiftly to business.

"Your Excellency," said the Mighty Monk, "I must ask how long you intend to keep my friend without trial. Your ships have long ago sailed for England without him and you must intend to pass judgment upon him here. I am afraid that this unwonted delay is occasioned by my presence."

The governor took some snuff and sneezed, "You ask audience to criticize our justice? God's blood, priest, that's the true brass of a Nor'Wester."

"I must remind you, Your Excellency, that priests have no politics other than the dictates of God and the saints—and as I have never seen any saints among either the H.B.C.s or the Nor'Westers, and probably never will, you must accept my presence as wholly impartial."

"No saints, eh? God blind me, but you're very bold, priest."

"Bold, how so? You happen to be an emperor of a domain three times the size of Europe, but since we have somewhat disproved the divine right of kings, I cannot accept your belief that your power of life and death over your men can be made to extend to all peoples of the continent. You must know by now that this youth you have penned up is, by rights, a subject of the United States of America, a member of a powerful and warlike tribe and a gentleman in his own right by birth which—begging Your Excellency's pardon—can hardly be matched by any member of the Nor'Westers or Hudson's Bay Company either."

"If you were not a priest—"

"You would hang, draw and quarter me without burial, eh? But I am a priest and I have already laid before you the true facts of this crime."

"I have scalps, affidavits, testimony by Motley—By the devil, priest, I'm not likely to take your word against that of my own men."

"You're taking the word of the Nor'Westers."

"Damned if I am."

"Damned anyway, Your Excellency. You can hold despotic sway over the luckless fools who quitted England to come under your tyrannical rule, but this issues you no license—"

"The Charter states—"

Marc rumbled out a laugh. "The Charter? Signed by a king more than a century dead? You still cling to the powers written on that scrap of parchment which expired one hundred years ago? You still claim your right to punish, expel, and even hang all trespassers on your poaching grounds? St. Anne save me, Your Excellency, but you English are stubborn fools. Never mind, I come to demand immediate trial before the prisoner dies of want and exposure. For months he has shivered and starved—"

"Serves the murderer right! He cost us dear, priest, and we'll charge off his suffering as part of his punishment."

"Then it is intentional!"

"Ah—er—well, now. We're civilized, of course. But

no trial, priest. You are wasting my valuable time with this nonsense. In fact, it just now comes to me that there is an Indian canoe tied on the river. The supply officer will issue you provisions."

"With winter almost here?"

"Easy trip. Not a thousand miles to Fort William. You can make it in a month or two or three. I'll give you passports to our posts and you can draw on them for food."

"Worthy of the English," said Father Marc with an amused grin. "You fear my testimony will make your vengeance less complete and you ship me off to get me out of the way and to hope that alternate freezes and thaws will prevent my ever arriving at Fort William. Ah, well, Your Excellency, it is most revealing. I never would have thought it of you. 'Lords of the Outer Marches,' eh? Let's hope you know a trick or two about walking on coals in the hereafter."

With a roar of laughter Father Marc quitted the room and left the shaken governor sitting fatly in his chair, wondering fitfully about the soul he had forgotten these many years.

But his determination was not at all shaken by Marc's reproaches. He was so anxious to proceed that he personally upbraided the supply officer and the brigade leaders to make them aid the monk's departure in every possible way.

Father Marc left the next day in a gloomy, soggy rain, his big muscles bulging as he thrust the prow of his light canoe up the Nelson River toward Lake Winnipeg.

His baggage was identical with that he had taken from Fort Chesterfield and included Yellow Hair's war sack, clothing kit and weapons. Marc knew that, if he left these things at York Factory they would only be appropriated by H.B.C. and Yellow Hair would be allowed to have none of them and, furthermore, Father Marc needed them himself.

He was very sad because he was convinced that he would never see Yellow Hair again.

CHAPTER 18

THE FRIENDLY ELEMENTS

This same rain, falling as it did from lowering gray clouds upon the outhouse in which he was confined, set Yellow Hair to pacing uneasily across the six feet of mud allowed him.

The roof was open in many places and dreary streams dropped through to form spreading puddles in the dirt. The muck was so soft that the tattered fragments of his moccasins were soon caked with the mire.

There was not one dry place in which he could lie down and, as evening came, the fluidity of the mud increased until even walking was rendered impossible.

Miserable and cold, he thought hungrily about White Fox's tall lodge seventy days' hard travel to the southwest. He remembered how the fire in the center sputtered and flared when rain fell through the small smoke hole. He wistfully recalled the softness of warm dry robes and easy willow beds and the feeling of happiness and security that came from the sizzle of frying steaks mingling with the sweet aroma of Indian tobacco.

The thought of a bounteous supply of food almost unnerved him. His stomach felt raw with emptiness and for the long time it had been that way he had never been able to get used to it. There had never come a numb period because the sparse and filthy food he was offered was just enough to maintain the craving.

During the day he had seen a dog sniffing about the yard. Through a crack he had watched the beast for more than two hours.

Once he had heard of men eating dogs and the thought had been very distasteful to him then. But now he remembered how he had watched the beast with intent and eager eyes. He had not wondered how the raw flesh would taste, he had only had a recurring mad thought that there, within ten paces of him, was the wherewithal to satisfy the despotic demands of his hunger. He had wanted to reach out and throttle the animal with his bare hands and bolt down the still warm flesh until he could eat no longer.

More than once he had been tempted to chew the ragged buckskin of his sorry hunting shirt. On one occasion he had gnawed at the grimy fringe. But there was no food there.

Hunger is a demand that swallows up all other thoughts. He had no worry about his immediate fate. He only knew, sleeping and awake, that he had to have food.

Tonight, chilled by the drizzle that flooded the place, starved and weak and gaunt, so weary that he finally laid out full length in the muck, he could not get his mind focused for long on any thought but food. He would start out to think about rain, doggedly striving to keep on thinking about it, but his thoughts would treacherously slip into the memory that this rain would swell the streams and that when the streams flooded, buffalo which tried to swim them would often drown, and the visualizing of the brown bodies brought the fantasy of broiling meat agonizingly upon him.

He would start out again with determination. He would consider escape. He would remember the guns of the ever-pacing guards outside, and guns meant the wherewithal to kill game and game again meant food.

Striving to escape that torture anew he would instantly clamp on Father Marc as thought material, but into his head came the vision of Father Marc sitting at a rough table carving a slab of venison.

Writhing, he would make a great effort to choose a new line of thought, cursing his imagination which insisted on running whether he wanted it to or not, craving sleep to still it.

He thought about Bright Star and wondered if she knew where he was and if she still waited for him. He achieved some success in this, which was a tribute to the love he bore the slender, graceful girl. He had a vision of himself in a big lodge with robes stacked all about him. He thought of what he would say to Bright Star and how she would answer him.

"Give me my pipe, beautiful one," he would say.

"Here it is, my lord, packed and fired for you. Do you wish me to send Magpie to invite White Fox and Bear Claws in for the evening?"

"No. I like to sit here and smoke and watch you. I could do nothing all the rest of my life but look at you."

"Ah, my great warrior husband, but if you did that how would we gain our food? If you did not hunt . . . ?"

Instantly the pleasant hallucination was shattered. He could see a cooking pot simmering over the coals and smell the racking odor of the boiling meat. He writhed and turned over, shivering as he let his left shoulder sink into the clammy muck.

He concentrated hard and brought the pretty vision back.

"Did you think I would never return?" he heard himself say.

"I knew you would come back to me. I waited and though the time was long it is nothing now that you are here. They urged me to take Long Bow for a husband but I would not hear them. He had robes and horses and he is handsome—"

"Handsome? Long Bow handsome? When he drinks from a stream he has to close his eyes."

She laughed at that and came across the lodge to sit down beside him and lay her head peacefully upon his knees. Her hair was soft as he stroked it, sweet as it caressed his face.

"You will never leave me again, my warrior."

"Never. I promise it on the sacred Beaver Roll. I cry out so loudly that the Above Ones will stop and listen and hold me to my promise. How could I ever leave you? When I went away I thought I would return by the Falling Leaf Moon but the whites detained me and sent me up a long river and held me within a miserable lodge without sufficient *food*."

There it was again, knifing through him like chilly steel. He turned over and sat up, shaking with cold. Presently he sank down again and artfully resumed his pleasant dream.

"There is a dance tonight," he said, "and White Fox and I are going to act out the battle of the white fort. We will make it very funny. Antelope has gotten some white clay from the river and some red paint and three Lone-Fighters have volunteered to act as the whites."

"I know," said Bright Star, "I have already found

some clothes tattered enough for you. And I have mixed some black paint. You don't think it will rain tonight?"

"No, it won't rain," said Yellow Hair.

"But if it did even a little bit it would spoil the show."

"A little bit wouldn't hurt."

"But wouldn't it ruin your guns so that you could not fire powder charges?"

He sat up and sprang to his feet and stood there quivering, his sunken eyes on fire with hope.

Although the thought, because he had made it all up himself, had been wholly his own, it seemed a wonderful omen because, in fancy, it had come from the lips of Bright Star.

She was so real to him in that instant that he was certain she stood beside him.

Hoarsely, he whispered, "I'll come back to you. Wait a little longer. I'll come back! I swear it."

The drizzle which fell inside was nothing compared to that which beat down out-of-doors. He pressed his face to the wall and watchfully searched the grounds.

His two sentries were there, pacing, a lantern on the ground at the point where they met. The flickering tongue of the candle flame, harassed by wind and water, showed up only their boots.

But by looking closely as they turned and went away from each other, Yellow Hair could see how they carried their weapons: on their shoulders, locks up, uncovered.

It was neither required nor wanted that these vassals should use their brains. Their orders were brief—to pace around the outhouse, carrying weapons. Until they heard more than that—and they had not for some months—they would continue to do so fair weather or blizzard. They met at the lantern, exchanged a few remarks, about-faced and walked away from each other, met behind the outhouse, finished the sentence they might have started, about-faced and went back to the lantern their separate ways.

"Hi wager 'e don't myke it."

Meeting behind the house, the other one said, "Hi bet the bloke does. 'E's brawny and . . ."

Presently, behind the house, he concluded, ". . . 'e's got a lot of beef to tide him over."

At the lantern the other said, "Hi think 'e'll need more'n 'is own fat, Roger. Hit's . . ."

Behind the house, ". . . more'n a thousand bitter miles to Fort Will'm. 'Ow much?"

At the lantern. "Hi got five shillin's says yes."

Behind the house. "Not even Gawd'll give that barmy priest a 'and. Five shillin's says 'e won't."

At the lantern, "Hit's a bet and Hi'll love drinkin' hit up."

This had been going on for so many weary days, this constant, interrupted argument, that until now Yellow Hair had paid little heed to it. Now he was shocked by the intelligence it gave him and, by listening impatiently for two hours more, he managed to understand that Father Marc had that day left for Fort William.

First there had been Bright Star's voice.

And now the example of Father Marc.

He could not fail in this!

Weak and gaunt as he was, excitement made him forget the cold and gave him fitful strength.

He reached up to a beam and swung his length over it. He jabbed tentative fingers at the leaking roof and found the shingles to be as rotten as any trading policy.

Eagerly he thrust his hand through and pushed sidewise, widening the gap. He balanced himself on the beam and thrust his head out into the dripping night.

A shingle came loose and very easily slid down the slope.

Yellow Hair's heart stopped beating until it hit the ground.

The mud softened the noise but it had been heard.

"Roger! Something dropped!"

"Coming!"

The guards looked carefully over the ground, bending low beside the lantern. They found the shingle.

But Yellow Hair had no desire to wait for their comment upon it. He was all the way out through the rickety roof and had gripped the soggy ridge-pole, lowering himself on the other side and down.

Quietly he dropped to the wet earth and stabbed about in the blackness trying to locate the inner palisade.

He knew then, with swift orientation, that his back was toward the main building and that he would have to circle the shack to get to the palisades.

Within a few seconds it would leak into the English skulls of Roger and his mate that they had better look inside the outhouse. It was therefore asking quite a bit of Yellow Hair that he had to map his whole strategy for the next hour in the same length of time that it would take the guards to realize that he was gone.

But Yellow Hair had not trained on beer and cold mutton pie and nobody had ever tried to convince him that the less a soldier thinks the better the soldier.

When every instinct told him to run, he made himself creep. He slid around the edge of the house like a greased shadow and saw Roger gripping the shingle, his mate holding the lantern and both of them holding their guns and staring at the door before them.

Just why great generals and strategists like the York governor and Napoleon Bonaparte give their sentries lanterns to carry has always been something of a mystery to Cree scouts. It was a startling blunder to Yellow Hair and he took advantage of it on the instant.

A man staring into a fire is blind to the outer darkness. A sentry carrying a lantern limits his view to about ten circular feet of ground and all else is covered by a black wall that shuts down abruptly at the yellow border.

Yellow Hair stepped out of his cover and sprinted so silently that his feet scarcely touched the ground. He was in full view of the sentries and one of them was staring right at him, but past the flicker in the lantern.

"M'ybe the blighter 'as hescaped," said the intrepid Roger, his blinded eyes fixed in Yellow Hair's direction.

"Gawblin'me!" croaked his mate. "M'ybe we better look in and stir 'im up, wot?"

"Hit's a go. Three bob he an't there!"

"No bet, Roger. Hopen the door."

Yellow Hair reached the gate which opened toward the river, slid around behind a sentry box and ran questing fingers up the nail-studded face. The top was fifteen feet high, about nine feet over his head and six feet higher than he could ever hope to reach without help.

He attempted to get his moccasins to grip on the nails but while the rain had done him one good turn it now decided that it had overreached itself and promptly did him a bad one. The water-greased planks offered no footholds or handholds.

He was pressing himself against it, bludgeoning his

brain to give him a way out, when the alarm was sounded.

"Sergeant of the guard! He's gone! Turn out! Turn out, the renegade's gone!"

Even a deaf person could have heard that shout all the way to Albany.

A yell came from the garrison's bastion. Curses ripped from the officers' mess. The sentry leaped awake in his box and grabbed up his rifle—in which the priming, being covered, was dry.

This man was not blinded by any lantern and he leaped forward so suddenly toward the gate that he grazed Yellow Hair in passing.

Acting with remarkable understanding, the sentry lashed out with his hand and touched the torn buckskin and knew what he had.

A seasoned campaigner on many far-flung fronts, this soldier knew better than to advance. He leaped back to raise his rifle.

Yellow Hair snatched at the muzzle. It exploded. The tongue of red sparks lanced over his head.

Yellow Hair shoved hard and then quickly gave the barrel a twist and a pull. It came free.

The guard reacted again with amazing speed. He knew that the butt would hammer down the instant he loosed it. He leaped backwards, spun about and raced toward the bastion braying the alarm.

Lanterns danced out of the doorways, catching up the polished steel of an officer's saber.

Yellow Hair saw them coming. He cast a despairing glance at the top of the gate and then gripped the muzzle like a club, ready to go down like a warrior should—fighting.

That there was something odd about the long-barreled weapon came to him on the instant. As a military rifle it had a sling swung from the underside.

The lanterns were sweeping in upon him. Brazenly he used their swiftly approaching light to see what he was doing. His fingers found a metal buckle. He undid it from the muzzle end and then cast the sling loose. The buckle itself caught in the stock swivel, giving, with the leather, a reach of about seven and a half feet.

He knotted the strap, stepped away from the gate and made an upward cast toward the spike-trimmed top.

"There he goes!"

"Shoot him!"

"'E's armed!"

"Knock him down!"

The knot caught between two spikes and held. Yellow Hair braced his feet against the nail studs, gripped the muzzle and, leaning far out, walked like a fly up the gate.

He snatched at the spikes on top, dangled for an instant and hoisted himself up halfway.

Two rifles blasted at him from below.

A pistol roared.

His right arm was knocked forward and he slipped back on the inside, hanging by his left hand.

The rain changed its fickle mind and helped him again. Three locks snapped futile sparks into drenched priming.

An officer leaped ahead waving his saber, bawling a command to follow, looking and feeling just as heroic as a general leading a thrilling charge straight into the slavering fangs of the enemy. The officer paused an instant, unable to resist the pose of pausing to wave the charge signal, dramatically pointing to the wounded, starved, scarecrow who hung helplessly on the gate.

The saber swished. Yellow Hair saw it coming and made a pendulum out of himself. Steel clanged on the soft wood and bit deep, not an inch away from severing his leg at the thigh.

But Yellow Hair was not so far gone that he forgot his ritual of battle.

"Hyai, you redcoats! Thanks!"

He stepped on the blunt side of the imbedded saber before the officer could wrench it free and, with that as a boost, went straight up and over the spikes and fell free into the blackness on the other side.

He hit as limp as possible but the fall made his bones rattle and he had no fat for padding. But the mud was soft and the approach was an incline and he took the force out of the impact in a slide.

With great foresight, since the French had so easily taken them many decades before, York Factory kept its gates bolted and double-locked.

And with at least fifteen men clawing at the bars all at once, not one of them succeeded in taking them down.

Yellow Hair did not wait to find out what would happen. He remembered where the landing was although he had only seen it once. Skidding through the muck, he plunged down the bank and almost into the stream.

He tripped over an inverted canoe and scrambled about it for the paddles. These, he soon learned, were in a small boathouse close by.

Providentially he located the door in a hurry and fumbled through the blackness until he encountered the stacked oars.

A slight hysteria had him in its grip and he laughed

jerkily at a thought which occurred to him.

His right arm, he discovered, was very much in his way and so he tucked it into his belt and used his left to gather up all the sweeps.

With these as a battering ram he opened the door on the river side and swiftly consigned every oar in the place to the Nelson and, subsequently, the wide reaches of Hudson's Bay.

He took two paddles he had salvaged and reached the canoe just as the fort gates crashed open. The swinging lanterns showed up a host of running legs. The murmur of the stream was swallowed up in the profane orders which laid out the attack.

Yellow Hair stuck the bow into the stream, gave a running shove on the stern, went waist-deep into the water and then floundered into the bottom of the frail and skittering craft.

"He's got a boat! Man the barges!"

"Get into that water! Drown him if you can't bring him back!"

"Where the hell has he gone?"

"There he is! Fire!"

Again locks snapped without result and men bellowed curses at the rain.

For the moment Yellow Hair felt safe enough as far as the fort was concerned. But the current of the Nelson River was calmly carrying him out to Hudson's Bay—on which many a luckless H.B.C. trapper had sacrificed his life for the winter overcoat of a beaver.

There were two difficulties.

It is almost impossible to paddle with only one hand.

And no Pikuni-bred gentleman ever saw any necessity for using water while there were horses to ride. In fact the Pikunis went so far as to scorn the eating of water-fowl and fish and believed—along with the Greeks, English sailors, and famous explorers—that there was such a thing as an underwater people, governed by a sort of Neptune who took the form of the beaver.

Yellow Hair had had some slight experience on the river but as H.B.C. used clumsy barges with oars instead of canoes and as, even then, Yellow Hair had been lying in the bottom of said barge, his experience was very limited.

But it attests to his ready adaptability that the mechanics of his unusual problem should be so quickly met and defeated—in some measure.

He wedged one paddle, blade up, into the stern gun-wale and held it there with his left leg. He laid the other paddle in front of this improvised peg and shoved forward upon it after the fashion of the Norwegian —though Yellow Hair knew little and cared less about these hardy Nordics.

He made enough progress to overcome the current and advance a little, but the bow was very erratic and he found himself stabbing toward the right bank with great frequency.

The rain and cold sawed into the wound in his arm. His starvation-diminished strength was on the knife edge of breaking. He was without food, blankets or weapons and the weather was shifting from the chill of late fall into the horrible vigor of early northern winter. Indeed, even now, ice was coating thinly along the more gentle reaches of the stream.

Tenscore men had perished before him on this watery highway through the wilderness. That rough, hardy Nor'Wester, Frobisher, would be ordained to die of weakness and starvation making this same trip within the decade.

Yellow Hair knew that Father Marc's mighty strength could drive a canoe like an arrow through the water and yet, to live, he had to catch up with Father Marc who already had a half-day start.

The impossible was only improbable to Yellow Hair. He was one of those rare beings who never find out, this side of death, that there is such a thing as being whipped by men and destiny. Such ignorance is divine. His eyes were fixed upon an object so far in advance that he had only impatience for all the hurdles which intervened —which is probably as good a key as any to his restlessness.

He might be wounded, starved and hunted in an alien land.

But he only knew one thing. He had to catch up to Father Marc.

CHAPTER 19

McGlincy Departs

Father Marc and Yellow Hair were not the only two expeditions in motion at the moment.

Eight hundred miles southwest of York Factory, bobbing along on the undulating bosom of the Saskatchewan, were McGlincy's brigades.

Major Alexander McGlincy himself was in the largest canoe, and the sight of him was most inspiring.

He knew how to travel, did McGlincy. It was raining so hard that the voyageurs were soaked through, but did McGlincy get wet? The spray spattered along the gunwales and into the men's faces, but did McGlincy get spattered? It was gruelling work even though it was downstream, but did McGlincy spare the whisky to keep his spirits up?

No, he had a fine canopy just big enough to cover him—which was fairly large, at that—held up by four poles lashed to the gunwales. He had the cloth, which normally was used to keep the spray from swamping them over the bows, stretched between the first two of these poles. This was very useful as a sail, but the wind happened to be ahead—though McGlincy would not let a small thing like that stand in the way of his speed. The men simply paddled harder and that was that.

With ruffles and braid he made a very imposing figure, sitting there with a bottle clutched and balanced upon his knee, with the Union Jack behind him—too wet to float, however.

Now and then he would bellow encouragement at some voyageur, bidding him sing or perhaps plow the water with more briskness.

He appeared very comfortable, but he was not. The cares of statesmanship weighed upon him. It was not for nothing that he was setting forth so late in the year. It was not for nothing that he risked having to walk part of the way over frozen streams.

As there is a deep policy and much prudence behind the moves of every great emperor, it is only fair to delve into the tangled skeins of diplomacy which were drawing McGlincy away from Fort Chesterfield.

It began in the Pikuni camp on the Marias between one barbarian named Bear Claws and another blood-thirsty savage called White Fox.

A certain maiden named Bright Star had forlornly brought the tidings of Yellow Hair's supposed death a long time before this and the news had been received in horrified silence. In Yellow Hair's lodge there were no women or children to mourn for him. Only White Fox was there and he remained several days staring at his fire, thinking about the boy he had raised to the estate of a warrior and man, and contemplating the brutal destiny of death.

White Fox had once had sons and daughters and wives but that had been long, long ago and they were all waiting for him in the nebulous land of the Sand Hills, watching over his fortunes and perhaps, now and then, interceding for him with the Great Spirit.

With the coming of the whites on the Saskatchewan there had simultaneously arrived the first Scourge of the Red Death. This had swept the continent and had caused the death of at least fifty percent of the Indian population. It had wiped out whole villages, whole nations. Young men had stabbed themselves through the heart rather than face the horror of having their strong young bodies become pitted and emaciated. For three years afterwards empty lodges, with worn skins fluttering in the dismal wind, had stood abandoned on the plains. But there had been no furs found in them after the first few months. White scavengers had stripped the awful dead of their beaver pelts and had shipped the tainted pelts into the east without comment on their origin.

White Fox, having suffered so much before, was now trying to reconcile himself to the death of Yellow Hair, brooding over the unlucky advent of the traders.

Being savages and barbarians, the Pikunis were slightly puzzled by the fate of Yellow Hair, and as they were not endowed with the reasoning powers of civilized peoples they naturally suspected that the white fort had some connection with this catastrophe.

But with all this provocation, in spite of Bright Star's constant effort to stir them into attack against the fort, the elders restrained their thousand warriors, saying that there was no actual proof that the death could be laid at the fort gates and that a general attack would be both foolish and unnecessary.

Bright Star had asked a favor of her father's brother and it had been granted. Although much pressure was brought to bear upon her, she did not wish to immediately marry Long Bow. She finally achieved a reprieve for a whole year on the grounds that sorrow lay too heavily in her heart.

Only one result came instantly from the report that Yellow Hair was dead. Word was spread by courier and scout throughout the land that no white trader would be allowed to set foot in the Pikuni domain on the pain of death. This domain, it is right to note, extended from the North Saskatchewan River southward for six hundred miles to the Yellowstone River and from the Rocky Mountains eastward for an average distance of four hundred miles. The three tribes kept this region properly policed and governed and, mistakenly supposed that they had a deed of title to it by common consent of the other, bordering Indian nations who, in their turn, held like dominions.

It would have taken a man three and a half months of constant riding to have completely circumnavigated this territory.

Unluckily, the area contained fine beaver country and the broadcast order, which was made in the hope that it would keep traders from entering and killing Blackfeet, was handsomely disregarded.

The situation, then, was heightened by the act of two trappers named Potts and Colter that should be briefly noted. They invaded the Blackfoot country, laid their traps by night, caught many beaver and tried to escape with their loot, well knowing they were trespassers.

They were stopped on the Jefferson River by an expressly despatched party of warriors. When ordered to pull into shore the trappers obeyed. To prevent bloodshed the Pikunis demanded that they instantly surrender their guns.

Briefly, Colter snatched back the rifle belonging to

Potts and Potts instantly tried to shove off in his canoe. On order a warrior fired a cautious arrow to prevent Potts' departure. Potts raised his rifle and shot the warrior dead.

Colter was sportingly given a chance to run for his life and he killed a young brave and then escaped by hiding under brush in a river.

The provocation was not nearly sufficient, of course. The Pikunis had only lost half their tribe by smallpox brought by the whites and three warriors at the hands of trappers and Lewis. In return they had killed one man—Potts.

All this was rather heightened by Yellow Hair's supposed death and even the elders began to get worried and restless in the belief that these traders meant them no good.

And then, by grapevine, came the stories which were being told about Yellow Hair's atrocities and Bright Star eagerly clutched at the belief that she might have been wrong in her supposition that he was dead.

Yellow Hair had vanished out of Fort Chesterfield. This was the one clear fact that was debated. Posted scouts on the heights had been able to gain no trace of him about the fort and so, when the tribe went to trade in the fall (Falling Leaf Moon) White Fox and Bear Claws were directed to interrogate the white chief.

A saner and more more civilized people, such as those in Europe, would have killed half a million men by this time. But the Pikunis were only savages and although they knew they could wipe out every white within a thousand miles without half trying, they parleyed and debated and wanted to be sure.

White Fox and Bear Claws, dressed in clean elkskin

and their regalia for state occasions, somehow managed to get an audience with McGlincy.

White Fox, through a French-Canadian interpreter, inquired, "We have come for tidings of our little chief. Would the mighty white chief give us any news of Yellow Hair?"

McGlincy scowled, hiccupped, coughed and belched and heartily damned their impertinence and ordered them to be thrown out on the spot. No filthy savage was going to affront *his* dignity with such impertinence.

Bear Claws bore up and quietly said, "The white chief, whose dignity we salute and revere, must know something of Yellow Hair. Could we prevail upon him to give us the slightest tidings of his fate?"

McGlincy squirmed and was about to damn them heartily again and order up the guard when Luberly whispered that McGlincy had better glance through a loophole toward the bluffs.

McGlincy was much affronted by this suggestion but as Luberly seemed to be thoroughly scared, McGlincy complied.

What he saw made his blue nose turn to the color of rotten meat. A slight tremble came to his hand and he had to take six quick shots in succession to steady his nerves.

Along the top of the bluff he had seen something which he would not readily forget.

Seven hundred and fifty warriors were quietly sitting their mounts along the crest. Their coupsticks waved gently in the wind. Their lances were couched. The fringe of their buckskin shirts shivered when their mounts moved restively. Outlined against the blue sky, the well-trained and splendidly-equipped cavalry looked

162

like so many bronze and pedestaled statues.

Of the same stock as Timur the Limper's chagateurs (who conquered all Asia except Cathay), carrying the same weapons as Bayazid the Thunderer (who made all Europe tremble), trained in the same tactics as their ancestors who made up the spearhead of Genghis Khan's mighty host, these seven hundred and fifty troopers presented a picture that would have made (and indeed did make) many a general turn slightly sallow with apprehension.

McGlincy was instantly the heart and soul of courtesy. A critical observer would have attributed this to wretched terror but it was, of course, only the policy and quick-wittedness to be found in all truly great men.

"He is gone to the country of the whites," groveled McGlincy. "Tell them quick. He's all right and he went east."

White Fox, repressing a cynical grin, replied, "When will he return?"

"Oh . . . aw . . . er . . . ah . . . Presently! Presently!"

"Then he is safe and well?" said Bear Claws.

"Damme, yes! Of course he is. Why only this week we had word from him that he was in fine condition, having the time of his life. He . . . uh . . . ulp . . . sent his very best regards to you . . . um . . . ah . . . gentlemen. Bless me if he didn't!"

White Fox and Bear Claws withdrew and when they were out of the fort Bear Claws signaled with his hand and the cavalry wheeled in good order and disappeared.

White Fox told Bright Star, "There is something bad in all this. The white chief was frightened into lying, but I believe that Yellow Hair must still be alive and that at least a portion of this story we have heard is true."

Bright Star eagerly seized upon this fragment of hope. "We'll build a medicine lodge and I shall make my vows. And the Above Ones will return him safe and tell him that he must come back before spring is over next year. He's alive, White Fox! I know he's alive!"

White Fox knew how deeply the girl felt about it and he tried to hope, for her sake, that Yellow Hair would return. But White Fox had known too much suffering to remain optimistic about anything. He realized that it would certainly fail to help matters if Running Elk's brother, Big Wolf, exerted his authority on this marriage matter.

But White Fox could say nothing. Running Elk's goods, wives and children had become Big Wolf's property and Running Elk's authority was now his brother's.

Long Bow was handsome and he had wealth and, in selecting a husband for a girl, the head of the house must of necessity exert much caution. Although this situation sometimes brought unhappiness to the girls, in the long run it worked out for the best.

Long Bow's brother was a good provider and had some goods and was very acceptable. This was important because, in the event of Long Bow's death, all his household would become the property of that brother and Big Wolf did not want Bright Star to become destitute and homeless if her husband died. Yellow Hair, by the same reasoning, was not a good selection because he had no kin.

No one, much less White Fox, would dare say a word to the head of the house in which Bright Star lived. Big Wolf had already been very reasonable to delay by granting a reprieve until spring.

White Fox, then, had to content himself with matters

of state, but for all his stoney face he was not insensible to the daily walks Bright Star took along the ridge. He knew she was watching the north, hoping to see a lone horseman appear on the plains.

The tribe laughed about the sudden departure of McGlincy because they were not schooled in the ways of diplomacy and strategy and naturally thought that McGlincy had left because he had been frightened away.

Perhaps, they reasoned, McGlincy had gone to hasten the return of Yellow Hair. McGlincy might possibly wish to restore the friendship between the tribe and the fort and thus prevent the burning and sacking of the place.

But White Fox did not laugh. In McGlincy he saw only evil and the more he pondered the strange occurrences, the more he became convinced that Yellow Hair had somehow fled the fort and McGlincy might be tracking him down and not running away.

If Yellow Hair happened to be on the river he would meet McGlincy.

White Fox shut his eyes tight and prayed fervently for the accuracy of Yellow Hair's rifle.

CHAPTER 20

THE CHIPMUNK

Yellow Hair had no thoughts to spare for McGlincy.

He hated the river because the current was striving relentlessly to carry him back to York Factory.

Already the English would have made oars and manned their barges. With the glee and questionable mercy of fox-hunters the English had been quick to take up the chase and their long sweeps were driving their boats upriver at a speed which curled white froth on the cannon-mounted bows.

At York Factory the governor had been worked up into puffing rage and sweating activity and the word was gone on the roar of the snow-laden wind that Hudson's Bay Company would pay, in cash or trade goods, the sum of fifty pounds—a half year's wages—for the presentation of Yellow Hair's scalp at the factory.

As a sort of apology for this barbaric cry, the governor added that the sum of seventy-five pounds would be paid for Yellow Hair's return alive.

The word, traveling mouth to mouth, post to post, river to river, did not take long to hit the Rockies and echo back. It was astonishing to note that the news went farther in one day than a brigade could travel in a month. But then, in the world's every wilderness there have been swift and wholly unaccountable communication systems so mysterious and complete that nothing short of mental telepathy could account for them.

In this case there were visible means of relaying the offer and the orders. Posts along the Nelson, the Saskatchewan, Lake Winnipeg and Lake of the Woods were very close together in one long network. Numerous hunters' cabins were between each pair of posts, and all hugged the river which was the grand highroad of travel.

Added to this was the presence of roving bands of Cree hunters who had, themselves, a complete communication system.

Before Yellow Hair was one day out of York Factory the word that he was on the river had leaped two hundred miles ahead of him and H.B.C. brigades all along the banks were on the alert to intercept him.

It has ever been a weary task to try to outguess and outlast the English. Such thoroughness is laudable and scarcely to be escaped by one man. The trap was open before him, ready to snap shut and the fox-hunters were shouting "Tally-ho" behind him.

Yellow Hair knew all this because he had more than once witnessed the speed of spreading news on the plains.

The problem had to be squarely met and Yellow Hair was never one to dally over a decision.

At noon, with everything washed out by the fall of snow that had changed places with the rain, Yellow Hair ran his canoe into the beach.

Deliberately he burned his bridge by rolling it over and knocking a hole in the bottom of it with a large rock. He thrust the sinking craft back into the stream and resolutely turned his face inland.

The forest was silent and gloomy, filled with thickets and windfalls and darkness. It was not much like the clean timber of the Rockies and it weighed in upon him.

He had been going for hours on nervous reaction and now that he felt himself momentarily safe he probed the wilderness for a hiding place where he could inspect and treat his wound and prepare weapons with which to kill much-needed game.

It was in this search that he started up a chipmunk.

The little, rust-colored bit of fur was much disturbed. It had been preparing for a long snooze in company with the Mrs. and it did not take very kindly to such intrusion.

Bristling with fear and ferocity it sprang up on a limb and started to swear in a jerky, high-pitched voice which left no question as to its meaning.

Yellow Hair, weary as he was, was so glad to hear something besides the roaring drone of silence that he looked up and managed a grin.

The chi-chi-chi-chi of the chipmunk rose to new heights and then abruptly ceased entirely.

It flirted its tail, spun about and raced along its sky-highway until it was out of sight.

Yellow Hair thought he had frightened it away and the gloom settled heavily over him again.

Abruptly, the chi-chi-chi-chi started up again some distance away.

Yellow Hair stiffened.

The chipmunk was barking at another intruder!

Without even a knife to protect himself and in a very sorry condition, Yellow Hair realized that he had to act.

Boldly he strode forward toward the sound, heart

drumming in his throat, knees buckling under him from weakness.

The chipmunk soared into falsetto profanity.

Yellow Hair parted the branches to face the target of its wrath.

CHAPTER 21

REUNION

For an instant Yellow Hair regretted the brash impulse that had caused him to head toward the intruder, but he knew that escape would be useless. If he could be located so easily after he had tried so hard to put off all pursuit, there was little chance of him getting across eight hundred miles of wilderness to the Pikuni nation.

Through the thick boughs he could see a pair of Crees. They were armed with trade rifles and wore three-point H.B.C. blankets and were quite obviously closely associated with the company. They were therefore in the search of the reward.

As quietly as Yellow Hair had approached, they had heard him. They stood now w.th their rifles ready, their dark eyes fixed upon Yellow Hair's haggard face.

For several seconds the two Crees neither moved nor spoke and then one turned and beckoned to someone Yellow Hair had not seen.

Twigs cracked and brush whipped and it appeared that a silver tip grizzly was on his way. But it was only Father Marc Lettau trying to squeeze his mighty bulk through the thickets.

Yellow Hair's face flared into an expression of joy and then, as suddenly, stiffened up a trifle.

"Hello," said Yellow Hair.

Father Marc's joy was not held in check by the presence of the two strange Crees. He lunged forward with a great laugh and jerked Yellow Hair toward him and almost suffocated the warrior.

The wound hurt like a hot poker but Yellow Hair showed no trace of it. He grinned and listened to Father Marc retailing his pleasure in a voice which reached half a mile.

Finally Father Marc became intelligible. "How did you escape?"

"Never mind that. How did you locate me?"

"Locate you? That was easy. You think a man on the river can hide? Last night I camped late and a few hours later I was awakened by these two Indians. They told me the news and I immediately hauled my canoe into the brush and backtracked. We've been watching the river for hours and when we saw you head into the bank we made our way to the place and tracked you—or rather, they did. I wouldn't be able to track a buffalo in a swamp. But good God, my boy, you're wounded and here I've been—"

He broke off, reached down and picked Yellow Hair up in his arms as though the boy had been a pigmy instead of a very tall man.

The two Crees broke the way for them and after a few minutes of floundering through the brush, they came to a camp pitched in the shelter of a large rock.

A third Cree was sitting there over the fire. He was an old man and he did not glance up at their approach. In silence he watched Father Marc bustle about getting medical supplies, boiling water, fumbling and fussing and puttering and talking all the while.

The two scouts drifted off presently at a sign from the

old one and Yellow Hair knew that they had been ordered to watch for the English. He could not understand their friendship in view of their weapons and H.B.C. blankets but he asked no questions. Indeed, he could not have made himself heard above the constant niagara of Father Marc's words.

At last Yellow Hair was bandaged and propped comfortably on blankets against the rock. He drank the brimstone brew Father Marc had made and, out of courtesy, pretended he liked it. The stuff did warm him.

"Now for our route," Father Marc was saying, bending over a square of bare earth with a stick and looking like a big, shaggy bear. "We can't go through to your country. There are too many forts and the Hudson's Bay men will be on the watch all winter. But we can strike straight south and get to Fort William without running into the H.B.C.s."

"I want to head west," said Yellow Hair.

"And get shot down on sight? No! I also have my neck to consider in this. I have to go to Fort William and make a full report of all this and clear myself and you, too. Old Simon MacIntosh will see how wrong McGlincy was. Old Simon will send you back to your country in a canoe in company with half a dozen brigades. Don't think all whites are bad, my boy."

"Oh, I don't!" said Yellow Hair, but with a smile.

"Then we head for Fort William. We can make it in two or three months overland now that it's freezing. The river will be solid in a few days and we'll have to abandon our canoe anyway."

"If you think I want to see the inside of Fort William's butter tub, you're a madman."

"But they won't do anything like that after I tell them

about you. By the saints, man, you can't thumb your nose at the H.B.C. posts like that. They'd pick you up and send you right back to York Factory."

"As long as I stay this far away from my own nation," said Yellow Hair, "I am in danger and in trouble."

"But you'll get back," pleaded Father Marc. "I promise you that they won't harm you at Fort William."

"I think it very foolish," said Yellow Hair. "I have no dislike for a good round fight, but when the odds mount up like they have, I begin to see some reason in the things White Fox has taught me. 'Never attack an enemy unless you have done everything possible to make your position good and his position bad.' "

"What do you mean by that?"

"What I said."

"You mean Fort Chesterfield . . ."

"I didn't say that."

"You mean you'll attack—See here, Yellow Hair, this has all been a big mistake. Don't let it sour you on all your own people."

"My people are the Pikunis."

"Oh, come now. There's a call you can't deny. If you see the whites, you won't think they're so bad."

"I've seen the whites and I'm now sitting altogether too close to white country."

Father Marc heaved a sigh which shook the ground around him for thirty feet. "Be reasonable, Yellow Hair."

"That has never been one of my virtues."

"But, by St. Joseph, my boy, down at Fort William they'll cover you with honor and glory for the runaround you gave the H.B.C.s."

"In Pikuni country I will get honor and glory for being smart enough to save my neck and come back from the whites alive."

"Do this for me," begged Father Marc, holding out his big hands. "Come to Fort William and return to your country with the brigades next summer."

"I'm not anyone to choose."

"But look! If we clear you of all guilt at Fort William, the H.B.C. will never bother you again. Otherwise you may visit death and war upon your own people."

Yellow Hair had not thought of that before. It troubled him now and he sat for a long time nursing the warm cup between his cold hands. At last, "You think it would be bad for me to go back and have everyone think I did all they say I did?"

"It would be horrible."

"That settles it. I go to Fort William and take the chance of getting killed. My people would never thank me for bringing them a war. I have no right to cause men to be killed on my account."

Because, out of habit, he had been talking partly sign with his hands, Yellow Hair's words had been slightly understood by the Cree.

He sat up straighter now, his fine old eyes looking closely at Yellow Hair. In sign he said, "If the Spotted Robes are your people—and I see that from your moccasins and the three lines on the toe—it would be wise for you to return. The whites swarm through this land, very mad that you have escaped."

Although his shoulder bothered him a little, Yellow Hair opened up his signs to make his meaning plain.

The Cree brooded upon this for some time and finally

signed, "You are right. The longer you can keep these English dog-faces out of your own nation the longer your people will be happy."

Yellow Hair's curiosity prompted him to ask, "Why have you tried to help me?" And, "Are your people not the servants of the English?"

To the last question the Cree gave an emphatic and angry "No." To the first he signed, "My people have heard them talk of you and we thought you were one of the western tribes. For many years your people and my people have been at peace. We have no interest in dog-face justice as we have suffered from it ourselves. Our people have been bought by a metal cooking pot, a three-point blanket and a few bad guns. But we can do nothing. We think we need these things and so we hunt beaver and skin them. Your people were once called slaves. No man has ever dared call my people slaves, but we are and you are not."

He went on for some time, but as the Cree and Yellow Hair rapidly found out that they were wholly understood to each other in signs, their hands came down in front of them, closer and closer to their chests and the graceful movements became smaller and smaller in scope, more and more abbreviated until Father Marc could gather not one wave of it.

Feeling left out, Father Marc laid out Yellow Hair's baggage and weapons which instantly put a stop to the conversation.

Yellow Hair was very glad to see them as he had thought them long ago lost. He had good reason to be anxious about them as they were considerably better than the run-of-the-stock weapons of the Nor'Westers.

The rifle had been Many-Guns' last acquisition but it

was still excellent and would be for many years. It was a Robert Woods, fifty-seven and a half inches long. It had an octagonal barrel forty-two and a half inches in length, shooting forty-two balls to the pound. A beautiful rifle, having a full maple stock brass-mounted with a brass patch box, and it was very well balanced and sturdy, weighing eight and a quarter pounds.

The pistol had also been the property of Many-Guns. It was a .69 caliber flintlock shooting an ounce ball and could do work at short range.

Yellow Hair caressed these and finally laid them down to sort out his clothes. He took a heavy elkskin hunting shirt that was brightly worked in porcupine quills, a pair of boot moccasins with the fur turned in, and a pair of long, form-fitting leggings and was presently more comfortably dressed.

"Within a few hours, after I get some sleep," said Yellow Hair, "we will travel. I see your provisions are few—after the dent I am going to make in them they will be fewer—but I can hunt what we need and this Cree chief can give us pemmican. We can make the journey, English or no English, but I still do not feel right about approaching Fort William."

"You'll get a fine reception," said Father Marc.

"Most likely," said Yellow Hair with an ironic grin.

CHAPTER 22

YELLOW HAIR PERSUADED

To attribute the underlying causes of Yellow Hair's decision to go down to Fort William to petty and mean revenge is the most vicious kind of slander.

It has been said by men whose reputations are beyond cavil that this was the one and only motive for such a foolish move.

However, judging the man by the actions which have already been related, and by the light of his early training and environment, the foolhardiness becomes minute and even the most biased observer could not help but see something of heroism in his decision.

The length of his deliberation occupied minutes and much wiser men have yammered and harangued for hours to decide some greatly inferior point.

But Yellow Hair had never been one of to resort to the subterfuge of parley to cover up the fact that he lacked intelligence. As the greatest military commanders in history have been noted for split-instant decisions, so was Yellow Hair.

In the gap between the Mighty Monk's last remark and Yellow Hair's abrupt tack, and ready answer, many thoughts had sped through his mind, had been sorted out and the result had been most clearly indicated.

He had to go to Fort William, not to his own country.

He had seen enough of trading tactics to know that a single beaver pelt was worth the lives of many men—or at least it seemed that way. Although he did not know what use these traders had for animal fur, he understood the great value they set upon it.

He knew that Pikuni country was fine beaver country and that the wilderness to the east was rapidly becoming depleted of all fur-bearing animals except wolves.

He had seen the soldiers at York Factory and understood to a small degree that there were many more of these whites than he had at first supposed and that all of them were ready for war.

Then an apparently unrelated thought had come to him. He remembered Running Elk and Wolf Plume and the sorrow which attended their deaths. This had been occasioned by these whites with no provocation whatever.

The fact that he was very badly wanted for an execution had long been driven home to him.

In spite of the consequences to himself he knew that he did not dare immediately return to his people because that would give these traders an excuse to declare war on the Blackfeet. His fairness must be here remarked. He supposed that any manner of man needed an excuse for war.

An Indian has a fierce nationalism which would make any European's patriotism look like treason.

Yellow Hair's nationalism dictated that he first settle with the whites and demonstrate his innocence and then, with that danger to his people eliminated, return to them.

The Cree chief appreciated all this. Father Marc attributed it wholly to curiosity to see more whites and to his own gifted eloquence and, in some measure, to gratitude.

Accordingly they made ready for their journey. The canoe was now out of the question and they left it in its cache. It would be impossible to carry all their baggage upon their backs as Yellow Hair plainly could not stand the burrowing of a pack-strap into his still-open wound, even though he pleaded that he could use a headband.

Father Marc worried and sweated about their baggage transportation. He had never become quite used to the casualness with which a Cree or Pikuni sets out upon a jaunt which will take months to complete.

The Cree chief had already been of great aid to them. To Father Marc's surprise, even more favors were forthcoming.

This man's exact identity will forever remain indistinct. It is unlucky for a warrior of any rank to pronounce his own name aloud and the two scouts offered no introductions. And as this Cree chief seemed to feel himself obligated to aid Yellow Hair's destiny, Father Marc knew better than to inquire deeply into the motives. The Cree had come silently to them from the forest, had helped them, and would go silently away.

Yellow Hair made no comment because in fact and effect he himself was an Indian. He did not see a man in a three-point blanket. He saw authority, a war record, much wisdom and much philosophy. Without remarking it, audibly, Yellow Hair understood that the Cree had no use for the H.B.C. reward. That sum was small compared to the reputation which would attend the man who had aided Yellow Hair's escape from the English.

The Cree now came forward with a toboggan he seemed to have produced straight out of the earth. As the snow was thickening with each passing hour it would soon be sufficient to support the sledge. He threw in a set of harness but no dogs, saying that since the English had come, game was often scarce and during the past year the Cree dog population had suffered for the general good. He did not say that this was the reason for a certain false chronicle which states that Indians eat dogs whenever they wish a great delicacy, probably because the Cree chief thought straighter than the men who write up the customs of people they have neither seen nor appreciated.

The dogs could be found en route, perhaps. Possibly, he added with some amusement, at an H.B.C. fort.

And this, indeed, was the way Yellow Hair got his dogs.

He was deep in the conquered territory of the whites, no matter how wild it was, no matter the lack of deeds in white hands, and the whites were roaming all through it.

A man of Yellow Hair's reckless and incautious temperament sees high adventure in such a situation and now that his decision was made, something like abandon gave impulse to his actions.

Father Marc might weigh many stones more than the adopted Pikuni, and he might be able to break wood as thick as Yellow Hair's body, and he might be able to laugh at anything, but he could never match the scout's gallant daring.

Thus they started on their long and dangerous journey, their game of fox and hounds with the English where the stakes were the gallows vs. Fort William.

CHAPTER 23

THE DANGEROUS TREK

To attempt a trip from the ice-glazed regions of Hudson's Bay to the northwest shore of Lake Superior, through nine degrees of latitude, through dense woods and across plains, down rivers and across frozen lakes, with mercury so far below zero that it did not even reach into the tube, attests the hardiness and the spirit of any man.

But when, added to that, there is the constant need for hiding, scouting, backtracking and generally avoiding the thorough and systematic effort of the English to bring Yellow Hair to justice, the magnitude of the voyage is impossible to conceive without making the trip itself.

It was long and tedious and grueling. The English were bad enough but added to that was howling winter in the north, impenetrable forests, the glazed ice of paralyzed rivers, the scream of blasting storms, chill camps with scant protection—and the wolves.

The English might have tried to slaughter all the available game but they had made no dent upon the wolves.

At each campfire there they were, a waiting, starved ring of green eyes against the outer darkness, jaws slavering, insane at the prospect of easy meat. Their howls quavered and broke in the stillness of the snow-stifled world and the dogs replied in whimpers as their wolf ancestry stirred uneasily within them.

The camps were too various for mention. Men traveling on foot across a thousand miles of wilderness make many camps of many kinds. In abandoned hunters' cabins, in windfalls, under rocks, against frozen banks, beside towering trees, deep in brittle thickets of brush, they made their small fires and hoped the smoke would not call down the wrath and fire of the still-searching H.B.C.s.

The food they ate ran the whole scale of diet from the buffalo hide trail markers (no food for weak teeth, that) to juicy tenderloins from fresh-killed elk. The latter was in the minority as Yellow Hair did not dare fire his rifle and had to depend upon a badly seasoned bow he had fashioned and upon arrows which still contained stiff sap.

The escapes were even more varied than either their food or camps: one night lying in a drift listening to the growls of searching English who had crossed their trail; a day spent in the very shadow of a post trying to pirate a much-needed trace dog; hours expended in a careful backtracking to mislead three hunters who could think of nothing but fifty pounds; two minutes spent in petrified surprise at meeting a post factor face to face on a trail, two hours carrying the factor close to his post so that he would not freeze in his bonds.

Track and counter-track, scout and escape. They plowed southward, ever southward toward Fort William on the shores of Lake Superior.

From Hudson's Bay to the Great Lakes in the misery

of winter would be a saga under the most favorable conditions—much less when pursuit and imminent death were added.

On the face of it the pursuit was too unequal. The pursued had every item in the catalogue of Pikuni tracking and hunting at Yellow Hair's fingertips. The English were hampered by the feeling that Yellow Hair would only be uncovered in an ambush that would most likely prove fatal to the loyal Lords of the Outer Marches—or at least to one or two of their servants at eight pounds bounty in the Orkneys, a sum which bad business made considerable.

The English were in their "own" country, it is true, but a matter more vital than that was at play.

There are varying degrees of education. No Englishman would have stated that Yellow Hair was educated in the slightest degree as he knew no Latin, could not balance a teacup on one knee and a muffin plate on the other and had never heard of a minuet. Yellow Hair would never have considered an Englishman, possessing these doubtlessly invaluable attributes, an even faintly worthy opponent in the art of woodcraft and therefore, to Yellow Hair, these English were not educated in the slightest degree.

When father Marc's enormous white fangs were not castanetting in tempo to the wind's scream they were parted in hearty laughter. He began to appreciate this matter of variant education.

Week in and week out (or rather storm in and storm out), Yellow Hair persisted in making the worthy English appear in a very foolish light and did it with so much savage glee that a more sober man than Father Marc would have grown hysterical.

Half of one night Yellow Hair lay on the fringe of an H.B.C. fire listening to the strange jargon of the Orkneymen and the snarls of a brigade leader who had once been on Bow Street. Yellow Hair had howled with the ringing wolves, egging them on, but never once becoming involved with the wolfish economic problem that hunger that means either meat or death. The sleepless Orkneymen, vowing they'd get very drunk on the reward, never once suspected the proximity of that reward's object, and never once connected the loss of their dogs with the object of their quest.

Until he ran across the right explanation, Father Marc more than once reflected upon certain legends about werewolves. He was led into this channel of thought by the seeming affection Yellow Hair had for these cadaverous and glowering brutes. Not even Father Marc's friendship for the scout nor his religious beliefs could argue him out of the werewolf theory. It cost him several bad nights until Yellow Hair, upon discovering and ferreting out this uneasiness, explained with several grins—well-repressed—something about Pikunis and wolves.

The Pikuni name for "scout" is sometimes "wolf." How this affinity originated is a matter of much learned conjecture which has no place here. Whether it originated when the Pikunis—and all Blackfeet—were forest people on the Great Slave Lake in the long ago or when they came to the plains is of no moment.

But the Pikuni has a saying, "The gun which shoots a wolf will never shoot straight again," and he lives up to this maxim in spite of possibly spurious records that show a large number of wolf pelts traded into the posts for goods. If the records are genuine, then the pelts were garnered in raids.

The Pikuni signal is a wolf howl so accurate that the wolves themselves are misled by it. The sacred wolf song starts with a howl which, when yipped and blasted out of a thousand throats, is rather more compelling than the milder tune and bloodier sentiments of "La Marseillaise," or even "God Save the King."

And so, while Father Marc grinned away his uneasiness at these carnivora, Yellow Hair grinned at them with friendliness, appreciating their intelligence, their swiftness, and if not their courage, at least their cunning. Countless times Yellow Hair scared Father Marc half out of his cassock by suddenly emitting a yipping bark in the direction of a new set of eyes which had joined the waiting ring about the fire, throwing the wolf song in that direction as though telling the animal to keep its distance, that here was a kindred spirit.

Thus the winter and the distance wore away and, suddenly, the two found themselves on the bank of the Kaministiqwia. They left the toboggan, made travois for the dogs, and proceeded down the stream to Fort William with spring in the air, with breaking ice gnashing its glassy teeth out in the current, to arrive and face adventures much more intricate and dangerous than those of the journey.

CHAPTER 24

THE RECEPTION

God built Lake Superior.

The Nor'Westers built Fort William.

The recipe for the place called for stone, lead, logs, rum, logs, mud, rum, knives, rifles, rum, nails, cannon, shot, rum, pelts, traps, canoes, rum, mud, water, axes, logs, paint, augers, rum, pegs, rum, mud and, of course, plans.

This, however, was merely the crust. The filling consisted numerously of sweepings from the Montreal jails, Frenchmen, Englishmen, Irishmen, Scotchmen; sweepings from the London jails, Swedes, Indians, half-breeds, De Meurons, voyageurs, bullies; sweepings from the Quebec jails, women, children, boys, girls; sweepings from the New York jails, partners, "rangers of the burnt woods," *coureurs des bois,* all shot through with intrigue.

Well baked in summer and frozen in winter, the place presented a scowling slab palisade on every side eighteen feet high. Over the gate was a guardhouse in which sat a sentry. Between this and the river were countless log huts inhabited by the people who made the fur trade an actuality but who did not deserve the protection of the cannon—the Indians and half-breeds.

Inside these palisades were housed from fifteen hundred to two thousand people—families, traders, clerks, voyageurs, bullies, camp followers, partners and leeches. These inhabited the buildings within which sprawled out across a mammoth square, making quite a show, the whole resembling a muddy, crude Old World town.

There should be no surprise occasioned by the presence of white women—and one very beautiful white woman in particular—in this unwholesome atmosphere as orchids are grown in festering swamps and many pretty flowers have a far less delicate bed.

Fort William, after its accommodating move from the United States back to British territory following the Boundary Settlement, had discovered itself to be the actual dividing line between the northwest limit of "civilization" and the southeast limit of the raw domain which, according to H.B.C., belonged to H.B.C., and according to the Nor'Westers belonged to the Nor'-Westers and which, in reality, belonged to the Indians.

The backtrail of eighteen hundred miles to Montreal by lake and river was becoming fairly well settled as the incumbent Indians died off from various fatal illnesses visited upon them, according to contemporary church records, for their heathen beliefs and, according to state records, their stubborn insistence that they owned the country.

This, then, was not only the last outpost of the plow but the easternmost limit (which was a variable thing, depending upon the death-rate of buffalos) of the bison civilization.

Not only women had come west to the place, but also there had arrived in late years a few fur buyers, a fact which drives home the peacefulness of the region.

The winter had been very hard on the partners who

had remained. It had tried the temper of almost everyone except the Indians about the place who had been too busy trying to keep from starving and freezing to resort to the luxury of boredom.

Accordingly when a sloppy sentry sang out that two men and several travois dogs were arriving there was an immediate and excited flurry within the palisades. It was plain that this pair must have traveled the whole winter to arrive so soon after the breakup. It was hoped that they had news of the raiding Nor'Westers and the beleaguered English.

Strangely enough, news of all kinds—all of it counterfeit—surged through the fort, even though every man who was on the walls could tell that the strangers had not arrived, much less spoken. It is strange how the anxiety for news will lead to its instant manufacture.

The gates were flung open and there was an immediate rush for grandstand seats. At the sudden appearance of a party of three just outside the great saloon, the crowd held back its excitement for an instant to give this group the preferred place to the right of the huge portals.

One of these was a girl, not more than twenty-one years of age but for all that possessing the arts and graces of the most accomplished courtier. She was very blonde, very slender and very poised. The silk of her flowing gown shimmered below the limits of her encompassing cloak. She walked with the proud tread of an empress—which indeed was her position if not her title in the huge fort. When she paused to wait the coming of the strangers she stood so well that it appeared instantly that these men were arriving solely for her pleasure.

On her right stood her father, so bent over and warped and crooked that he only came to her shoulder. On her left was a man evidently destined to become her husband and a man who, because of his ultimate influence on Yellow Hair's destiny, deserves a great deal of introduction.

This man was tall, straight and slender. In fact he was so erect that he almost leaned backwards and so slender that many of his enemies accused him of wearing a corset. Haughty is the best word for him as the adjective "majestic" is wholly the property of McGlincy.

He had a sword and a cape and ruffles and gold buckles on his thin and delicate shoes. These last were in no danger of being soiled as a servant had very carefully laid a four-point blanket down in the mud to protect his lordship from the distemper that might result from any contact with so horrible a thing as mud.

This gentleman also had a mustache. But this is no incidental mention of that cherished article. It is reserved until last because the last thing said always makes the best impression—or the worst.

He was playing with this mustache when Yellow Hair first sighted him. It is an unseemly word, "playing," but "toying" does not put forth the idea of pleasure with any force. It is not to be construed that he was roughhousing with this mustache. On the contrary, he was stroking it as one strokes the head of a favorite dog. Not that the tender article of his love required any touching up, either. It was so carefully waxed and spiked and trimmed and waxed again that bullies with little respect often shook their heads over it, saying that a hard fall on the face would cause the thing to pierce all the way through his lordship's skull.

And so, beside his lady love, looking very fine, his lordship caught Yellow Hair's laughter square between the eyes—or rather, on both spikes of that mustache.

When a careless, incautious fellow has pushed himself a hundred miles past the last limit of his endurance, when his moccasins are all worn out and when his stomach is very empty, his most obvious characteristics erupt volcano-like to the surface. If he is irritable, beware. If he laughs there must be something very wholesome about him.

With all this pomp of greeting to amuse him, Yellow Hair did not at first catch sight of his lordship. People, before they began to show up as individuals, swirled in a colored pattern about the Pikuni.

Yellow Hair, with some satisfaction, sighted his buckskin-clad kind and then, in abrupt contrast, saw the haughty lord.

Quite ready to laugh from the sheer hysteria of exhaustion, the sight of a coxcomb standing upon a blanket affected Yellow Hair strangely. He grinned and nudged Father Marc. The Mighty Monk gulped and prodded back in alarm.

For the first time in his life Yellow Hair saw a mustache without any beard to go with it and the idea of a man wearing hair upon his upper lip and fondling it with so much love seemed very funny.

Marc's prod did it and there it was done.

Yellow Hair might have murdered every man in the place with more impunity. He might have laughed at his lordship's shoes and even gotten away with it. But he made the fatal error of stabbing ridicule at the most cherished thing his lordship possessed.

The sword came half out of its scabbard before his

lordship noticed that a knife, pistol and rifle were in Yellow Hair's possession. The sword clanged back. His lordship snorted like a bullet-struck horse and gave his head a toss in a most equine manner, practically upsetting himself and the girl beside him as he bridled.

Yellow Hair was very close to them both, almost standing on the blanket. When the girl's dodge (done with grace) away from the sword-fumbling was almost turned into a spill by the snort, Yellow Hair, his reflexes acting quicker than his head, snapped out a hand to steady her.

He stopped laughing. His mouth went slightly open and his hand swooped up to cover it in that time-honored Pikuni exclamation of surprise.

A white woman?

Now who would ever have believed there was such a thing as a white woman in this world?

Impossible. Some medicine pipe dream.

But there she was with her pretty gray eyes looking sideways at his handsome, if startled, face. She appeared to be rapt in contemplation of so pleasing an object, but in reality she took in everything about him. The face of a well-bred gentleman, the eyes of a gallant who would dare anything, even death, with a laugh, the well-sculpt body of an athlete, the strong hands of an artist.

She was pleased.

She narrowed her look and made it very sweet.

Father Marc, trying to avoid a possible massacre, jerked Yellow Hair away and hustled him in haste toward the porch where Old Simon was waiting for them.

"You fool," said Father Marc. "That was Lord Strathleigh! And that girl was Evelyn Lee, his sweetheart and future wife! And the old man was her father, Lee, the great fur buyer. You always get into more trouble! Why do you have to smoke on a gunpowder keg? Whether you see Heaven or the Saskatchewan this summer depends on which way the cat jumps and there's no sense in shying a stick at it to make it jump the wrong way! That lord is the best duelist in France or England and unless I cover up who you are, he'll challenge you for that affront and if I pretend you're a savage he'll have bullies kill you."

"For laughing at that thing on his upper lip?"

"He spends a hundred pounds a year on perfumed mustache wax. He'd lose his estates before he'd shave it off. By St. Matthew, youngster, that yellow scalp of yours will certainly never get gray at the rate you're going."

His voice was very harsh, which was not unusual for Father Marc. A glance at the merry, pleased expression on his face made a close observer conclude that the voice was harsh because it had to take such a long trip before it ever reached his teeth.

He would have said much more, but Old Simon MacIntosh was shouting a welcome to the priest and when gnarled and canny Simon learned the identity of this handsome young man, his wrinkled and cunning face almost broke apart he smiled so hard and brittlely.

"Good! Good!" croaked Old Simon. "The savage the damned English want so bad. Good work, priest! Good work! We've business for a good killer, I tell you that. Come in and get drunk, both of you."

This last was, of course, the highest honor Old Simon could present to any man.

CHAPTER 25

WHO IS YELLOW HAIR?

After a week had passed, Yellow Hair was still as bewildered by the continuance of his welcome as he had been the instant it was hurled at him.

He did not understand the partners and the partners did not understand him. Yellow Hair's lack of understanding was honest and ungarnished, but the partners covered theirs with amazing bits of statesmanship which would have done credit to a more inclusive cause.

The welcome was statesmanship and policy in itself. This should not be construed to mean that the Nor'Westers were wanting in generosity and cheer as no one can deny that they were open-handed in the extreme, always feeling called upon to prove that they, singular or plural, could drink more whisky per hour than anyone on the continent.

The attempt at wassail was calculated to make Yellow Hair believe that he could be quite at ease at Fort William and that he was regarded in no other light than that of a returning hero who had bested the H.B.C.s.

Not a word was said about the plan that had shot like hot grape into Old Simon's rather shrunken skull. Fort William knew all about Yellow Hair—or thought they did. In common with almost every man in the business, whether in St. Louis or Edmonton, they had heard those atrocity stories which had grown out of Yellow Hair's fight with Motley's crew. The Nor'Westers understood that they had a fighter in their midst and this much was all too true.

But they went further in their reasoning, overreaching themselves completely. Yellow Hair was plainly at odds with Hudson's Bay Company and who but the Nor'-Westers had more right to capitalize on that enmity? With visions of mountainous fur bales at their gates, put there without the added expense of trading anything for them, the Nor'Westers suffered double hallucinations—one from addled hope and the other from spirits. They handed out their whiskey and high wine with reckless abandon and, when they discovered that Yellow Hair would not drink a solitary drop of the stuff, they drank it themselves and charged it off to Yellow Hair.

He was much too severely schooled (though this does not mean by punishment as Pikunis never punish their children) in the doleful effects of spirits on Indians to wish himself so much harm.

But he ate well and began to look a little less gaunt and, having collected an offered purse from Old Simon, engaged a nimble-fingered old Algonquian woman to tailor him some clothing from beautifully tanned antelope skin, instructing her carefully in his tribal design.

He was a little puzzled by this stir, of course, but Yellow Hair had the happy type of mind which can take everything in stride and make decisions only when the last instant has arrived.

He did not realize that men who possess bad qualities and reputations are apt to make those honorable and good by causing them to be rewarded in others. If he had known this he would have quitted the fort instantly, English or no English.

So many new things had leaped up before him that he needed no depressive like high wine to make him dull enough to be amused. He bothered Father Marc every waking hour by asking questions and then following up with shrewd comments which made the mighty bulk of the priest rock for lack of answer, and then laugh at Yellow Hair's wisdom and his own denseness.

For instance, Yellow Hair saw a soldier returned from the Napoleon Wars and noted the string of medals on his chest.

"Why the brass and color?" said Yellow Hair.

"Medals," replied Marc, off guard.

"What are medals?"

Marc scratched his big, dark jowl and shut one eye thoughtfully. "Why, when a man attacks the enemy in a valiant manner or some such thing they give him a medal as a reward for his being brave."

"Is that so?" said Yellow Hair, a grin beginning to come down from under his ear. "We wear them on our head, not on our chest and I think they're much prettier."

"What are you talking about?"

With an innocent smile, Yellow Hair said, "If a man in my country is brave in battle the Council, after due deliberation, may award him a coup and he can wear an eagle plume in his bonnet. Much better than some of these high brass hats I see because they are not nearly so heavy and they show up better than these medals."

Marc boomed his laugh in appreciation.

Abruptly Yellow Hair changed the subject to something which interested him more. "Why does everybody tip their hats to that fellow with hair on his lip? Is it because of that mustache?"

"My goodness, no," said Marc piously. "He's a lord."

"And is this title 'lord' something like chief?"

"Just about."

"Then he is a good fighter, eh?"

"Well, yes. He's killed quite a few men in duels. They say that's why he came out here. Finest shot in Europe and a wonderful swordsman. But that isn't why he's a lord. His father was a lord before him."

"What's that got to do with it?"

Marc started blandly to explain with even a little superiority in his tone. But he suddenly gave Yellow Hair a baffled glance and gaped at him.

Yellow Hair followed through deftly. "I knew a chief of great reputation who had a son we had to dress in woman's clothes, he was such a coward. Because the chief was brave was no reason the son should be brave. Of course it helps to have a very brave father but sometimes the father shelters the son so much that when the boy grows up he can't stand on his own feet. I don't think so much of that practice. He duels, you say? What do you mean by duel?"

Marc was on better ground here. He had said a few last words over the stiffening bodies of several gentlemen who had been unfortunate enough to value honor more than life. He expounded at great length.

Finally Yellow Hair cut him short. "In the Pikuni nation, we put murderers on trial. The dead man's family can either choose to take all the killer's goods or require the killer's life."

"But this is not murder, this dueling."

"Why not?" said Yellow Hair with a frown. "You say that this lord is the best in Europe—whatever that is—and that he is deadly accurate with a pistol or a sword. He wants to kill a man for some reason or other and so he bullies him into accepting this challenge and then, because the lord is admittedly best with a sword or a pistol, he is the victor. Why isn't that murder?"

Father Marc raised his eyes to heaven as though to ask St. Joseph what a poor priest could do against a brain like that. If Marc had been a stubborn, opinionated man he could probably have argued it out to his satisfaction if not to Yellow Hair's. However, Marc, as is common with huge men, had very mild opinions about matters in the abstract and was even willing to recognize a gleam of truth when he saw it.

Perhaps Yellow Hair would not have been so complacent if he had known what was going forward in his quarters.

Old Simon had thought, as a precaution, knowing all men to be very evil, that it would be best to examine Yellow Hair's baggage to make certain that no bank notes were there to show that Yellow Hair was in the employ of the H.B.C.s as a spy.

Old Simon demonstrated a lot of humor with a beaver-trap mouth but not very much with his eyes. And when a roll of papers were swiftly brought to him from Yellow Hair's war sack and when he had posted a man to apprise him of Yellow Hair's approach if he came, his small and glassy orbs passed over the roll with a glance so calculating that the sheets were instantly icy to the touch.

In truth Yellow Hair himself did not know what was

in that roll. The Pikunis have a Beaver Medicine Roll which is sacred and lucky and show it much the same reverence as Marc showed his Bible. The stories of both are not dissimilar.

Yellow Hair, having been given this roll of documents just before his father Many-Guns had died, had always kept them close to him because his father, according to White Fox, had seemed to attach great importance to them.

Before his imprisonment at Fort Chesterfield Yellow Hair had not been able to read. Since that sorry event he had not thought anything new about this mysterious packet. It was lucky and that was enough for him.

But Old Simon's bony fingers—so thin they clattered when he moved them—wrapped avidly around the roll and his glassy chill eyes slid over the lines, first in amazement, then in interest and finally in as close a counterfeit to amusement as Old Simon could make.

The papers were various. One of them was an appointment to meet one G. Washington. Another was a commission in the United States Army, stating that one Lawrence Randolph Kirk was hereby created a colonel. There was a marriage certificate which lawfully united Beatrice Talbot and L. R. Kirk. Another was a letter from John Adams congratulating Larry Kirk upon the birth of a fine boy who he hoped would become as illustrious as his father. There was a small, black-bordered and age-yellowed clipping, a death notice regretting the passing of Beatrice Talbot Kirk, wife of Senator Kirk from Virginia. And then came several clippings giving a running account of a duel fought between one General Grossman and one Colonel Lawrence

Randolph Kirk, lately Senator from Virginia, which had occurred on an island near the Great Falls of the Potomac. Following this was a lament regretting the demise of the famous General Grossman. Following that came several bitter editorials which stated that the "murder" of Grossman was not justified no matter the false charges of high treason brought against Kirk by the late general, and no matter that the general was a challenger. This editorial also expressed surprise that Grossman should have been hit at all, much less killed, because of his fine reputation as a miraculous shot and Kirk's statement before the duel that he would not fire to kill—which was made to disarm the general's suspicions, of course.

It was plain, even to Old Simon, who already knew about the case, though the sad event had taken place a score of years before, that Grossman's friends had hounded Kirk out of Virginia, had caused the death of his wife through poverty and despair and had sent Kirk into the wilderness with his small son.

The letter Kirk had written to "My son Michael" contained an apology which the writer had hoped the boy could never read. Kirk had said that he could only leave a few weapons and half a dozen horses, that an estate of a thousand acres and four hundred slaves had long ago been swallowed up in lawsuits.

There was other information concerning the means which might some day be taken to clear Kirk in that duel as Kirk was certain that Grossman had been, all through the Revolution, in the pay of the British and the charges against Kirk had only been made to cover and discredit the fact that the treason had been Grossman's.

This made Old Simon MacIntosh grin very much and

there even appeared something which was almost humor in his glittery eyes.

Someone had entered the room while he was reading and he glanced up in alarm and then stood up in honor of his lordship. Old Simon did not let the honor last but an instant. He promptly seated himself and shoved an ever-present bottle at Strathleigh.

"What have you there?" said the lord. "Something interesting, I hope. Blast me, but this is the dullest place in the world for a man of my refinements. Fancy me coming to such a place. I thought it would be amusing, you know. Indians to be killed and all that. Why, damme, I haven't seen but three Indians killed since I been here and they were all roaring drunk. Don't they ever attack? By Jove, Simon, I don't think you're so much of a host at that. Can't we get an expedition together or something like that, eh? I've a new French rifle I'm anxious to try out. Aren't there any Indians close by that don't like you or some such thing? I swear, Simon, I've wasted my last shot on buffalo. When you kill them they simply fall over. I bagged a hundred and five last week and there wasn't a thrill in the whole of it. Now I've heard it was more sporting than that out here. Yelling fiends and all that. Of course everybody knows a redskin runs after the first shot, but can't we totter out and look us up a covey of them, what?"

"Did you tell the hunters where you'd killed the buffalo?"

"No, by God, so I didn't. Slipped my mind, it was such poor sport. They're still out there, I suppose."

"Never mind," said Simon, "there are plenty of buffalo. I thought I might have saved the price of ammunition on you."

"Ho, that's a jolly one, that is. A prudent man, eh, MacIntosh? What have you there, man?"

"You know that woods runner that came in here a week or so ago with Father Marc?"

"Damme, that I do. I've been wondering how I should have him punished for that unseemly conduct."

His lordship brooded over it and caressed his mustache as though to soothe its doubtlessly maligned spikes.

"I'm always careful, Your Lordship, and so I took a bit of a glance through his baggage and found these."

Strathleigh took the papers, yawned and shuffled carelessly through them. He tossed them back after a while with another yawn.

"The Kirk that shot Grossman, eh? Good shot, that Grossman. Almost as accomplished a duelist as I have become, so he was. I remember talking about it with the King but he agreed with me it must have been a fluke shot. Accident, you know. The King told me that, while Grossman was never as good as I was, he was still a fine shot."

"That Kirk's boy is this woods runner we've been hearing so much about."

"Devil take me, so he is according to this. A gentleman in the savage costume, what? Masquerade, no doubt, what? Trying to put something over, eh?"

"Perhaps. But no matter. The lad is as good a killer as—er—I mean he's built himself a fine reputation and we'll soon be using it. Partners are beginning to arrive from Montreal and the back country. Early meeting this year. There's work to be done. Something of a joke on this Larry Kirk to have us use his son this way."

"Right, right, right," smiled his lordship. "But the

blighter has been missing out of the col—I mean the United States these twenty years. No matter about that. What if he is a gentleman?"

"Ay, what if he is. Have a drink?"

CHAPTER 26

HIS LORDSHIP SEES

Yellow Hair tried every day to get the ear of Old Simon. There was nothing of real interest in this fort, and the amusement quickly wore off to be replaced by restlessness.

He wanted to have a hearing on the Fort Chesterfield affair, get everything straight about it, clear himself completely, despatch the findings to Hudson's Bay Company and then return home.

Bright Star was forever with him and as the delay increased he began to be apprehensive about her. Though he knew nothing about Big Wolf's decision and the choice of Long Bow and the limited time, he could nevertheless sense somehow that all was not right.

He had been gone so long he dared not think what had happened in his absence and so he tried to keep his thoughts in the back of his head.

He had dreams about a big lodge he would build on his return and how he would make it comfortable and keep it filled with meat. He would sit for hours in one place—which was most unusual for him—and think up conversations between himself and his beautiful bride-to-be.

And then a chill of reality would make him shiver. He

did not know whether she was waiting for him or not.

She had told him she would.

He could see her face when she had said that. Dark eyes downcast, masked by her long lashes, cheeks colored ever so little by shyness.

She had said that she would wait and watch for him, but the time had been so long.

At the beginning of the third week he began to pace up and down the river bank without his smile, his blue eyes cold and his nerves as edged as the knife in his belt.

He was all oblivious to the events taking place about him. He saw partners arrive and repair to the great saloon in the center of the huge fort. He had been there once and he would not consent to go again. ·

In the hall—which was sixty feet by thirty—were hung the painted likenesses of the more famous partners of the company. They were depicted in court costume, with beautiful ruffles and gold-buckled shoes. They made a line of severe but manly faces staring down upon the oaken tables, and it must be remarked that the painters who were bribed to paint them that way suffered so terribly that they had to dull their artistic senses by drinking up their all.

The partners who had already arrived had hilariously toasted the defeat of H.B.C. at the hands of Yellow Hair. They had swilled to Yellow Hair's cunning and to all those other gruesome virtues which they had gathered out of the broadcast tales.

Yellow Hair was no flawless prude. On the contrary. But there is something revolting in having liquor forced upon you by drunks and there is something horrible in watching grown men "shoot the rapids" using kegs for canoes as they shot down the tilted tables. The singing and drumming and fifing had been very off-key and, as soon as he could, Yellow Hair had slipped quietly out.

The next morning he found that quantities of rum had been freely distributed to the Indians outside the fort. And as an Indian has no great immunity to alcohol, the resulting brawl had caused the deaths of two men, three women and a small child.

Afterwards, the Indians who had found out what they had done had come, plunged in the black depths of grief, to the partners to plead that justice be done to them, the Indians, and that they be killed for their crimes because they could no longer bear to live with the miserable memory.

Yellow Hair had, of course, asked himself and Father Marc just why it was necessary to issue the rum in the first place, but there didn't seem to be any answer. While it is sometimes possible to puzzle out the problems of wisdom, it is impossible to answer folly except in its own terms.

Less and less reason could Yellow Hair find in Fort William. He saw that everyone bowed and scraped to this man Lee who appeared to be nothing more than a badly bent old man who suffered from a horrible case —according to his ever-present and dismal whine—of dyspepsia which, according to Yellow Hair's findings, was nothing more than a common bellyache and had its cure in eating less rare meat and drinking less high wine.

Out of curiosity he took an interest in both the old man and his daughter Evelyn, wondering how the girl stood him so patiently.

Then he observed that the old man was always talking about being swindled out of his money, being forced to pay too high a price for furs the X.Y.s (Nor'Westers) got for almost nothing, and realized that this "money" was the answer to the hypochondriac's power.

Because old Lee had this stuff called "money," he had power. But because old Lee was a most unpleasant fool, Yellow Hair could not connect the two at all and began to confuse the religious beliefs of these traders. The fort chaplain was accorded much less courtesy than Lee.

Because of this same "money," old Lee could keep his daughter at his side, in a way, bribing her, because she was the only one who could faithfully oversee the regularity of the medicine without which the old man would undoubtedly die.

Then Yellow Hair saw something else. This lord did not love this lady he was to marry because he was much more solicitous about the old man than he was about the girl. Yellow Hair quite naturally concluded that the lord was also interested in this power called "money" and was willing to elevate Evelyn's position in life for a considerable number of these very odd scraps of paper which you could not eat or use to make clothes or hunt with, but which turned into all three with a mysterious alchemy Yellow Hair could not divine.

Just why the position of his lordship's wife was worth even more than this so highly valued "money" was quite beyond Yellow Hair.

He had stopped worrying about all that now, knowing it to be beyond the analyzing ability of any man he knew, but while his attention to this problem had brought no result to his reason it had brought a very definite result to his security, by taking it away.

He had watched the girl Evelyn.

She had seen him doing that.

Evelyn, being both bored and a woman, had misconstrued the meaning of the glance.

Yellow Hair was very good to look upon, as he was all tricked out in white antelope clothes wonderfully beaded and fringed and colorful. The leggings were tight to his legs all the way up and he had a fine pair of legs. The beautiful mane of hair he wore was very attractive to the girl who was tired of wigs.

The grace of the man as he leaned thoughtfully on his rifle—with the muzzle as high as his shoulder—staring up at the hill behind the fort or across the stream and lake was very picturesque.

And presently, dressed in her best with her eyes trying hard to stay modest, the English maiden paraded twice a day along the wall.

That made Yellow Hair grin once when he noticed it. He understood instantly and was greatly amused when he saw that this lady was trying very hard to look as pretty as his Bright Star.

The wrong pair of eyes saw that grin.

Lord Strathleigh received a jolt which caused a clink in his money-bag mind.

But Lord Strathleigh showed no sign of it at the moment. He trod the path with dignity down from the gate and to the river ahead of a considerable crowd who poured forth.

Yellow Hair glanced out to see what had caused this commotion and sighted a single canoe rounding the bend.

Old Simon screeched, "It's Alex McGlincy!"

Yellow Hair recoiled and his grip around the rifle tightened.

Paddles straining, bottle aloft, McGlincy swerved in for a landing.

CHAPTER 27

TIDINGS OF WAR

Alexander McGlincy looked very haggard. He had not exactly lost weight but his chest had dropped somewhat. There was a new brightness to his puffily shapeless nose, a certain depth of blueness under his eyes and a certain weary droop to his misshapen mouth that all betokened great strain.

This occasioned no surprise in the partners. They too well knew the toll exacted by the heavy and harassing business of state.

McGlincy's canoe made the landing and stopped there like a shot arrow hitting stone. The voyageurs were dripping with sweat and dropping with weariness, showing they had come far very fast.

McGlincy leaped out from under his canopy—the edge of which almost knocked his hat off—spread his feet apart to keep from weaving and struck an heroic pose, holding the bottle at present arms.

Plainly he was a courier with tidings of disaster. You could almost visualize the thundering horse, the flying pennon, the backward glance at close pursuit as the valiant bearer of news and the only hope of a besieged garrison's salvation came to the destination for succor without which hundreds would die.

McGlincy hiccupped.

McGlincy looked steadily at them as though unwilling to part with such momentous news after undergoing so much suffering to bring it home.

It was a dramatic moment, comparable only with the arrival of the runner from Marathon, though McGlincy looked more like Bacchus than a Greek athlete.

"God's blood!" cried McGlincy, following it with a loud belch that rocked him as though he had been hit by canister.

The crowd hung on that in hushed suspense.

"Murder! Fire and damnation!" roared McGlincy.

The crowd leaned tensely forward, mouths gaping, eyes bulging.

"We're lost!" cried McGlincy.

While a tremor ran through the mob, he sloshed some high wine down his throat to grease up his voice.

"We're undone!" imparted McGlincy and then he too leaned forward confidentially.

"The God damned English!" snarled McGlincy.

With that he evidently felt that he had done his duty because he rocked a trifle and Old Simon and another partner quickly fastened upon his arms to lead him swiftly toward the great saloon and the ten gallon kegs.

McGlincy had been much too preoccupied with the effect of his landing to notice that Yellow Hair stood on the outward edge of the crowd. He was much too busy trying to get through the twenty-foot opening of the gate to see anything now.

Not one syllable more would McGlincy say before he had been safely ensconced upon a chair and a whole forest of bottles had risen up like Hindu magic before him.

He was saving of his news because, like all great men,

he knew the value of keeping everyone waiting for long periods of time to heighten the importance of both self and tidings.

Finally, after sampling something of everything, he looked down the long table at the closely and tensely gathered partners who had the various expressions of men all ready to do or die and damn the enemy.

"Gentlemen," said McGlincy, intending no sarcasm. "Gentlemen, I'm come from the Saskatchewan. I've walked my legs to pegs, I've blistered my hands, starved and froze to carry the horrible news of the catastrophe to you without delay."

They had to wait for a hiccup and a belch and they filled in the gap with harsh, "Dammes!" "Gawd blind mes!" and just plain, "Awrrh!"

"I've starved and froze. I've not spared man or boat to hasten my arrival."

And this, in his favor, was only too true.

"The English are in possession of the Saskatchewan!"

He took a loud gulp, banged the bottle on the table, reared half up and roared, "The English have taken the Saskatchewan!"

The news created a terrific stir and the walls shook with the fusillade of oaths that volleyed from the score of throats.

McGlincy could not hold himself upright more than a minute and so now he sank back, glowering and looking terrible in his black wrath.

He began to talk, using hiccups for commas and belches for periods. He told them about the descent of Motley on the fort; the awful destruction which resulted in spite of his own heroic defense of the place, the attack by thousands of savages and barbarians; the cunning

intrigue of the English which had made the Blackfeet
turn against the Nor'Westers in favor of the H.B.C.s.

He told them until they could see gore running down
the oaken table and spreading in pools upon the floor,
until they could smell the smoke of flaming cannon, until they could hear the ear-splitting, falsetto yip-yow-yip
of the Blackfeet in full charge. He told them until they
could see the great McGlincy wrapped in a death grap-
ple with a savage, naked, bloodthirsty chief, until they
could almost count the uncountable dead which were
strewn about McGlincy's feet. He told them until they
could hear the screams of the dead and dying (so he
said) above the rattle of rifle fire.

He finished grandly, "And I caught the damned
English spy (hiccup) and at the sight of me (hiccup) he
became so terrified that he told all! (Belch)." McGlincy
looked very fierce and leaned forward to glare down at
the miserable, begging captive. "And he said (hiccup)
that it was true! (Belch) The English are hiring the
Blackfeet to drive us out of the Saskatchewan! Nor'-
Westers! To arms! (Belch)."

This was not something that had happened between
Yellow Hair's release to the H.B.C. and McGlincy's
arrival at Fort William. This tale McGlincy told was as
correct a version of Motley's call and the Blackfeet
request for Yellow Hair as McGlincy could possibly give.

Consistency is one of the most valuable virtues in the
world and McGlincy was certainly consistent as well as
everything else noble and great.

He had to have a reason for departing so abruptly
from the fort and this was it. His voyageurs were
accomplished and talented in this same art and he had
nothing to fear from them. Besides, there was a practical

side to it and McGlincy, like all famous statesmen and conquerors, was completely practical. He did not want to go back to Fort Chesterfield without a heavy guard and this was a highly laudable way of procuring one. Further, he did not want the true story of Yellow Hair's capture from him ever to be known to the other partners because that might occasion some embarrassment in accounting for the lost furs that would never show on any Nor'Wester tally sheet and only in McGlincy's Montreal account book.

With tales of terror and warfare between the brigades becoming current and common, any Nor'Wester would believe anything about an H.B.C., and vice versa, a situation that did much to aggravate the murderous attacks, raids, and thefts that were echoing from the MacKenzie to the Hudson.

If they had looked up McGlincy's time of departure from Fort Chesterfield and his time of arrival at Fort William, they would have discovered that he must have loafed a great deal on the job in spite of his avowal of speed.

In all fairness, let it be said that these Nor'Westers might have gone so far as to have examined the story carefully had they not been so very anxious to keep on believing it true.

McGlincy had spent most of the winter at the new Fort Gibraltar at the Forks, some distance from Fort William up near Lake Winnipeg. When it had become necessary to sled the canoes, McGlincy had discovered that his weight made the runners bog down and he had called a halt.

As Gibraltar had been built since McGlincy had last passed that way, he considered it his duty to go over and inspect it. He had found MacDonald of Garth putting on the finishing touches and he had also found that a cellar there had been well-stocked with wines and high wines. As the red-headed Highlander of a famous family was most hospitable to a brother Nor'Wester, McGlincy had spent the winter in a very pleasant manner, singing and beating the drum and, of course, drinking. He always afterward intended to write about the peculiar and livid species of animals which he had minutely studied there at the Forks as nothing like them was ever contained in any text he could find on zoology. This streak of learned ambition was quickly lost, however.

Neither suspecting nor caring to suspect this tale of McGlincy's, Old Simon promptly spat out a long string of oaths that greatly excited the admiration of everyone and then vowed he'd have the Hudson's Bay Company know they couldn't do that to any Nor'Wester and get away with it.

At the moment it completely slipped everyone's mind to tell McGlincy that Yellow Hair was in and about the place and the kind fates which look over the lives of great men let McGlincy find it out that night, very quietly, without the least stir, when an incident of great bearing upon Yellow Hair's life occurred near the gate.

CHAPTER 28

Duel Without Code

At teatime in Lee's quarters, the old man, his daughter and Strathleigh were all gathered together. Teatime was always something of a strain because the old man, between enormous bites of cake, muffins, cookies and various meats and loud gulps of tea flavored with rum (or rather rum flavored with tea) made many complaints about the digestive organs that had been delivered over to him by his Maker.

These complaints, stated in a high-pitched whine, had to be answered with sympathy. If they were not, then the old man would instantly begin to sob that nobody appreciated him and that the only reason any attention was paid to him was because he was rich and everybody wanted his money—a fact which was uncomfortably close to the truth.

Having gorged himself, the old man would lay his twisted and warped frame on a couch and, propped up, would scowl and glower and sneer for hours on end that the X.Y.s were ruining him with their high prices and that a man couldn't make an honest living among thieves.

This, too, was true in a measure, but Lee underrated his profits. While the Nor'Westers sent out trade goods to the value of three thousand dollars a load and received in return ten to a hundred times that much in beaver, Lee forgot that there was some little risk and danger involved and some little expense necessary to the maintenance of forts and personnel, to say nothing of life.

Lee complained that he made as little as fifty percent per pack and had to take the brunt of a fluctuating market.

He objected very strenuously to the prodigality of these Nor'Westers because, it seemed to him, that they were spending Lee's life blood.

The H.B.C.s shipped most of their take to England, but the Nor'Westers depended upon buyers in Montreal, Quebec and New York, and these buyers cared very little whether the pelts were stamped X.Y. or H.B.C. or anything else as long as they got their profits.

Lee, while he regretted the sorry tangle of affairs, played against anyone any time he could make a dollar, following the prudent precepts of John Jacob Astor who built his wealth on the bones these traders left in the wilderness.

As in all great wars of any kind, the general staff was only slightly concerned with the men who stood the brunt of the skirmishes. At the moment Astor was laying plans to found Astoria on the mouth of the Columbia to snatch away the new northwest trade from the British and Canadians, using as capital the money he had made out of the sweat of these same people—and even the blood.

Presently David Thompson would go shooting across the continent, through blanks on the map no one could fill, to receive the surrender of Astoria from the hands of M'Dougal, Astor's man, who had been a Nor'Wester and became one again instantly after the surrender of the post.

Plot and counterplot. American companies in death throes with Canadian and British companies which, in turn, fought each other. Good men were dying alone in the unmapped fastnesses, but the general staff, as usual, forgot that privates were, after all, people.

Accordingly, Lee lay on his sofa and complained about being robbed until both Strathleigh (a true diplomat, that lord) and Evelyn strove desperately to keep their faces from stiffening in an agreeable expression.

But this day, old Lee had taken one slug too many in his tea and he was presently snoring. Unfortunately for Yellow Hair, his lordship and Evelyn were practically alone.

Evelyn had a deal of finesse about her but she had been occupying her time by remembering just how Yellow Hair had looked leaning on his rifle, staring at the far horizon.

"You aren't riding to the hounds," she said.

His lordship did not quite catch up to this remark and he twisted his mustache, stalling for a little time to think it over.

"That English hunting coat you affect when you go after buffalo and Indians and such things is hardly in keeping with the country, Roger."

Strathleigh thought this over cautiously. After he had married the girl the time for caution would be over but just now, remembering he had no estate or anything else, his lordship looked very intelligent and deftly balanced his teacup. He answered to several names including Roger. His right and full name was Lord Sir

Roger Mortimer Strathleigh-Strathleigh—which his enemies wrote "Strathleigh2."

"Hunting coat, m'dear?"

"Yes, hunting coat. And boots, too. And a top hat. Really, Roger, have you no taste for the fitness of things?"

"Taste, m'dear? Why the King himself recently told—"

"Bother the King!"

"M'dear, don't you think that's beastly strong of you?"

"I am talking about hunting coats," said Evelyn firmly.

"Yes, yes, yes, yes. Quite! Hunting coats! Oh, yes, yes, of course."

"It's a wonder you don't carry a French horn with you to blow tally-ho or something."

"French horn? Really, m'dear, it would be cumbersome no end. The French gave the King and I—"

"It's bad enough to see you moving off with three Indians carrying your guns and a hunter packing your lunch. But a hunting coat of all things!"

"Really, m'dear. . . . Oh, you're objecting to the coat? Why it cost a pretty penny, so it did. Damme, it was made by the King's tailor himself, so it was. Beautiful coat . . ."

"You never heard that 'in Rome you do as the Romans?' Roger, I think that the coat is in horrible taste. You should have some of these women outside the fort make you an Indian costume. A hunting shirt with fringe and all that."

"Indian?" blinked his lordship. "Did you say Indian? M'dear, do you think I would stoop so low as to clothe myself like one of these savage barbarians? Really, m'dear, I should never live it down if it got to the ears of the King."

"But," said Evelyn, sighing deeply, "buckskin is so handsome, so manly."

His lordship sharpened a mustache spike and began to frown. "Whatever put that into your head? Just last month you and I were both howling with laughter at these brutes who went around clothed in animal skins. Really, m'dear, you can be trying at times."

"You should have one," she said with decision. "In the morning I'll order one for you. And a pair of those long leggings which reach all the way from the moccasin to the belt. And you should hunt with one of those long American rifles, too, and . . . and lean on it."

His lordship began to sense on the instant that something was very wrong here. His brain was very quick and he instantly remembered seeing Yellow Hair doing just that thing not five hours ago.

His features took on a feline cast and he looked down at his carefully polished claws. "By any chance, you wouldn't want me to look like that renegade?"

She felt the edge in his voice. This was the first time he had ever showed any real jealousy or interest in her and more than once she had deplored the lack of it. A sudden craving for excitement took hold of her. Was he not the greatest duelist in Europe and England? Had anyone ever fought a duel over her? No! And it was high time.

"He's not a renegade!" she replied haughtily. "He's a very fine gentleman himself. He . . . he told me so last night."

"Last night?"

"On the wall."

His lordship already had one score with Yellow Hair and he saw instantly that he had another. He did not see through this lie.

"So you walk with a renegade at night on the wall?" snarled Strathleigh. "You walk with . . . ah, very well. We shall see about this."

She looked very frightened then and a great deal of it was genuine. "You won't kill him?"

That crystallized his lordship's exact intentions. He stood up very boldly and whipped his mustache into line and gazed gallantly down upon her.

"I mean just that, m'dear."

She pleaded with him one way and another but his lordship had also been bored. Now a good, quick duel would be exciting and nobody would be the worse, except maybe Yellow Hair.

He remembered that the fellow was a gentleman-born and therefore eligible to be challenged by a man so high in the social scale.

His lordship summed it up when he said, "M'dear, when I tell this to the King, what a splendid story it will make."

"But you won't really kill him?"

"M'dear, where honor is involved there is only one recourse for the gentleman who holds honor more dearly than he does his life. Besides, I've never lost one single duel out of forty-one."

He left then, and went to his rooms. He took down his pistols and loaded them with great care, unwilling to trust such an important task to a servant or second.

They were excellent pistols, having served well many times. Built by a famous French maker, they represented the ultimate in accuracy and beauty. Their long barrels were chased with gold and their butts were gleaming silver.

This took him some little time and when he had finished he laid the case away and was about to leave when it came to him that it might be safer to carry one in his belt. He hid the butt in a fold of his shirt and walked forth.

Yellow Hair was foolishly feeling fairly safe at this time. He had understood, finally, that from one motive or another the Nor'Westers intended neither to kill him nor imprison him and he supposed that McGlincy cared little about his presence at Fort William.

There were many high-caste Indians in the fort itself and there were several *bois brûlés,* the "runners of the burnt woods," and Deschamps, and many *coureurs des bois.* Although none of these had savory reputations because of their long employment by the X.Y.s, they were nevertheless people of the woods and plains and wilderness and Yellow Hair understood them.

With twoscore of these sitting about a blaze large enough to be dignified by the term "council fire," Yellow Hair was hurling back banter as swiftly as it came his way, using both words and sign. Someone suggested a song and Yellow Hair picked up a short stick from the pile of wood and began to beat time against his rifle stock.

Presently they all were singing. Gone were the looming and scabby palisades. Gone were the buildings of the whites. With "civilization" shut out by the black curtain which stood at the limit of the fire's light, they gave way to the wildness of the music.

Suddenly on the far side from Yellow Hair, men stopped singing. An Indian youth opened his mouth slightly and slapped his hand over it. Silence swept around the circle to Yellow Hair.

A foot prodded Yellow Hair's back.

Scowling, his lordship grated, "Stop that ungodly caterwaul. You're disturbing the whole fort."

This was not exactly the truth as many voyageurs had wandered over to the blaze to join in the song and even these loud voices could not have reached half across the area between the palisades. But his lordship knew, with that knowledge given to and employed by the superior people of the world, that to stop joy and laughter abruptly is to immediately replace it with a sullen sense of wrong.

Yellow Hair did not like to have his back prodded. He turned halfway around and looked up, the smile replaced by a chill in his blue eyes.

"Have you voice enough to drown us out?"

"Add 'sir' to that when you address me!"

Yellow Hair turned back toward the fire, crossed his legs and picked up his stick. "Where were we, warriors?"

His lordship laid a hand none too gently on Yellow Hair's shoulder. "You dare to affront *me*?"

Wearily, Yellow Hair said, "Please go away. Can't you see we're busy?"

His lordship puffed on that one. He grew very tall and he spat out an oath. "God's blood! You insolent savage, I'll have your life for this!"

Evidently despairing of starting the song, Yellow Hair uncoiled himself and stood up. His lordship was somewhat surprised to see that the other was the taller man.

"Get out of here," said Yellow Hair, "before you say something you'll regret. I have no fight with you and I want none. It is not my habit to pick on weaklings. Go off some place and twirl your mustache."

This stabbed into his lordship's shocked ears like red pokers. He had come to start this very fight and he found himself out-generaled. He lost his temper.

Father Marc was rushing up, but he did not arrive soon enough.

His lordship was carrying a gauntlet and he slapped it against Yellow Hair's face. This was not a code and routine to Yellow Hair. It was a sudden declaration of war and he acted accordingly. With his right hand open, he swung with unerring aim.

The pistol-shot crack of the impact was instantly followed by a second.

Stung on both cheeks, slammed backwards, the lord's fall was aided by a third blow.

Into the mud went Lord Sir Roger Mortimer Strathleigh-Strathleigh.

Fearing that Yellow Hair would finish his lordship off on the second, Father Marc snatched Yellow Hair's arms and pulled him back. But Yellow Hair was grinning in delight when he saw the thing he had done to the cherished mustache.

The *bois brûlés* came up as one man, cheering their lungs out. Voyageurs bellowed their mirth, seeing something very funny in the immaculate lord's now muddy condition.

"I challenge you!" roared Strathleigh.

"Looks like you're already whipped," grinned Yellow Hair.

His lordship struggled to his feet and gnawed at his lips from rage. In a saner condition he might have been more diplomatic but he had such a hearty contempt for all things not straight out of court that he failed to remember he was dealing with a man who had more real pride than all the lords in Christendom.

"I challenge you to a duel to the death!"

"Come ahead!" said Yellow Hair. "Give him a knife, somebody. I've got mine."

A partner came up that instant and in Strathleigh this partner saw Lee's favor. He bawled, "Let me kill the damned half-breed!"

Father Marc, on the instant, saw the responsibility he had in holding Yellow Hair. He quickly released him.

"Come ahead," said Yellow Hair with delight.

"I've challenged him to a duel!" choked Strathleigh. "A duel at dawn! My seconds will wait upon you this very night."

"Afraid to come yourself?" said Yellow Hair in a taunting voice.

"Choose your weapons!" shrieked his lordship. "A duel, I say to avenge my honor!"

"Why the delay?" said Yellow Hair.

Three more partners came up and then Old Simon who began to explain to Yellow Hair that the proper procedure for a duel was to first choose seconds, then weapons, then the ground and the hour. Old Simon said that they would each have one shot. . . .

"What do I care about all that?" said Yellow Hair. "If he wants to kill me so badly, why doesn't he do it right now?"

They could make no headway against this logic and, indeed, they could give Yellow Hair no satisfaction as to just why killing men had to be done in such a systematic manner.

In a condition known as high dudgeon, his lordship stalked from the scene.

He was about forty paces from there and within light which fell from a window. Yellow Hair's back was to the fire.

Yellow Hair called, "Don't run away now! You started this! Haven't you got enough courage to see it through?"

Exasperated at such ignorance, Strathleigh lost all control of himself. He whirled and his hand gripped his pistol butt. He crouched forward and aimed at the clear silhouette.

Yellow Hair had seen neither pistol nor movement. But he saw the flash of sparks from the flint, the glare of the pan, the flash of the muzzle and while all this was happening Yellow Hair was going sideways and down.

The bullet missed him and thudded into a log across the fire.

Yellow Hair waited to make no parley about this. He did not know how many pistols his lordship might have, and furthermore he didn't care.

His long rifle was in his hand before the shot had echoed. He flopped over, jabbed the stock into his shoulder, sighted and squeezed.

He yipped, "The pistol!"

The Woods rifle ribboned the night with sparks.

The glint of bright metal in his lordship's right hand jumped skyward and sailed to the left. His lordship screamed as the bullet tore through the muscles of his wrist.

"Any more?" shouted Yellow Hair. "Come back and have it out, you coward! Come back where I can see what you're doing! Maybe you're afraid when the light's not in your favor, eh? Come back!"

But his lordship showed no signs of obeying. He was

behind a house, well on his way to his rooms, holding his wounded wrist and swearing monotonously between his teeth.

A great burst of laughter reached him. He heard the voyageurs cheering Yellow Hair. It was a bitter dose to take.

CHAPTER 29

A USE FOR THE RENEGADE

The Thunder Moon came and found Yellow Hair still at Fort William. This month, July, was the time of the annual meeting of the Nor'West partners. Brigades a thousand strong came sweeping grandly out from Montreal, up rivers and across lakes to the jumping-off place, ready to launch out into the wilderness and conquer H.B.C. and the fur trade and the wilderness itself.

All the wintering partners except one or two who had been detained by H.B.C.s had come from the interior, and with the good partners from everywhere assembled, Fort William began to take on the complexion of a battlefield.

The bullies, encouraged, bragged and blustered and fought. Even clerks and partners matched muscle in howling brawls. The rule of the day was to get drunk and to fight and to get drunk again and the old palisades shuddered under the impact of *régales*.

Every night and every day crazed men fought and died and generally enjoyed themselves. Father Marc, though not the fort chaplain, wore out his mighty strength confessing the dying, absolving the dead and keeping peace in a place where peace was as foreign as the mention of H.B.C. without an accompanying oath.

Yellow Hair had met with subterfuge and delay at

every turn. More apprehensive than ever about affairs in his own country, impatient to find out what had happened to his friends and almost crazy himself when he realized that Bright Star might long ago have married Long Bow under orders.

Father Marc was too busy to be consulted and Yellow Hair felt isolated and alone in all this noise and confusion.

He suspected strongly that McGlincy was staving off any chance of a hearing on the Fort Chesterfield affair and, satisfied that any further stay was useless, Yellow Hair prepared to leave for the upcountry, H.B.C. or no H.B.C.

The girl Evelyn Lee had not lost interest in him. His brawl with Strathleigh had made Yellow Hair seem very much a knight fighting for her honor and she lost no opportunities in thrusting herself in his way. He was handsome and he had proven himself a better man than his lordship and, title or no title, it amused Evelyn to play at a highly dangerous game.

Yellow Hair was far too preoccupied in wondering what had happened to his Bright Star to notice anyone else, but to Strathleigh's way of thinking, Yellow Hair was trying his best to cut the lord out of old Lee's wealth.

In McGlincy, the lord found an ally. McGlincy, one night while drunk, agreed very heartily with Strathleigh that the young renegade was a "bad 'un" and ought to be stood up against a wall and shot. This was not very consistent with the policy McGlincy had adopted upon seeing that Yellow Hair was within the fort. McGlincy appointed himself an authority on Yellow Hair's entire history and, though deploring the fact that the renegade was a terrible liar, stated a thousand times that no man could fight like the renegade could.

To McGlincy's way of thinking, it was best to keep talking about Yellow Hair, thereby preventing Yellow Hair from receiving any credence for anything he might say in his own behalf. The policy worked out very well, though it made Yellow Hair even more notorious than ever. McGlincy told about attacks Yellow Hair had made on H.B.C. and made those attacks such gory and savage things that he held even the blood-sated partners spellbound with them.

Old Simon was very puzzled as to the best course to pursue in chasing the H.B.C.s out of the Saskatchewan and removing the hostile Blackfeet, or at least making the tribe look favorably upon the Nor'Westers.

Old Simon used the means employed so often by men in high places; the best way to gain respect and obedience is through fear instilled by a campaign of cruelty or at least force. He did not doubt that such methods would obtain instant result from "a crowd of naked, ignorant barbarians."

To get all reactions on this problem, Old Simon called a meeting.

When the bottles were all lined up in front of the partners in the great saloon, Old Simon rose and stated his problem, requesting any solution that might occur to the gentlemen present.

A long silence followed, cut only by a gurgle here or a belch there. Finally his lordship (who had a sort of standing because of his friendship with Lee) stood up.

His arm was in a sling, though it was long ago healed. With his left hand he wound his mustache up and scowled up and down the long board.

"I think," said his lordship, "that we might find use for this renegade. I have heard a great deal of talk about his influence with the Blackfeet and I also understand that he is not above price. Of honor he has none—as you can witness from the treacherous attack he made upon me."

He sat down and cued McGlincy. There was an understanding between these two. They had talked about it into the long hours of the night.

McGlincy stood up, grasping the bottle and thereby supporting himself. Impressively he said, "Gentlemen!"

This held them for quite a little while, so he said, "Gentlemen, this is a grave problem."

In possession of this profound observation, the partners all nodded thoughtfully, rubbed their chins and looked very wise at one another in agreement to what McGlincy said.

"His lordship has stuck his paddle in the right river," said McGlincy. "The renegade, that arch enemy of the H.B.C.s, that scourge of fire along the frontier, that bloodthirsty savage and barbarian, can be persuaded to accept a proposal that we make to him."

He had to pause there because his hat kept jolting over his eyes every time he hiccupped. He laid the hat on the chair.

"The policy I am about to outline is profound and strategic. Damme, if it ain't. I propose we concentrate our brigades on the Saskatchewan, that we occupy Fort Chesterfield with force. We fight fire with fire, blood with blood and we never say die!"

These sentiments were cheered and there was a pause while everyone toasted McGlincy. That personage accepted the praise which undoubtedly was his due and presently continued.

"We call out these damned savages. We tell them to send their chiefs into council with us. Then as soon as we get the fools inside the fort we lock them up!"

Everyone was stunned by the sagacity that was here displayed. McGlincy, greasing his lungs with a quick drag at his bottle, indicated them with its mouth.

"We hold them as—hic—hostages! If we get attacked we tell them we'll kill their chiefs to a man. Then, to insure peace and good trade at the fort, we bring all the chiefs back here to Fort William under heavy guard and we lock them up and hold them as long as we need. A lifetime if necessary!"

His lordship suggested the toast this time and it was uproariously given. McGlincy bowed.

The thin voice of doubt through the mouth of Old Simon said, "What if these chiefs are too smart to come inside the fort?"

"That's just what they'll do," replied McGlincy. "I've thought all that out. When they see we've got so many men in the place, they'll balk. And *that's* where this renegade comes in."

"Right there," said his lordship warmly.

"Yes, right there," said McGlincy. "We stand him up on the runway and he sings out that the whites are all for peace and there ain't any danger at all in coming in. They've got faith in him and in they come and there we've got 'em. Damme if we haven't."

Old Simon scratched his bald head. "Maybe he'll say something we won't want him to say."

"We bribe him first. Then we have an interpreter there to tell us if he says right and finally—"

"Finally," interrupted his lordship with an eagerness he took no care to hide, "Finally, I stand there behind him with a pistol at his back. One false move and the devil is dead!"

This was too much thinking all in one piece for the Nor'Westers. They cheered and stamped their feet and rolled out the kegs and sang McGlincy's praises. Was there ever a greater man?

Was it not now possible to make these Blackfeet turn against their "present employers," the H.B.C.?

Was it not now possible to possess the pick of all furs from Edmonton to the Missouri?

Would not the Hudson's Bay Company be driven from the field?

Yes, a million times yes!

Indeed, they told each other, this McGlincy was certainly a great man.

CHAPTER 30

YELLOW HAIR SEES

There *is* honor among thieves.

They honor thievery, knavery, cunning, hypocrisy and prevarication—when these are not used among the brotherhood of villains, but directed against a common enemy.

If such a plan as that put forth by McGlincy and echoed by his lordship had been promulgated to thwart the designs of the Nor'Westers instead of furthering them, McGlincy would have been strung up in the gateway within the hour.

It makes a great deal of difference which target a marksman uses. If he shoots at and kills an animal not linked in any way with either the sympathies or affections of the bystanders, that marksman is instantly a wonderful fellow. But if the shot be directed at the bystander, no matter the beautiful accuracy of it, then the marksman is instantly a villain, a murderer and the cry goes up that he be hanged.

Therefore, it makes a great deal of difference which side a man takes in a fight, how his actions are measured.

If Benedict Arnold had deserted from the British to the colonials, he would probably now have countless statues erected to his memory and history would applaud him through the ages.

The Nor'Westers, therefore, considered this bit of treachery of McGlincy's to be the most laudable and heroic thing which had yet come before their notice. In fairness, the same thing can be said of any great general employing strategy to win his battles.

Yellow Hair himself was amazed to discover that he had suddenly risen to a new estate. Heretofore the Nor'-Westers had thought him interesting and clever, but now, shining in the reflected sunlight of McGlincy, Yellow Hair took on new value and was accorded respect in vast quantities.

This man gave him a pistol and that one presented him with a powder horn. This one handed out a scarlet headsilk and that one a Toledo-bladed knife.

Everyone was very kind to him and spoke to him cordially whenever he passed and invited him here and there and remembered that he was a gentleman and not a "damned savage."

Yellow Hair, had he not suffered so very much at white hands, might have taken all this in stride, with perfect ease and poise and he might even have contracted the disease known as "brag."

But when Father Marc commented on all this, Yellow Hair looked soberly at the Mighty Monk.

"They're ready to go upriver," said Yellow Hair. "They're launching many more canoes than usual for Fort Chesterfield. They have issued out many rifles more than they need and have much powder and shot. These, Marc, are the indications and implements of war."

"You needn't worry," boomed the Mighty Monk. "It means that the H.B.C.s are in for it."

"I wish I thought you were right. I've heard that dog-face who calls himself a lord—which is also the term you use for God—swank through the place talking about the sport of killing Indians. He told Old Simon he was anxious to try a special ball of a peculiar pointed shape. He said that that would stop the 'damned redskins.' He talks about shooting Indians as you and I might talk about shooting skunks, and if the man had as much regard for taste as he has for that mustache, he would bother to inform himself that Indians are quite as good as he is—indeed, much better."

"Oh, now, don't let that popinjay get on your nerves, lad," laughed Father Marc. "He's a windstorm without rain."

"I'm not sure of that. He's killed twoscore men in duels and he tried to murder me. But that isn't what's worrying me."

"No?"

"No! There's this talk about Indians. And then there's a sudden show of interest in me. Judging by the reputation they have handed out to me all cut and tanned, they should have nothing but contempt for one they call a renegade—though the Above Ones know I'm as good a Pikuni as White Fox."

"You think they're getting ready to fight your people?"

"I'm not saying what I think because I have no evidence of any real value to back it up. I cannot understand why they would want to fight my people because my people have never done a single thing to them. On the contrary, the Pikunis have aided these whites time and again with provisions, horses and pelts. And so I cannot bring myself to believe that any people like these would want to fight when there has been no provocation, only kindness."

"You have very slim evidence that this is the case," said Father Marc. "I think the H.B.C.s are the goal. There has been enough friction during the past year to start fifty wars."

"There's more to it than that. There's this sudden burst of fondness for me. They give me things and ask me around and show me off like I was a fine saddle or something of the sort. There's reason behind that."

"Why," grinned Father Marc, amused that anyone should object to offered glory, "they know you're a fighter and they need fighters to whip the English. That's all."

"Marc, there's a certain difference in treatment. There's the honor accorded the warrior. This is not it. Then there is the attention paid to a buffalo horse when the owner feeds it and grooms it and pets it."

"What's the matter with that?"

"Why, nothing, except that this never happens unless the owner wants the horse to be in fine shape so that he can ride him to death."

"Oh."

"And I've seen these whites fattening chickens before they kill and eat them—though why anybody should want to eat a chicken I don't know. It stands this way to me. I'm wanted for some underhanded purpose or other. These Nor'Westers are going against my people. What else can they want of me but to have me play traitor to the Pikunis?"

"If you think that, leave the fort and escape."

"Not me," said Yellow Hair. "I think the Pikunis are involved here and I can do them more good while I'm inside the white ranks than upon a horse charging them. We have many horses, but we have no friends among the whites."

"You may be very harsh," said Father Marc.

"And I may be very right. I don't like the way that lord keeps looking at the small of my back. He's thinking about bullets when he looks at that spot. Come lightning or hail, Marc, I'm sticking with these brigades and if there's treachery afoot there'll be a few of these whites to tell it in their Sand Hills—if they have any."

"But maybe it will mean your life," said Father Marc, at last very alarmed.

"Maybe," said Yellow Hair with a bitter grin.

CHAPTER 31

BRIGADES WESTWARD

It took seventy days for the brigades to reach the rich wilderness of the Saskatchewan from Fort William.

A long and hard journey, rendered dangerous by the ununderstandable conduct of the Sioux, who, for some reason no Nor'Wester could understand, objected to this constant traffic, and occasionally gave vent to their irritation with a present of arrows and bullets.

The way was, of course, by water. These traders would never have been able to exist had it not been for the crisscross chain of rivers that ran like incisions back and forth across the continent, laying it wide open to the indifferent doctoring of the whites and prematurely exposing the flanks of the Indian nations.

No man would be mean and narrow enough to didactically state that this business of harvesting the riches of furs in a land as large as the Russian Empire did not require some degree of bravery.

Solid animal courage, daredevil tactics and feats of beef and brawn were as common to these traders as their rum. Flags flying, with songs rolling out of their throats, paddles flashing, headsilks fluttering, the voyageurs drove through this unfriendly land with as little seeming care as though they were on their way to a *régale* where all the rum was free.

While the settler and pioneer drove inland with the feeling and declaration that they owned the country, the Nor'Westers sped through this maze of waterways with an air which clearly said they didn't give a damn who owned it.

Furs meant untold wealth and furs they would have. For a keg of whisky costing two pounds they received beaver pelts to the value of sixty pounds. But danger cut down their profit and they had the overhead of forts and a fair-sized army.

Even the devil demands credit for some things and any man who has the slightest idea what these thousand dangers consisted of would be both blind and foolish if he failed to appreciate the spirit that catapulted these wild legions into the unmapped whole of the northern continent.

Five hundred canoes started out from Fort William with several destinations for the several brigades. Laden with trade goods, arms and men, bound for points months apart, facing a winter which might bring wealth and might bring death, these voyageurs and bullies, no matter their immediate past and their moral standards, exact the admiration of any thinking man.

It was not the bullies and the voyageurs who formed the policies and dictates of the fur trade. It was not for them to think, but only to obey. Each was a small part of a mighty machine, under the direct and despotic rule of the Nor'West partners.

With H.B.C. insisting that the monopoly of the trade was their own and with the X.Y.s stating to the contrary that the North West Fur Company owned the monopoly, these partners were determined to fight it out to the last pelt and the last bullet.

Each one of the wintering partners was speeding north and west to resume the command of empires within empires, individually to become the tyrants and overlords of territories the size of several Germanys.

Furs. That was the byword. Furs. Anything was lawful, any policy was good as long as it got furs.

Up the Kaministiqwia. Through Lake of the Woods. Past the granite gap that was Portage of the Rat. Down the foaming torrent of the Winnipeg River, flowing north into Lake Winnipeg.

Five hundred canoes abreast, lashed by pairs, gunwale to gunwale, wafted by the wind with bright wakes behind them, with blue skies above them and with the amber shores and green trees mirrored on the quiet surface of the water.

North to the mouth of the Saskatchewan, past Horse Island, around the Grand Rapids and ahead lay a thousand miles of unbroken and navigable waterway.

Brigades had dropped off. To Pembina on Red River. To Swan Lake. To Athabasca. To Grand Forks. To the Mandans. To the Assiniboine. And to the vast region of the Saskatchewan.

The main part of this great army, speeding in their light canoes, meeting and jeering the H.B.C.s, trading, stopping to patch canoes, stopping at forts, racing the clumsy English barges, but all the while pouring in a torrent that darkened the water up into the land of the best and most plentiful pelts—the Saskatchewan.

Yellow Hair was uneasy and impatient but he had to accept his lot. He hated the labor of paddling as his whole conception of travel had to do with the horse and, as long as he did not have to wield a blade, he took out his restlessness in hunting on the way, in sign talking with Crees until his arms ached, inquiring for news of the Blackfeet.

In the canoes and out of them, he never for an instant relaxed his vigil. He watched McGlincy and distrusted McGlincy's seeming friendship. He watched the lord and made very certain that he never presented his back for the shot he knew would some day come.

McGlincy, he noticed, was always inspecting the arms of the brigades, always issuing strict orders about the stowage of the powder, always quick to blast and damn the soul of any luckless voyageur who failed to bail with enough speed or failed to mend any seam.

This confirmed Yellow Hair's suspicion that the unwarranted number of bullies in the brigades were there for war and war alone. Bullies were all brag and bluster. They worked but little, considering that beneath their dignity. It was their portion to fight and that they expected to earn their money before fall was gone was clearly understood from the way they talked about the ease with which any competent man could kill a dozen Indians.

His lordship had been sour on the first part of the journey. It was not at all to his liking to go so far into the land of trees and plains, though he never failed to vow that it would make a priceless story to tell the King.

His lordship continued to exact respect and McGlincy was very ready with it.

The voyageurs and bullies, thought Yellow Hair, fawned upon men like Luberly. The Luberlys fawned upon the McGlincys. And the McGlincys fawned upon the lords. The lords, supposed Yellow Hair, groveled before a thing they called a king and the king, if he was a man, probably fawned upon some courtesan and she—well, it was all very round, at that.

Father Marc, returning to his old post at the fort, evidently with all forgiven, was one of the busiest of men. With a prayer book in one hand and a fist in the other, he kept the voyageurs fairly well in line so that they would arrive at their destinations without too many broken heads or unconfessed souls.

Although many men solicited Yellow Hair's conversation, he was very saving with his opinions. He was too restless to long remain seated at a fire or in a canoe, and a kind of thick dread had hold of him that would not let him sleep.

What of the Pikunis?

What of Bright Star?

What part would he be asked to play in this coming war?

No one had any answer for those questions.

His lordship, as the rigors of the trip began to take away the paleness of his face and replace it with "detestable" brown, and as his man servant had forgotten to put in a sufficient quantity of mustache wax, grew less sour and more morose.

This trip, thought Strathleigh, was the height of folly. But he had had to make it. The magnet which had tried to keep him at Fort William had been unable to overcome the reasons he should go to the Saskatchewan and perhaps spend a winter in the wilds.

First, there was the girl Evelyn. Although Yellow Hair had seldom looked in her direction she had whetted his lordship's appetite for revenge to a keen edge that demanded action. She vowed that Yellow Hair was his rival, principally because she had no great taste for Strathleigh and liked to anger him. Thus, Yellow Hair had to be put out of the way.

Second, there was the matter of the "duel." Yellow Hair had tended to prove that Strathleigh was a coward and had, with one well-placed shot—which had been accurately called before it was made and could not be attributed to luck—completely wrecked his lordship's reputation as the best of duelists. Thus, before that reputation could again stand without criticism, Yellow Hair had to be put out of the way.

Third, there was the request—which amounted to an order—from Lee, who respected no position not held by sheer power of money, to the effect that the Nor'-Westers were ruining him—Lee—by charging him too much. His lordship, as Lee's agent and friend, was to look into this matter. As his lordship had a financial interest in this himself, he had had to go.

And then, too, there was the smaller consideration that it might be sport after all. With three fine hunting weapons to try out, his lordship expressed great desire to try them on fair game like Indians.

Yellow Hair knew something like this was going on in Strathleigh's mind and he never failed to miss those eyes on the small of his back.

McGlincy's kindness was too thin for even a fool to fail to realize it.

McGlincy had suffered something in prestige when he had been frightened out by the Blackfeet. He wanted to even up that score a little. He had never ceased to worry that someday it would be discovered by the other partners that the fiasco at the fort had come out rather on the blue side of McGlincy's personal ledger.

Someday Yellow Hair might talk.

Yellow Hair could not be allowed to live that long, especially when his usefulness would be over just as soon as he had been used for the betrayal and seizure of the powerful Blackfoot chiefs.

McGlincy knew he would be successful. If a pow-wow after that seizure did not bring results and if the Blackfeet did not immediately express a desire to attack the H.B.C.s and the Americans and turn the proceeds over to the Nor'Westers, then McGlincy had the means to carry out those demands by ample force of arms.

The fort, on the rebuilding of the trade room, had been much enlarged, much strengthened. There was nothing to fear from that quarter—not with a hundred and fifty bullies, all well armed, and another hundred and fifty voyageurs.

An expensive campaign but it could result in nothing short of complete success.

McGlincy had every reason to be kind to the man who, though he did not know it, would soon be of great use to the Nor'Westers.

The seventy days were drawing to an end. Yellow Hair began to brighten as they entered country he knew. He cried out at the sight of every recognized bluff and stream and as they came nearer and nearer to the confluence of the South Saskatchewan and the Red Deer River, his excitement could not be suppressed.

One ingredient of that excitement was the expectancy of coming battle and his anxiety to somehow warn the Pikunis that war was at hand.

He was closely guarded now, though none of his actions were hampered. He was too valuable to this plan of McGlincy's to let loose now.

But Yellow Hair had other ways. He had already told Crees that the white men were on the war trail into Blackfoot country. Word might have passed in that direction.

Now he looked into his war sack and pulled out paint. He startled the voyageurs very much until he explained that this was the custom of his people whenever they were overjoyed at the prospect of coming home. He did not tell them that the red stripes he slashed across his face were the markings of WAR.

He did not tell them that there was a reason in the way he carried his knife and rifle. That meant WAR.

He let them think him very uncivilized when he wrecked the back of his fine antelope hunting shirt with the design $\rangle \langle\langle$. He did not explain that this was one goose flying against two geese and that it was the universal Indian sign for WAR.

His idle drawings of a hand clutching a tomahawk —though so crudely done that none but pictographers could read it—in the sands about the fires of their abandoned camps meant WAR.

And one evening when he was alone at a fire, he did not comment on the way he ruined his robe by throwing it over the coals, jerking it off, then throwing it over again and again. In exclamation points of smoke in the sky, he spelled out WAR.

And, shivering with excitement and apprehension, he gave no sign when he saw a Pikuni scout slide backward from a bluff. That wolf had read those signs and those signs spelled WAR BETWEEN THIS BRIGADE AND THE PIKUNI NATION—ASSEMBLE ALL WARRIORS!

CHAPTER 32

DEATH TO THE BLACKFEET!

The arrival at Fort Chesterfield was an affair of great importance and, as all affairs of state, required much ceremony.

McGlincy had been absent for almost a year and as it was now October he knew, of course, that matters of importance had been long waiting his attention. But this did not deter him from accepting the pomp that was his due.

He succeeded in getting solidly on the landing without upsetting his canoe and he stood there, waiting for his lordship to come up beside him and even shifted hands with his bottle to give his lordship his arm.

This arm of McGlincy's was not much help to Strathleigh but it did serve to keep McGlincy on his feet.

They went up toward the gate where Luberly stood and when Luberly saw that McGlincy was actually conversing and condescending like an ordinary man, he realized that the fellow with the fine hunting coat and the spiked mustache must be at least the King of England.

Luberly gaped. He wiped his hands uncomfortably upon the thick grease of his shirt, adding dirt to his fingers rather than removing it. He shifted from one foot to the other uneasily. He sniffled and swiped his black sleeve anxiously across his upper lip and then stood there picking at his beard, very frightened.

McGlincy's abrupt departure the year before had left Luberly, so to speak, to fry in his own grease. But, while he had pushed forward a great deal of work upon the defenses, he had not been molested. In fact, just that spring, he had collected over two hundred packs of beaver skins at forty pounds a pack, in return for which he had had to issue trade rifles and ammunition.

The people who had brought him these packs were, as far as Luberly was concerned, just a mob of savages and barbarians tricked out in finery. He mentioned them as "filthy heathens," but as Luberly had no religion whatsoever and he had never been called clean by anyone, the remark must be put down as a sloppy bit of profanity.

He knew vaguely, of course, that the people were Minnetarees and must be raiding somewhere to come north as far as Fort Chesterfield, but he had traded them the rifles and the whisky and had taken in the pelts.

Then another "mob of bloodthirsty redskins" had descended upon him with more beaver pelts, demanding rifles and ammunition and he had given them out. These were Snakes from the mountains.

Following this group came another. A large band of Crows who, following their namesake, appeared and disappeared with amazing speed. The Crows had wanted rifles and ammunition and seemed to possess untold wealth in pelts.

Shortly thereafter a fellow had arrived who called

himself White Fox and two other men who, the interpreter said, were named Low Horns and Lost-in-Mountains. These men did not seem to have the force which had backed them up on a former visit and so Luberly's treatment of them had been very abrupt.

They had made a foolish demand. They had said that the fort had done the Blackfeet a grave injustice by so carelessly handing out arms to every band which came along. As in any racial group, unbalanced power tends to work to the detriment of any weaker people and war was almost certain to follow on one frontier or another.

Luberly had no orders about this and so he had given them an emphatic curse and told them to be gone before he turned his rifles on them.

Strangely enough this same trio had come to them about the first of July, followed by a considerable troop of their people who carried a large quantity of pelts. They had demanded trade rifles and ammunition.

But by this time Luberly's stock was in a sad condition and he had not been able to wholly fulfill their needs, vainly urging whisky upon them as a currency.

Luberly did not ask where these pelts came from but a story, told very touchingly, about an American brigade entering Blackfoot country, gave him some clue which he did not bother to follow: This brigade had unsuccessfully attacked a small Blackfoot war party and had been, in return, hurried out of the country minus their illegally trapped furs.

And so it was that Luberly, when he saw the number of rifles and the amount of ammunition in the big flotilla, very agreeably supposed that he could now get the rest of those pelts from the Blackfeet.

But Luberly, who was not war-minded except when on the superior side and when the enemy had no chance whatever, received a rude shock.

The cannon went off in salute. The voyageurs and bullies in the fort cheered lustily.

McGlincy and Strathleigh came to a halt just outside the gate.

McGlincy raised his bottle for silence. An abrupt hush fell upon the place as every man breathlessly waited for the doubtless immortal words.

"Damme, my lads!" cried McGlincy. "Here's the answer to your prayers. Here's succor! We've arrived!"

Everybody cheered and cheered and cheered so that Yellow Hair's small "Huh!" of disgust was completely swallowed up in the bellow.

Now Luberly had not felt himself in need of succor but he now found it prudent to wring his hands and shout, "Thank God you've come!"

His lordship was very impressed, though he felt slighted at not having more attention paid to his noble person. He cleared his throat and wound up his mustache so hard that it would twirl for an hour without another touch.

"Yes, my brave lads," said his lordship, "we've come night and day to your rescue. Now let them attack!"

Luberly was mystified by this but he cried, "Ay, let them attack!" and promptly ordered another salute and a cheer. He wondered vaguely who would be attacking what, but that did not keep him from reverently bowing and scraping and muttering his happiness, his thankfulness, and calling on God himself to witness that he had only done his duty.

This rather encouraged McGlincy in a hallucination

which, interspersed with green lizards and orange buffalos, had been with him for some little time. So often had he told this story, so wonderfully did he paint and adorn it with blood that now, seeing Luberly agree with him perfectly, he believed himself implicitly and began to get really angry with the "damned barbarians" who would dare affront *him* with an attack.

His curses grew louder and more sincere as he progressed across the yard and to the trading post and he was fairly frothing when he entered and gave his lordship a seat.

He broke open a new case—which as usual followed close behind—poured out two cups full and drank, "To the extermination of those vermin, the Blackfeet."

To which he added with a belch, "Damme if we won't!"

Luberly had not yet thought it wise to mention a certain matter that had been in full view these many months, but when he saw that McGlincy had mellowed after an hour's steady pouring and when he observed that his lordship had begun to feel gay, Luberly sprung his surprise.

In the rebuilding, as long as the H.B.C.s were paying for it, the trading house itself had been raised considerably and a lookout tower placed on top of that. The palisades, running downhill somewhat toward the river, were therefore low enough so as not to obstruct a clear view of the highland on the opposite bank.

The newly built edifice across the river was not visible from the stream itself and the arriving brigades had been too glad to get to the fort to look around very much.

Now Luberly threw the door open and with an

apologetic sniffle to assure these two great gentlemen he had nothing to do with it, he pointed a dirty fingernail across the South Saskatchewan.

As all men who stray from the truth are apt to get tangled in their stories and forget certain things they have said, such was the case with McGlincy.

He had told the Nor'Westers, with careless enthusiasm, that the Hudson's Bay Company was building a fort, had incited the Indians against the X.Y.s and had stolen much trade.

While remembering the rest of it, through retelling, he had forgotten the fort.

But there it was!

An H.B.C. post on the top of a bluff with the British flag dangling from the pole in the slack air of the clear day, had only been there in fancy. Now it was there in reality.

"Bless me," said McGlincy in a weak voice.

For an instant he soberly recalled that he had been lying when he had first said that it was there. Then, on second thought, he realized that he had not been lying at all; That every word he had spoken, every attack he had outlined, was the white, ungarnished truth.

"We'll show 'em!" shouted McGlincy. "And we'll show these damned savages if they can attack us!"

He pounded the table with the bottom of his bottle, looked very fierce, growled and drank and then belched ferociously.

His lordship, knowing the story, now saw it confirmed perfectly and, anxious to try out those three new rifles, immediately began a long discussion of policy as to the best ways and means of conducting this campaign to make the plains safe for the Nor'Westers, to secure all the furs in the whole department and avenge the wrongs already suffered.

Yellow Hair, in the meanwhile, stayed with Father Marc. He saw the rebuilt trading house, the new quarters, the enforced palisades, the new cannon emplacements, and he shut his eyes to recall the blazing horror of that attack upon him in this very place.

He could cut and run.

It was not too late.

He was four days' fast travel to the Marias and there were his horses—his own horses—grazing just outside the post.

He shook his head as though something had blinded him. He could tell the Blackfeet that something was afoot, but that was all. He knew nothing more than what he could see standing right here.

No, not even the call from the south, the worry about the girl who would become his sits-beside-him woman (unless she already belonged to Long Bow), not even the memory of past treachery could make him go.

His place was here, inside the fort.

Here he was needed and could help.

And here he would stay.

CHAPTER 33

LET THERE BE WAR

The wolf hurled himself southward toward the Pikuni village, using up his last horse, riding so hard that the mustang's feet could not be seen and both horse and rider appeared to be canted over and detached from the undulating ocean of the limitless prairie.

Four mounted scouts posted on a knoll caught sight of the oncoming messenger.

Speed meant that a hostile war party might be close behind him. The four took no chances of having their town surprised. They began to signal, "Enemy in sight!"

White Fox and Low Horns, walking along in front of the lodges, glanced up and stopped. They could see the four mounted scouts silhouetted against the deep blue of the sky.

By pairs they were riding toward and past each other to turn and repass again and again. The signal could not be mistaken.

White Fox gave a shout.

Instantly the whole village was hurled into turmoil. Men dashed out of their lodges to stare at the scouts and as quickly raced inside again to snatch up weapons.

Horse herders, knowing their part, mounted and hurled the group of war ponies in toward the tents.

Shouting and yipping warriors crowded out into the streets. Dogs howled. Children screamed. Orders went rocketing the length and breadth of the big camp.

The wolf swept by the lookout post and raised his hand in a negative.

"I am not followed! I have important news!"

He was gone in a roll of dust and hoof-thunder to careen into a street and bring his mustang standing before the tent of Low Horns.

The signal had been relayed from the knoll. Men stood with saddles half cinched, with weapons half loaded. Quiet ripped through the place with the speed of a prairie fire.

Low Horns saluted the wolf.

The messenger hurled himself off and thrust his bridle into the hands of a herder. His face was without excitement. He walked with dignity through the oval door of Low Horns' lodge.

The leaders of various clans, throwing robes about them and putting their weapons away for the moment, strode toward the big lodge.

Low Horns sat down at the head. The chiefs ranged themselves in order about the smoldering fire. The pipe was lighted and passed in the direction the sun takes, but not past the door.

Low Horns nodded to the wolf.

With folded arms, the scout stood just inside the entrance. "Chiefs, I have seen Yellow Hair."

A shiver ran around the circle, almost imperceptible. There was no interruption.

"I have seen as many canoes upon the river as there are doves in a flock, loaded with as many men as half our nation. Two days' travel below the Big Forks I saw smoke. The next morning I found a symbol drawn beside the dead ashes.

"I rode swiftly and found a point of vantage on a bluff and there I saw the canoes.

"Yellow Hair was in one of these. He was not working with the other men. His face was painted with red stripes with circles on his cheeks. On the back of his hunting shirt he had made one goose flying against two geese.

"Being Pikuni he saw me on the bluff but he was the only one who did.

"These many canoes carry many rifles and men to shoot them. They are making for the white fort.

"Yellow Hair is telling us that they come for war against the Pikuni nation.

"I have finished."

The scout withdrew. Low Horns stood up.

"This is the reason the white trader gave guns to our enemies and refused guns to us. The whites want war. We have long known that we are not liked by the whites.

"Let there be war.

"I have finished."

The council broke up. The chiefs of the clans and societies went back to their tents.

Now that there was no need for haste, now that they knew they must travel far to the north, they made their preparations with great thoroughness.

Hunters were called in by swift messengers. Weapons were gone over, sharpened and polished. Because it was close to winter and because they might encounter storms before they could get back, they took out their quilted elkskin hunting shirts, their boot moccasins and included in their packs enough robes.

They gathered up sacked pemmican.

They detailed men to baggage, others to the horse herd. They sketched out their plan of procedure. They consulted Bear Claws as to any omens he might have observed.

And then, having prepared themselves with swiftness which would have been envied by any cavalry leader, they spread themselves out in the order of march and, with bonnets flowing, fringes dancing, weapons flashing, the host swept over the brown ocean of the plains, heading north.

They knew exactly what each man was to do, exactly how they should proceed. They had rear guard and advance guard and scouts on their flanks. They had left a detachment behind to guard their town. They had at least two relays of horses to a man.

The Pikunis were on their way to war.

CHAPTER 34

THE WHITE RUNNER

By this time McGlincy was so thoroughly convinced that the Hudson's Bay Company had taken over the Blackfeet and had bought their friendship for themselves and their hostility against the Nor'Westers that he divided his time three ways—frothing, swilling and preparing the fort.

The number of cannon had been increased to four and these, ready-loaded, were spotted in strategic positions. Two were aimed parallel with the palisades and mounted on a jutting bastion so that, loaded with shot, they could sweep the length of the wall and clear away any attacker there who was so foolish as to try scaling. The other two cannon, in a like position, commanded the length of the opposite palisade.

McGlincy, heartily cursing the Blackfeet for the benefit of his lordship and his own wrath, vowed a thousand times a day that this was Nor'Wester country and would remain so. He'd sweep out the Indians and then clean up their employers, the H.B.C. He'd raze that fort across the river, damme if he wouldn't!

His anger was increased to terrible heights when he found that the H.B.C. post was commanded by Robert Motley. That was very embarrassing because Motley might sometime find out about the swindle and the truth would come out about McGlincy's personal account.

It must be said of McGlincy that he was not without resource in matters pertaining to war. Otherwise he would never have stayed this long in his present exalted position.

While he did not doubt for an instant that his plan to capture hostages would work, neither did he neglect any possibility of the results which would attend failure.

The post was fortified. A plan in case of attack was mapped out. The trading house itself, being independently defensible, was prepared as a last retreat.

McGlincy, the day after his arrival, despatched a runner mounted on a swift horse to the south to look for Blackfeet and with orders to give them a message.

As this runner was a half-breed of the kind which made up the Deschamps, he was very well schooled in wilderness arts and could talk Algonquian enough to be understood by Pikunis and, if that failed, he could make it up with sign.

Eight days elapsed before this runner's return. He rode his horse straight into the gates and swung out of his saddle.

"What's up?" bawled McGlincy.

"I've talked with Blackfeet."

"Well, damme, out with it. Don't stand there and puff at me. What did you tell them? What did they say?"

"It was a raiding party."

"Raiding party? Gawd's blood, man, how many men in it?"

"Not half a dozen."

"What nonsense is this? Out with it! What did they have to say?"

The poor messenger tried his best to string his story

together but he was interrupted so much with questions and roared at so constantly and generally abused that he took some time to get it straight.

Yellow Hair, standing nearby, repressed a smile. He knew more about it than the messenger, and he wanted very much to know what the messenger had found.

Finally it was all out. The runner had come upon this small raiding party (advance guard a day's march ahead, thought Yellow Hair) and he had told them that the Great White Chief at the fort wanted to talk with their highest chiefs. The party replied that they were after Crows but that they would go back immediately and so inform the chiefs and that the runner need not bother himself further with the message. The runner had thanked them and returned with all haste (without knowing, thought Yellow Hair, that the Pikuni cavalry would have come up to him in a few hours).

McGlincy scrubbed his hands together. Matters were working out beautifully. Nobody suspected what the main design was.

McGlincy rushed preparations and his lordship looked to his three fine rifles and began to brighten up at the thought of the coming sport. The bullies swaggered around the fort and bragged about what they'd do to those "damned savages" when they arrived.

And that they could do plenty, Yellow Hair did not doubt. He knew that there must be few rifles in the possession of the Blackfeet in comparison to the vast number in the hands of these whites. The average number of rifles in Pikuni ranks would be about one to every thirty men. The fort was strong and well guarded by the cannon and an attacking cavalry force would face very serious losses if they attempted to scale the palisades.

But Yellow Hair also appreciated this situation from the viewpoint of his people. This fort, continuing to trade guns to Crows, Snakes, and Minnetarees, was a distinct menace to peace on the plains. And McGlincy had something in mind which even Yellow Hair could not fathom.

He grinned a great deal about the foolishness of that scout. On the face of it, a messenger would never have been able to find a Blackfoot raiding party. If the runner had used his head he would have known that he had been intercepted purposely to keep him from continuing further south.

Four days passed without either alarms or excitement. The rolling plains, brown and barren with winter's approach, seemed to sleep.

All the war there was at the moment was all in McGlincy's loud mouth, gargling around with the whisky.

CHAPTER 35

WOLVES

After sundown, the day before the battle, a wind had sprung up. It came down from the Arctic, bearing the chill breath of ice and storms, moaning desolately about the palisades with the tidings of winter's approach.

The night was black because there were neither moon nor stars. Muffled to the ears, sentries paced the runways and watched the bluffs.

McGlincy was growing very impatient. He sat in the trading house with a bottle in his hand, his face lit up by the flickering light of a piece of cotton burning smokily in a cup of grease.

A silence had come over the people around him. Luberly's eyes were large as he listened to the winds and a certain other sound which sent chills racing back and forth across his hunched shoulders.

His lordship was staring at the candle, listening, the tenseness of his nerves showing up on his thin mouth.

Yellow Hair was walking back and forth, back and forth along the wall, stopping now and then beside the casement as though listening.

Because it was cold and because the hard ground made hunting poor, the wolves howled. Their mournful, quavering voices rose and fell in long and dismal howls all along the line of bluffs above the fort.

Over and over again the voices started from a broken guttural whimper, rose upward, quavered there, rose again to mock the storm, hung dolefully at the top, broke and stumbled slowly down below the note which had begun the awful howl.

Over and over rolled the echo of the gloomy hunting song, seconded and swallowed by the hoarse moan of the storm.

Strathleigh had listened longer than he could stand. He banged his glass on the board and sprang to his feet, glaring at the casement.

"Shut up! Shut up, I tell you!"

But the gray wolves of the plains knew nothing of the authority of his lordship. The unending symphony of terror went on.

Feeling a little foolish, his lordship sank back.

"It's just the wolves," said Father Marc with a grin. "The wind makes them sad. If you stay here this winter you'll have to get used to it because they do that all the time."

"I don't see why," said his lordship peevishly. "Isn't there any way to stop them?"

Father Marc's grin broadened and he jerked a thumb at Yellow Hair. "On that long trip south from York Factory last winter, I heard Yellow Hair shut them up."

"Damme," snapped McGlincy. "I always thought he was half wolf anyhow."

"You don't mean," said his lordship, looking carefully at the tall shadow against the wall which was Yellow Hair, "that you can actually talk to the beasts!"

"Why not?" said Yellow Hair gently.

"I don't believe it," muttered Strathleigh.

Yellow Hair grinned at them from the shadows. He turned and threw the casement open. The burning rag flickered in the blast of chill wind which stabbed at them.

In that eerie, dancing light, Yellow Hair leaned on the sill. From his throat rose a breaking guttural moan. It rose higher and higher. It broke and rose again to a falsetto note which shook the room. Slowly he came down the scale again. With a malicious yip that shattered the nerves of every man in the place, he finished.

The only sound after that was the rasp of wood as the casement closed.

The wolves were not howling anymore.

McGlincy clutched the edges of the table and turned greenish-white as the wick flared.

"God damn me! 'Od's blood! He . . . he did it!"

Yellow Hair grinned. "They'll answer me when they have an answer ready. Listen!"

Presently came a long-drawn howl and abruptly it too ended in a savage yip.

"J . . . j . . . j . . . just like him," whispered Strathleigh. "It . . . it yipped! I heard it!"

"I told you so," said Father Marc, grinning.

Yellow Hair passed it off and went to the door. "It's stuffy inside here. If you gentlemen will pardon me, I'll take a walk along the runways."

"By all means," said his lordship, gladly. "By all means!" And when Yellow Hair was gone Strathleigh and McGlincy sat staring at each other across the flickering light. Finally McGlincy raised his bottle to his mouth. His hand was shaking.

Yellow Hair went up a ladder to the runway. He

spoke to the bully on guard and then paced along the cold walk, his shoulders at the height of the top of the logs.

He could see nothing but blackness at every hand and yet as he went silently along, occasionally speaking cheerfully to the sentries, he kept a close watch on the night.

He made a complete turn of the palisades and that was a very long walk in itself. He had started around again when he heard a scratching sound.

Instantly he was at the edge. He touched a hand briefly and glanced sideways to spot the guards.

With his face less than a hand's breadth away from another bronzed visage, Yellow Hair whispered, "The fort is very strong."

The other whispered back and, with a jolt, Yellow Hair recognized Long Bow. The Pikuni was standing on his saddled mount and the wind swallowed up any sounds the pony might make.

"We know that. All day we've looked over the place from the bluffs. Can we take it? Will it be necessary to attack immediately?"

"I don't know. I can only tell you what I see. These whites have come for war against our people and it is best to bring the war to them."

"You had better slide out and come with me, as I have staked a horse for you a little way up the river."

"No, it is best that I stay here."

"Yes, it is best. But have you thought they would kill you?"

"That is my risk. I can tell you nothing more."

"You will not leave?"

"No."

Their hands touched briefly again and there was a long pause.

Yellow Hair whispered, "And Bright Star?"

"No. She vanished from the camp during the Grass Moon."

"You cannot find her?"

"No. We do not know if raiders . . ."

They fell silent.

Long Bow touched Yellow Hair's shoulder. He vanished.

The wind grew louder and again up on the bluffs resounded the wavering moans of the wolves.

Yellow Hair went back to the trading house and opened the door.

He looked steadily for a long time at McGlincy.

CHAPTER 36

CHARGE

No matter what the traders' appellations for them: "bloodthirsty thieves," "treacherous savages," "ignorant barbarians," and others, the Pikunis did not feel themselves obligated to verify these spurious titles by attacking the fort without real reason.

Accordingly, when dawn streaked the east with yellow and white, the lines of mounted warriors strung themselves out along the bluffs, motionless silhouettes against the gray sky, and waited for the chiefs to approach the fort for parley.

McGlincy, although he did not realize that he was belying his own statements, had known that this procedure would take place, although he was rather startled when a hasty count assured him that well over seven hundred fighting men were drawn in a wide semicircle just out of range around the fort.

However, a great man like McGlincy is quick to grasp and control any situation. He saw that one of the chiefs was carrying a branch and that the group wished to discuss matters, and he therefore primed himself with a swig and gave vent to a grin.

"It's working out," he told Strathleigh inside the trading house before going forth. "I told you it took a clever man and a brave man to handle these brutes. Now, we get them inside, bottle them up. The rank and file may attack but we shatter them with cannon and rifles and before they can re-form, we tell them that every single one of their chiefs will be killed if they attack us again. It will work perfectly. Bless me if it won't!"

"Maybe," said Strathleigh, soberly, "they won't want to come inside. I grant they haven't much sense, but you know how cautious wild animals are in general."

McGlincy grinned. "You've seen me being nice to Yellow Hair, but you've forgotten why we brought him along."

"That's so."

"Jacques," barked McGlincy at a voyageur, "send that renegade in here!"

Jacques went away and presently Yellow Hair entered. His lordship had retired to his room to collect his rifles with the help of his servant and Yellow Hair did not even know that Strathleigh had been in the house.

Very tense and impatient, Yellow Hair snapped, "What do you want now?" He had no trust for this McGlincy and less respect and McGlincy knew it.

But McGlincy permitted himself a hearty belch and a broad and friendly smile. "My boy," said McGlincy expansively, "you have been of great service to the Nor'Westers and, as you may be gone from here before night, I wish to give you this as a token of my appreciation."

He pulled forth a thick roll of bank notes and slid them over the table. He felt so certain of the power of money that he did not bother, fortunately for his peace of mind, to read the sudden threat in Yellow Hair's chilly eyes.

"And what am I to do for this?" said Yellow Hair.

"Why, we have few enough here who understand this Blackfoot language. I want you to mount the wall and sing out that those chiefs are to come in for a nice, quiet parley."

The request was not unreasonable. In fact it was very much in order. Chiefs had come into the fort many times before and no man would be mad enough to try anything while he stared at that line of warriors along the bluffs.

Yellow Hair said, "Is that all?"

"Why, yes, of course, that's all. We all like you, Yellow Hair, and we think your influence with these people will aid us a great deal. You've proven yourself a man of mettle. Bless me, if you haven't! These Blackfeet were worried about you last year and they'll do what you tell them. Now, like a good lad, just step up there on the catwalk and sing out that I want to talk with them."

Yellow Hair was smiling, and that smile was not very nice to see. He spread the bank notes out in front of him and stirred them up with a casual finger.

He knew McGlincy's love for this queer stuff called "money." McGlincy would never part with such a large amount of it unless he expected to get it back very shortly—and the one way he could retrieve this was to kill Yellow Hair or at least hold him there. Thus, Yellow Hair saw his own doom in the pound notes.

He knew that at least three men among these whites could talk good Blackfoot and that one of them was Father Marc.

McGlincy knew the Pikunis would obey what Yellow Hair said. Therefore there was some great reason for wanting them to enter the fort. Treachery was here in this pile of paper.

He knew that McGlincy coveted trade and furs and was now afraid of the H.B.C.s across the river.

He knew McGlincy wanted a war and he knew that McGlincy wanted no loss to himself.

Yellow Hair's smile broadened like a wolf's. He picked up the bank notes, wadded them in his hand and abruptly hurled them into McGlincy's puffy face.

Taken aback, the great Nor'Wester instantly saw menace to his own person and he yanked at a pistol in his belt.

A .69 caliber flintlock was leveled at the center of the red coat.

"You want to lead those chiefs into a trap," said Yellow Hair so quietly that his words were like saws hacking off McGlincy's ears. "You have played your last trick, dog-face, and now—"

A pistol prodded Yellow Hair's spine.

Strathleigh said, "How now, my pretty renegade. What's this? What's this? Drop that gun, please."

He had been standing in the doorway at Yellow Hair's back. His finger was now coiled hopefully around the trigger of a silver-mounted pistol.

Knowing that his lordship had long wanted such a chance, Yellow Hair refused it to him. He could not fight back. Not just now. The flintlock dropped to the table.

"We've wasted enough time!" snapped Strathleigh.

McGlincy was getting some color back into his face. He scooped up and pocketed the roll of money and then turned to the door. He bawled, "Pierre!"

Pierre, a *bois brûlé* and a veteran in the Saskatchewan country, came running. He had been the runner to the Blackfeet and he spoke that language a little.

McGlincy quickly possessed himself of his pistol, slapped his hat sideways on his head, caught up a bottle and motioned with it toward the door.

To Yellow Hair McGlincy roared, "You'll give 'em that message, you God damned murderer. You'll give 'em that message or you're a dead man. March!"

With three bullies assisting and with his lordship's pistol at full cock behind, Yellow Hair was forcefully taken up the ladder to the runway and posted at the wall with his head showing.

Heads down, the bullies and Strathleigh were there to watch him. Behind him was a drop of ten feet to the ground.

The interpreter, Pierre, was posted beside Yellow Hair but also out of sight, and all the Pikunis could see was Yellow Hair, apparently alone on the wall.

"Now, damn you," snarled McGlincy, "you sing out, 'The Great White Chief desires to know why you come prepared for war. He wants to tell you that there is no occasion for war. He wishes to pow-wow with you and give you presents and the gates are open to you to show you his good faith.' There, you've got that? Now, damn your soul, put it into that heathen lingo and spew it loud! Pierre will know what you're saying and unless you say it right—"

"I'll be right here to put a bullet in your back," said Strathleigh, who did not add that he would do it anyway, though at a later date.

Yellow Hair looked long at the lines on the heights.

The sun was there now, shining on the upheld lances, flashing from knives, letting the war bonnets glare in the proud glories of red and white.

With shields ready over their breasts, the host sat with impassive faces, waiting orders to attack or withdraw, all eyes fixed upon Yellow Hair.

Warriors all. Equipped with the weapons that had twice conquered the eastern world; blood brothers to the valiant troopers who rode at the stirrups of Genghis Khan, of Tamerlane, kin to the Samurai. Drawn up, waiting orders, erect and haughty in their saddles, afraid of nothing.

A savage mob, this?

Rather, one of the finest bodies of trained cavalry that ever swept the Great Plains or the plains of any continent.

Yellow Hair looked proudly upon that martial host.

He looked back at the loud rabble crouching expectantly before the loopholes, rifles in hand.

Yellow Hair sang out in a voice which carried to the heights far beyond the chiefs he addressed a hundred paces from the gates.

"Pikunis! Warriors! Charge and do not leave a man alive!"

Those ringing words struck down like doom itself upon Pierre. It took him seconds to collect his wits and realize that McGlincy still thought Yellow Hair had given the right message.

Pierre screamed, "He ordered attack! We'll all be killed!"

In the instant which remained before the alarm, Yellow Hair whirled halfway about.

But Strathleigh had waited too long for this chance.

He aimed at Yellow Hair's face and fired.

Yellow Hair, on the instant, dived straight at Strathleigh. The bullet and flaming powder hit.

In a struggling ball of humanity, the entire group spilled earthward. But McGlincy stayed on the wall. Without looking down, to the right or left, McGlincy screamed, "KILL THOSE CHIEFS!"

Ponies trained to the chase of war and the hunt needed but a slight signal.

Yellow Hair's words had sent Low Horns, White Fox and the rest whirling about and hurtling back toward the bluffs.

The volley struck Lost-in-Mountains' mustang. White Fox and Big Wolf reached out with one accord and lifted the man from the somersaulting mount before he could strike the ground.

With only the dead horse lying behind them, the chiefs reached the limit of rifle fire and whirled again.

Low Horns raised his hand and dropped it.

The whole front had seen the shooting of Yellow Hair. They believed him dead. It only required this to whip them into a rising roar of rage.

From seven hundred throats and more came the war cries. A yip-yip and then, with voices soaring upward to a shrill, screaming falsetto which ripped through the eardrums like so many knives, the host streaked down from the heights in a thundering charge.

CHAPTER 37

HYAI, PIKUNIS!

Fully half of the three hundred rifles leveled through the loopholes in the palisades were discharged before the Pikunis were within range. The eddying, red-stabbed clouds of white smoke from the black powder hung like a fog outside the log slabs, momentarily hiding the enemy from view.

The war cry was coming near, mingling with the kettle-drumming of hoofs. Every warrior shouted his own way—giving rise to the belief that the tribe had an individual cry—and the racketing, undulating volley of those combined voices, heightened by the crack of rifles, made such an ungodly, soul-searing sound that the men in the fort who faced it for the first time went to pieces.

Unable now to see the charging host, unable to find out the distance that still remained between the hammering hoofs and the screaming, head-splitting yell and the smoke-shrouded fort, chaos reigned momentarily within the walls.

Out of a tangle of fighters rushing from one palisade to another emerged Yellow Hair.

Strathleigh had disappeared. Pierre was gone. Only the bullies and voyageurs and the far-off bellow of McGlincy made an impression on Yellow Hair's dazed senses.

He knew he was covered with blood. The bullet had ripped across his throat without touching the jugular vein, and his face was on fire with the burn of the powder.

Stunned by his fall, still wondering where his lordship had gone, without a single man in the place paying any attention to him whatever, Yellow Hair staggered ahead a step.

The war cry hit him like a tonic. He was instantly quivering, poised, ready to help.

Through the fog of smoke he saw the two cannon that had been loaded with shot to rake the palisade. The main part of the charge was coming from that direction.

How close were his warriors now?

The gunners up there on the bastion could not be distinctly seen.

A voyageur, screaming the names of a hundred saints but scurrying backward from the battle's tide, ran into Yellow Hair.

A quick blow to the jaw, a jerk at the fellow's belt and Yellow Hair had his rifle and pistol and knife.

Dropping to one knee he sighted upward at the bastion through the smoke. He fired and a gunner dropped. Casting the rifle away and gripping the pistol butt, Yellow Hair raced up the ladder and dashed along the runway, knocking gunners sprawling in his charge.

McGlincy heard the yell from another quarter. He roared to a rifleman and a bullet snipped bark just behind Yellow Hair.

Other bullets followed, all of them wild. He was moving too fast to be hit.

He sprang up to the level of the bastion. A gunner spun and caught a pistol ball in his teeth. Yellow Hair lunged over the falling body and stabbed down with his bright blade, swooping to grab the punk before the dead man hit the planking.

A thud of horses striking up against the log slabs shook the whole fort. The Pikunis gripped the tops of the wall and started over.

Bullies were hurled back and down from the runway to the ground. Other bullies loomed up to take their places and savagely contest the wall.

This was no time for indecision or thought.

Yellow Hair grabbed at a cannon, slashed its ropes, slammed it completely around, depressed the muzzle at the gate and applied the match he held.

The cannon thundered and hurtled backward and off the bastion.

The shot blasted through the gate, tearing it half off its huge hinges.

Yellow Hair yipped and shouted, "To the gate, Pikunis! The gate!"

Three bullies rose up directly in front of him, rifles raised to batter him down. He leaped backward over the second cannon, slashed at a rope and slewed the gun sideways, applying the match.

The bullies were on him again. He stepped backward and into space, falling free fifteen feet to the ground outside and into the cover of rolling smoke.

The cannon went off above him before he struck. Everything was spinning. He brought himself to his knees and shook his head to clear it.

Pikunis were being driven down from the wall. Riderless horses were rearing and charging back and forth, screaming when they were hit.

Yellow Hair stabbed out a hand and caught a bridle.

Without stopping the horse, he grabbed the high horn and vaulted into the saddle.

He turned his mount and raced beyond the smoke.

Face to face he met White Fox.

The old man's eyes went wide with pleasure, but otherwise he gave no sign.

Yellow Hair shouted, "The gate!" and then realized that he had to explain. "This was into the fort! Recall our people! Follow me!"

The order lashed like a blacksnake whip about the fort. Pikunis drew off, wheeled and sped after their chiefs.

In the lead Yellow Hair threw the weight of his mount against the sagging gate. It caved inward and smoke rolled out.

Into this maelstrom of flame of acrid fumes dashed the riders. Their shrill, blasting cry drowned out the rifle reports.

The bullies and all the rest whirled from the wall to face a fort full of warriors.

With a shout of terror the defenders fled toward the only other spot where a defense could be made. Many of them reached the trading house and dashed inside, slamming the door and shutting out their own friends.

But McGlincy was there. And his lordship was there all safe and sound. His lordship somehow didn't think so much of hunting Indians just now.

"Man the loopholes!" bawled McGlincy at this handful of his troops. "Shoot them down!"

His voice did not reach far. It was swallowed up in the uproar outside.

Yellow Hair shouted to Low Horns. Low Horns relayed the order to the milling throng of fighters.

Bullies and voyageurs were going out of the fort as fast as their bullets had ever sped. They left by the walls and they scattered across the fields to run squarely into an iron ring of Pikunis posted there.

They were rounded up because they were without weapons and because they knew this was their end. To their surprise they were not instantly slaughtered, but bunched like so many horses.

Inside the fort, the clamor subsided by degrees.

CHAPTER 38

TRIUMPH

McGlincy began to be apprehensive. Everything was so very silent when things had been so loud such a short time before. His men refused to fire through the loopholes in the trading post because, they said, such a movement would cause the Blackfeet to roast them alive by burning the place.

McGlincy was very shaky and he resorted to his bottle.

Strathleigh, in a very uneasy tone, said, "My God, they're . . . they're rolling up cannon!"

McGlincy instantly looked through a loophole and saw that it was true.

There were four cannon in the fort. Two of them had not been fired. And now all four of them were standing in a neat line squarely in the middle of the stockade with their huge muzzles pointing straight at the trading post.

Yellow Hair had seen them loaded before this and he directed the work now. The Pikunis had carried them bodily to this position and they now stood beside their mounts, armed with the rifles that had been so carelessly left about by the late defenders of the palisades.

Yellow Hair had something of a grin on his face, though his powder-blackened skin only let his teeth gleam through. To McGlincy these were very like wolf fangs.

It was too good a chance for Yellow Hair to miss. It was such a wonderful turnabout of the tables on McGlincy that it simply had to be done.

Punk in hand, Yellow Hair stood blowing gently upon it. Presently he looked up and studied the trading house.

With more humor than menace, he shouted, "McGlincy, come out of there!"

Nothing happened and Yellow Hair, who had found McGlincy's hat in the rubbish along the walls, now put it on, cocked it at an angle and shouted, "Damme if I don't blow you up! Come out of there or bless me if I don't!"

The punk crept near to the cannon touchholes. Yellow Hair's grin looked diabolical. Those four cannon, all fired at once, would blow the house apart and everything in it.

The door slammed inward.

McGlincy was catapulted out into the dust, evidently thrown out.

Instantly he picked himself up as far as his hands and knees and, his coat all stained with powder and dust, his hair in his eyes and his jowls flapping limply as he tried to talk, McGlincy stared at Yellow Hair and the painted host behind him.

Suddenly he began to blubber. McGlincy covered his chest with his hands and whined, "Please, Yellow Hair, please! I've never done anything. I've just tried to do my duty. Spare me! I'm a godly man, Yellow Hair. I never meant any harm. I . . ."

The punk was still near the touchholes and McGlincy was almost looking into the muzzles. His teeth began to chatter and he shook so hard he could not talk.

"Spare me," he whined.

"Don't kill me!" he shrieked.

"Please, for God's sake, have mercy on me!"

But Yellow Hair refused to do anything but grin at him and McGlincy's heart was ice within him.

He whimpered and groveled and walked forward by shifting his knees. His hands were held prayerfully under his upraised chin and his eyes sought heaven—though what he expected to find there is questionable.

"Come out, the rest of you," bawled Yellow Hair.

His lordship came first. His mustache was drooping with neglect and his hands shook so that the lace about them quivered.

The bullies and voyageurs who had been inside lined up and then Luberly limped forth trying to make himself as small as possible.

"McGlincy," said Yellow Hair, "I've heard you talk about an Indian torture that consisted of roasting a man alive over a fire."

"Oh God," shuddered McGlincy.

"And your lordship," said Yellow Hair, "has often stated that he wanted to shoot Indians. Now, perhaps he'd like to see how accurate Indians can shoot by letting them fire at him?"

Strathleigh gulped convulsively.

Yellow Hair's grin broadened. "You'd like that?"

"Oh, God, no," moaned Strathleigh. "Look, you're a civilized white man, Yellow Hair . . . er . . . Michael Kirk. You wouldn't—"

"You've said otherwise, Strathleigh."

"Oh, but really—"

"McGlincy," said Yellow Hair, "you've been a lot of

trouble to me and you really deserve something worse."

"Please," pleaded McGlincy, in the dust.

"So I'm going to give it to you. McGlincy, prepare to meet your doom."

"Oh, God."

"I'm going to send you to Edmonton."

"What?"

"You can make it before ice. I'm going to send you to Edmonton and I'm going to make sure you arrive there and that you'll have company. His lordship—"

"Me?" gulped Strathleigh, perking up.

"Yes. All of you and this other scum. McGlincy, death would not cure you, but above all else you love glory. I'm sending you north without arms, without baggage, without pelts, without this cocked hat, without that red coat, without a single drop of whisky. And you're there in the dust. I want your partners to know you were in the dust and to make sure they know and to make certain no lies are told, I'm sending his lordship along if he gives me his word to tell this straight."

"Oh, gladly," cried Strathleigh. "Oh, really, I will."

"Yes. Yes, I know you will. You can tell it to the King!"

McGlincy went very pale and he struggled to his feet. It struck home that his dishonor would be completed.

"But your lordship can't—"

Strathleigh snapped, "Get your filthy hands off me, you fool. Whatever I'll give you, you'll deserve."

"Luberly," blubbered McGlincy. "You—"

"Not me," said Luberly. "I've had enough of your stinking carcass, I have."

McGlincy sagged and then looked at the voyageurs

and bullies. He saw their contempt for him at last come to the surface now that his power was gone. He would never have another command, never another brigade or post. His partnership would be stripped from him when the whole of his iniquity came out.

"And," said Yellow Hair cheerfully, "I think Father Marc knows the story of those stolen H.B.C. furs, but I'm not sending Father Marc with you. I'm keeping him here to show him how a clean people can live.

"Also, I'm going across the river to call on Motley to let you confess to him."

"Don't!" cried McGlincy.

"What?"

"All right," said McGlincy in a whipped voice. "All right, I'll tell him."

"Strathleigh," said Yellow Hair, "these Blackfeet are finer people than any of yours. And this country we have here is wholly ours. You can tell the Nor'Westers to spread the word that we mean what we say. I have just talked with the chiefs and they tell me to communicate to you the ultimatum that no white shall set foot in the Blackfoot domain on the penalty of death. Too long we have remained idly by while you robbed us. Here in this fort we have the guns we need, the ammunition, the knives. We take them as the spoils of war. Whatever else we need we will trade for to the Hudson's Bay Company across the river.

"Through you and your men and friends I have received much harm even unto the loss of the woman who was to become my wife.

"Tell them that, Strathleigh, and I'll say no more about murder. You others, prepare to be gone. Take only your personal baggage, all else is forfeit to the Blackfoot nation and the families of the men who died bravely fighting here today. Your canoes are waiting for you."

CHAPTER 39

THE GRAND COUP

Before the sun was gone that day, the fort had burned down into a pile of smoking black embers. The goods were piled at the water's edge awaiting the manufacture of travois to carry them.

Motley and the rest of his post had pledged their good faith and Motley, after McGlincy's confession, harbored no ill will.

Not even a ripple remained on the South Saskatchewan to show that McGlincy's great flotilla had touched that sparkling waterway.

It was quiet as the twilight came on and Yellow Hair had slowly lost all elation of his victory. Ay, he had triumphed over McGlincy. He had delivered his tribe's ultimatum to the whites. He had secured the guns and ammunition he had originally been sent for, and a great deal more than anyone had expected.

Yes, the Council would give him what honor it was in their power to bestow. His bonnet would be flowing with grand coups and his lodge would be great.

But it was all empty.

He had come home, but that which he sought the most was no longer there.

Ay, he could wear out a thousand horses searching.

He could sweep the plains with fire to find her.

But that did not give her back and revenge is a useless thing.

Knees drawn up, arms around them, his sun-colored hair cascading down over his shoulders, he listlessly watched the river below.

White Fox had greeted him home. White Fox had made a funny spreading motion with his hands to show that Yellow Hair had broadened to the mighty estate of man. But White Fox had said nothing. He had known.

Father Marc, glad to be with the Pikunis and out of McGlincy's way, had talked to him for a little while, complimenting him upon the mercy his people had shown the whites who had caused them so much grief. But Father Marc had known what was wrong and he, too, had gone away.

Low Horns had come to him to spread a favorite painted robe that had been Low Horns' prize and which was now given freely in the hope that it would ease Yellow Hair's heart.

Long Bow had told him that he could have a favorite buffalo horse and offered to give it to him now.

But he had said nothing.

The long years he had been away flitted fitfully across his mind. Bad years they had been. But they might serve at some future time.

Gaunt years. Sobering years.

He was glad they would not come again.

Ay, he had returned. To an empty lodge. Too long he had been gone. Too long.

Ay, he knew what had happened. Bright Star had vanished just before she was to marry Long Bow. She had chosen the plains and possible death before she would marry without the consent of her uncle.

A sensible rule on the whole, of course, but some-times—sometimes maidens killed themselves as Bright Star had done.

Ay, gone too long, but that would not bring her back, this sorrow.

No, he would have to go on alone, his lodge empty save for the equipage of war.

He could not sit here through the night. He could not show them the darkness of his spirits. . . .

Something touched his shoulder.

Hands were sliding down his arms.

Abruptly he was pulled backwards and into the soft grass and there—there against the sky! There was Bright Star!

She was laughing! She was pummeling him!

And then Yellow Hair reached out and grabbed her and pulled her down in a heap beside him. He rolled her over and she pretended that she was trying to get away.

His face was smothered in her hair. Her voice was muffled and happy against his breast.

Suddenly he was crying.

Hyai! How she laughed at him! How she crowed over her own exploit! She mocked him, saying that she was as mighty a warrior as he was. Hadn't she hidden out on the Marias for months and months? Hadn't Magpie and a girl slave and herself done all their providing? Hadn't she seen the warriors leave?

Hyai! What a wife she would make him! She would become the greatest sits-beside-him woman in the whole Pikuni camp!

Hyai, but let him try to stop her.

Father Marc, his uneasy conscience prompting him, stood before them spouting the Latin that made them Christian man and wife.

But they cared nothing for that.

They cared nothing for anything as they stood together in the twilight, those two.

And then Long Bow, laughing, threw a buffalo robe at them and ran away to carry the tidings to the camp.

Black night but stars bright in the sky—the gentle whisper of the river down below—

He had come home.

THE END

APPENDIX

Compiled from the journals of the Lewis and Clark Expedition:

"Saturday, July 26, 1806. . . . At the distance of three miles we ascended the hills close to the river side (Marias), while Drewyer pursued the valley of the river on the opposite side. But scarcely had Captain Lewis reached the high plain, when he saw about a mile on his left a collection of about thirty horses. He immediately halted, and by the aid of his spyglass discovered that one half of the horses were saddled, and that on the eminence above the horses several Indians were looking down toward the river, probably at Drewyer. This was a most unwelcome sight. Their probable numbers rendered any contest with them of doubtful issue; to attempt to escape would only invite pursuit, and our horses were so bad that we would most certainly be overtaken; besides which, Drewyer could not be aware that the Indians were near, and if we ran he would most certainly be sacrificed. We therefore determined to make the best of our situation, and advanced towards them in a friendly manner. The flag which we had brought in case of such an accident was therefore displayed, and we continued our march slowly toward them.

"Their whole attention was so engaged by Drewyer that they did not immediately discover us. As soon as they did see us they appeared to be much alarmed and ran about in confusion, and some of them came down the hill and drove their horses within gunshot of the eminence, to which they then returned as if to wait our arrival. When we came within a quarter of a mile, one of the Indians mounted and rode full speed to receive us; but when within a hundred paces of us, he halted, and Captain Lewis, who had alighted to receive him, held out his hand and beckoned for him to approach; he only looked at us for some time, and then, without saying a word, returned to his companions with as much haste as he had advanced. The whole party now descended the hill and rode toward us. . . . Captain Lews now told his men that he believed that these were Minnetarees of fort de Prairie. . . .

"When the two parties came within a hundred yards of each other all the Indians except one halted; Captain Lewis therefore ordered his two men to halt while he advanced; and after shaking hands with the Indian, went on and did the same with all the others in the rear. . . .

"Captain Lewis now asked them by signs if they were Minnetarees of the north and was sorry to learn that his suspicion was too true. He then inquired if there was any chief among them. They pointed out three; but though he did not believe them, yet it was thought best to please, and he therefore gave to one a flag, to another a medal, and to a third a handkerchief. They appeared to be well satisfied with these presents, and now recovered from the agitation into which our first interview had thrown them, for they were generally more alarmed than ourselves at the meeting.

"In our turn, however, we became equally satisfied on discovering that they were not joined by any more of their companions, for we consider ourselves quite a match for eight Indians, particularly as these have but two guns, the rest being armed with only eye-dogs and bows and arrows.

"As it was growing late, Captain Lewis proposed that they should camp together near the river; for he was glad to see them and had a great deal to say to them.

"They assented; and being soon joined by Drewyer, we proceeded towards the river, and after descending a very steep bluff, two hundred and fifty feet high, encamped in a small bottom. Here the Indians formed a large semicircular tent of dressed buffalo skins, in which the two parties assembled, and by means of Drewyer the evening was spent in conversation with the Indians.

"They informed us that they were part of a large band which at present lay encamped on the main branch of the Marias River, near the foot of the Rocky Mountains, and at a distance of a day and a half's journey from this place. Another large band were hunting buffalo from the Broken Mountains, from which they would proceed in a few days to the north of the Marias River. *With the first of these there was a white man.* . . .

"Captain Lewis in turn informed them that he had come from the great river which leads toward the rising Sun; that he had been as far as the great lake where the Sun sets; that he had seen many nations, the greater part of whom were at war with each other, but by his mediation were restored to peace . . . that he had come in search of the Minnetarees in the hope of inducing them to live at peace with their neighbors. . . .

"They said they were anxious of being at peace with

their neighbors the Tushepaws, but those people had lately killed a number of their relations, as they proved by showing several of the party who had their hair cut as a sign of mourning. . . .

"Finding them fond of the pipe, Captain Lewis, who was desirous of keeping a constant watch during the night, smoked with them until a late hour, and as soon as they were all asleep he awoke R. Fields, ordering him to arouse us all in case any Indian left camp. . . .

"Sunday, 27th of July, 1806. This morning at daylight the Indians got up and crowded around the fire near which J. Fields, who was then on watch, had carelessly left his rifle near the head of his brother who was still asleep. One of the Indians slipped up behind him and, unperceived, took his brother's and his own rifle, while at the same time two others seized those of Drewyer and Captain Lewis.

"As soon as Field turned 'round he saw the Indian running off with the rifles, and instantly calling his brother, they pursued him fifty or sixty yards, and just as they overtook him, in the scuffle for the rifles, R. Fields stabbed him through the heart with his knife; the Indian ran about fifteen steps and fell dead.

"They now ran back with the rifles to the camp. The moment the fellow had touched his gun, Drewyer, who was awake, jumped up and wrested her from him. The noise awoke Captain Lewis, who instantly started up from the ground and reached to seize his gun, but finding her gone, drew a pistol from his belt and turning about, saw the Indian running off with her.

"He followed him and ordered him to lay her down, which he was doing just as the two Fields came up and were taking aim to shoot him, when Captain Lewis ordered them not to fire as the Indian did not appear to intend any mischief. He dropped the gun and was going slowly off as Drewyer came out and asked permission to kill him, but this Captain Lewis forbid as he had not yet attempted to shoot us.

"But finding now that the Indians were attempting to drive off horses, he ordered three of them to follow up the main party who were driving horses up the river and fire instantly upon them; while he, without taking time to run for his shot pouch, pursued the fellow who had stolen his gun and another Indian who were trying to drive away the horses on the left of the camp.

"He pressed them so closely that they left twelve of their horses but continued to drive off one of our own. At the distance of three hundred paces they entered a steep niche in the river bluffs, when Captain Lewis, being too much winded to pursue them any farther, called out, as he did several times before, that unless they gave up the horse he would shoot them.

"As he raised his gun, one of the Indians jumped behind a rock and spoke to the other, who stopped at the distance of thirty paces, when Captain Lewis shot him in the belly. He fell on his knees and right elbow, but raising himself a little, fired, and then crawled behind a rock. . . . Captain Lewis, who was bareheaded, felt the wind of the ball very distinctly. . . and . . . retired slowly toward the camp. . . .

"We, however, were rather gainers by this contest, for we took four of the Indian horses and lost only one of our own. Besides which we found in the camp four shields, two bows with quivers, and one of their guns, which we took with us, and also the flag which we had presented to them, but left the medal 'round the neck of the dead man, in order that they might be informed who we were."

GLOSSARY

Reading is easier when one understands the words. To make this novel more enjoyable, the following unusual words have been defined.

Algonquian—(al ′gän kwē ən) A widespread and important family of over twenty languages used by a number of the North American Indian tribes, including the Arapaho, Cheyenne, Blackfoot, Chippewa, Fox, Shawnee, Ottawa, and others. Also refers to a member of the Algonquian tribe who lived in the area of the Ottawa River, Canada.

All Friends Society—See *Societies*.

Almost-whites—Indian tribes of the deserts, such as the Apaches, whose skin was lighter in color than that of the Blackfeet.

American Fur Company—Fur company established by John Jacob Astor.

Astor, John Jacob—(1763–1848) U.S. fur merchant and financier, born in Germany. Founder of the American Fur Company.

Bateau—(ba′to) A lightweight, flat-bottomed river boat used chiefly in Canada and Louisiana. Also, a man who steers a bateau.

Beaver Roll—A bundle of sacred objects used in Blackfoot ceremonies.

Blackfoot—Any member of the Algonquian Indian sub-tribes consisting of the Blackfoot proper, the Blood, and the Piegan of Montana, Saskatchewan and Alberta.

Bois brûlé—(bwä brü ′lā) A term used to refer to a "half-breed," half-Indian/half-white. From the French, meaning "burnt wood."

Boundary Settlement—By the Definite Treaty of Peace with Britain in 1783, the boundary between British North America and the United States west of the Great Lakes was a line from western Lake Superior to the most northerly point of the Lake of the Woods. This was known as the Boundary Settlement.

Brigades—Specifically, supply parties in the fur trade. They shuttled between headquarters and the posts, carrying supplies in one direction and furs in the other. They were sometimes used for raids on competitors.

Canister—A case filled with bullets or shot that is fired from a cannon.

Chagateurs—Members of a divided fourteenth-century Mongol dynasty which was reunited by Timur-i-Leng (Timur the Lame). The chagateur (jagatai) warriors, under the leadership of Timur, then embarked on vast conquests across Central Asia and created an empire that stretched from China on the east, to Turkey on the west.

Charter—In 1668, a group of wealthy Englishmen financed a fur-trading expedition to Hudson's Bay which was so successful that, two years later, they were granted a royal charter as the "Governor and Company of the Adventurers of England trading into Hudson's Bay."

Chinook—A dry wind blowing down the eastern slope

of the Rocky Mountains at recurring intervals.

Coulee—(′kü lē) A deep gulch or ravine, usually dry in summer.

Coup—An act of bravery where the enemy is directly struck. The courage stems from the proximity that is required. It would be a higher *coup* to hit or touch the enemy with the bare hand before any attack. Coup is also the award for such an act, such as an eagle feather.

Coupstick(′ku stik) —A stick used to touch an enemy (take coup) prior to killing him. Also a stick on which coups (such as plumes and scalps) are displayed.

Coureurs des bois—Canadian fur trappers. From the French, literally: runners of the woods.

Cree—A member of a tribe of Algonquian Indians who lived in an area extending from the southern end of Hudson Bay to northern Alberta, Canada.

Crows—A member of a tribe of Siouan Indians living in the upper basins of the Yellowstone and Big Horn rivers.

Damme—Another form of "Damn me!"

De Meurons—Members of a regiment of hired soldiers who were brought by the Hudson's Bay Company to Manitoba to protect a settlement.

Deschamps—In the 1600s, a few thousand Frenchmen immigrated to Canada. Some moved westward, living off the land as hunters and trappers and marrying local Indian women. After several generations, there grew in the Northwest a large population of French-Indian "half-breeds," or Métis, as they were more properly called, all sharing a small number of French surnames. In order to distinguish between various branches of these large "families," the practice of adding a descriptive clan name after the surname developed. "Deschamps" is a clan name meaning literally "of the fields," which is descriptive of where this clan lived.

Digger—A derogatory term for a member of any of several tribes of Indians in the western United States who dug roots for food.

Dudgeon—A feeling of anger, resentment, or offense; ill humor.

Eye-dog—A type of hatchet that traders used to exchange with the Indians.

Factor—A person who does business for another; an agent. The factors were in charge of the factories.

Factory—A fur-trading settlement in the Northwest.

Falling Leaf Moon—The Pikuni term for a month in autumn.

Fields Brothers—Joseph and Reuben Fields, brothers from Kentucky, members of the Lewis and Clark party.

Forks—Where the city of Winnipeg now stands.

Ghost-head—A skull.

Grape—Grapeshot; a cluster of small iron balls fired from a cannon.

Grass Moon—Blackfoot term for a month in midsummer.

Gunwale—(/gun əl) The upper edge of a boat's side.

Halyard—A rope for hoisting or lowering.

Hands—This unit is still used to measure the height of a horse. It is now equivalent to four inches. The measurement is from the ground to the withers. While sizes do vary, a Shetland pony is about ten hands high. An average horse is about 15 to 16 hands high. A horse that stood 25 hands high would be enormous.

H.B.C.—The Hudson's Bay Company became known by its initials which were used to marks its pelts.

High dudgeon—Very angry, resentful.

High wine—Distilled liquor.

Howitzer—A short cannon.

Hudson's Bay Company—A company chartered by the King of England in 1670 to trade furs to Great Britain. It was given considerable powers and had historic significance in the exploration, economic development and settlement of Canada.

Interloper—Any unauthorized trader. From interlope—to intrude on another's trading rights or privileges.

Jackstaff—A short staff, set on the bow of a boat or ship, to display a ship's colors.

Kitchi-Mokan—Pikuni term for a white man.

Kit-Fox Society—See *Societies*.

Laudanum—A preparation containing opium that was used primarily as a pain-killer or sedative.

Lone-Fighters—Those in the tribe who fought alone, away from a band or war party.

Loop—A hole or narrow slit in the wall of a fort for looking out or shooting through.

Louisiana Purchase—That territory which was purchased from France in 1803 for $15,000,000. It extended from the Mississippi to the Rocky Mountains, from New Orleans to Canada. It included the present states of Arkansas, Missouri, Iowa, Nebraska, South Dakota, almost all of Oklahoma and Minnesota, Colorado and Louisiana.

Mackinaw—A type of boat with a flat bottom, sharp bow, and square or pointed stern, formerly used on and around the upper Great Lakes.

Mandans—Indians who lived in the Missouri River Valley.

Metacarpals—Finger and hand bones.

Minnetarees—Also called the Hidatsa Indians or Falls Indians. Affiliated with the Blackfeet, Bloods and Piegans.

Nor'Wester—Short form of "North Westerner," which were those who worked for the North West Company.

Orkneymen—Men from the Orkney Islands, which are north of Scotland. The Orkneymen generally worked for Hudson's Bay Company.

Outer Marches, Lords of—These were simply those who were farthest into the wilderness, farthest from headquarters. It is taken from the English phrase where the Marches were the borders farthest from the central government. It was also the border areas under dispute. The phrase was being used sarcastically, as one was lord of nothing.

Palisade(s)—Any one of a row of large pointed stakes set in the ground to form a fence for fortification or defense.

Partners—The North West Company was composed of partners who had bought into the business enterprise and who shared its profits and risks.

Pays d'en haut—From the French, meaning, literally, "country of the above." In the Canadian fur trade, this was the country west of Lake Superior.

Pemmican—Meat that was chopped up, dried and often mixed with a fruit or berry and then pressed into cakes or small bags. It could last indefinitely as a concentrated, high-energy food.

Pikuni—A term used frequently in Montana as a substitute for Piegan. (See *Blackfoot*.)

Planting Moon—Time in the spring when planting occurs.

Popinjay—A strutting, conceited person. The word comes from the Middle English word *papejay*, which was a parrot.

Portage—The carrying or transporting of boats or provisions overland from one river or lake to another. Also, the place over which this is done.

Postern—A back door or gate; private entrance at the side or rear.

Pot au beurre—(pod ō'ber) French: tub of butter.

Powder horn—A container made of an animal's horn, for carrying gunpowder.

Punch—The male character of the puppet show Punch and Judy, a hook-nosed, humpbacked figure.

Quiver—A case for holding arrows.

Red Death—Smallpox.

Red Moon—A moon in late summer, about August.

Régale—(rə'gāl)A feast or party.

Runners of the burnt woods—See *bois brûlés*.

Shining Mountains—The Rocky Mountains.

Sits-beside-him woman—In those tribes that were

polygamous, the most favored wife sat beside the man during certain important occasions, thus earning this name.

Snakes—Snake Indians. They lived to the south of the Blackfeet.

Societies—The tribes were stratified into different age and social levels, each one having its own society which had its own value and importance—the Society of the Horns, the All Friends Society, the Kit-Fox Society, etc.

Society of the Horns—See *Societies*.

Trace dog—A dog trained to pull a sled or another form of carrier by means of a trace (a harness).

Thompson, David—Explorer and cartographer of the West circa the early 1800s.

Thunder Moon—The Pikuni term for the month of July.

Tibias—Leg bones.

Touchhole—In early firearms, the hole in the lower part of the barrel through which the charge was lit.

Tushepaw—Another name for the Flathead Indians.

Upcountry—The interior of a country.

Voyageur—(vwäyäzher) In the fur trade, one who transported goods and men by rivers and lakes to trading posts for the fur companies.

Wolf—Pikuni scout.

X.Y.s—Because the North West Company marked their pelts with the letters "X.Y." to distinguish them from those of the Hudson's Bay Company who marked theirs "H.B.C.," the Nor'Westers were often called X.Y.s.

About the Author
L. Ron Hubbard

L. Ron Hubbard's remarkable writing career spanned more than half-a-century of intense literary achievement and creative influence.

And though he was first and foremost a writer, his life experiences and travels in all corners of the globe were wide and diverse. His insatiable curiosity and personal belief that one should live life as a professional led to a lifetime of extraordinary accomplishment. He was also an explorer, ethnologist, mariner and pilot, filmmaker and photographer, philosopher and educator, composer and musician.

Growing up in the still-rugged frontier country of Montana, he broke his first bronc and became the blood brother of a Blackfeet Indian medicine man by age six. In 1927, when he was 16, he traveled to a still remote Asia. The following year, to further satisfy his thirst for adventure and augment his growing knowledge of other cultures, he left school and returned to the Orient. On this trip, he worked as a supercargo and helmsman aboard a coastal trader which plied the seas between Japan and Java. He came to know old Shanghai, Beijing and the Western Hills at a time when few Westerners could enter China. He traveled more than a quarter of a million miles by sea and land while still a teenager and before the advent of commercial aviation as we know it.

He returned to the United States in the autumn of 1929 to complete his formal education. He entered George Washington University in Washington, D.C., where he studied engineering and took one of the earliest courses in atomic and molecular physics. In addition to his studies, he was the president of the Engineering Society and Flying Club, and wrote articles, stories and plays for the university newspaper. During the same period he also barnstormed across the American mid-West and was a national correspondent and photographer for the *Sportsman Pilot* magazine, the most distinguished aviation publication of its day.

Returning to his classroom of the world in 1932, he led two separate expeditions, the Caribbean Motion Picture Expedition; sailing on one of the last of America's four-masted commercial ships, and the second, a mineralogical survey of Puerto Rico. His exploits earned him membership in the renowned Explorers Club and he subsequently carried their coveted flag on two more voyages of exploration and discovery. As a master mariner licensed to operate ships in any ocean, his lifelong love of the sea was reflected in the many ships he captained and the skill of the crews he trained. He also served with distinction as a U.S. naval officer during the Second World War.

All of this—and much more—found its way, into his writing and gave his stories a compelling sense of authenticity that has appealed to readers throughout the world. It started in 1934 with the publication of "The Green God" in *Thrilling Adventure* magazine, a story about an American naval intelligence officer caught up in the mystery and intrigues of pre-communist China. With his extensive knowledge of the world and its people and his ability to write in any style and genre, he rapidly achieved prominence as a writer of action adventure, western, mystery and suspense. Such was the respect of his fellow writers that he was only 25 when elected president of the New York Chapter of the American Fiction Guild.

In addition to his career as a leading writer of fiction, he worked as a successful screenwriter in Hollywood where he wrote the original story and script for Columbia's 1937 hit serial, "The Secret of Treasure Island." His work on numerous films for Columbia, Universal and other major studios involved writing, providing story lines and serving as a script consultant.

In 1938, he was approached by the venerable New York publishing house of Street and Smith, the publishers of *Astounding Science Fiction*. Wanting to capitalize on the proven reader appeal of the L. Ron Hubbard byline to capture more readers for this emerging genre, they essentially offered to buy all the science fiction he wrote. When he protested that he did not write about machines and machinery but that he wrote about people, they told him that was exactly what was wanted. The rest is history.

The impact and influence that his novels and stories had on the fields of science fiction, fantasy and horror virtually amounted to the changing of a genre. It is the compelling human element that he originally brought to this new genre that remains today the basis of its growing international popularity.

L. Ron Hubbard consistently enabled readers to peer into the minds and emotions of characters in a way that sharply heightened the reading experience without slowing the pace of the story, a level of writing rarely achieved.

Among the most celebrated examples of this are three stories he published in a single, phenomenally creative year (1940)—FINAL BLACKOUT and its grimly possible future world of unremitting war and ultimate courage which Robert Heinlein called "as perfect a piece of science fiction as has ever been written"; the ingenious fantasy-adventure, TYPEWRITER IN THE SKY described by Clive Cussler as "written in the great style adventure should be written in"; and the prototype novel of clutching psychological suspense and horror in the midst of ordinary, everyday life, FEAR, studied by writers from Stephen King to Ray Bradbury.

It was Mr. Hubbard's trendsetting work in the speculative fiction field from 1938 to 1950, particularly, that not only helped to expand the scope and imaginative boundaries of science fiction and fantasy but indelibly established him as one of the founders of what continues to be regarded as the genre's Golden Age.

Widely honored—recipient of Italy's Tetradramma D'Oro Award and a special Gutenberg Award, among other significant literary honors—BATTLEFIELD EARTH has sold more than 6,000,000 copies in 23 languages and is the biggest single-volume science fiction novel in the history of the genre at 1050 pages. It was ranked number three out of the 100 best English language novels of the twentieth century in the Random House Modern Library

Reader's Poll. Additionally, this *New York Times* and international bestseller was voted the #1 science fiction novel of the twentieth century by the American Book Readers Association. BATTLEFIELD EARTH is now a major motion picture.

The *MISSION EARTH*® dekalogy has been equally acclaimed, winning the Cosmos 2000 Award from French readers and the coveted Nova-Science Fiction Award from Italy's National Committee for Science Fiction and Fantasy. The dekalogy has sold more than seven million copies in 6 languages, and each of its 10 volumes became *New York Times* and international bestsellers as they were released.

The first of L. Ron Hubbard's original screenplays AI! PEDRITO! WHEN INTELLIGENCE GOES WRONG, novelized by author Kevin J. Anderson, was released in 1998 and immediately appeared as a *New York Times* bestseller. This was followed in 1999 with the publication of A VERY STRANGE TRIP, an original L. Ron Hubbard story of time-traveling adventure, novelized by Dave Wolverton, that also became a *New York Times* bestseller directly following its release.

His literary output ultimately encompassed more than 250 published novels, novelettes, short stories and screenplays in every major genre.

For more information on L. Ron Hubbard and his many acclaimed works of fiction visit the L. Ron Hubbard literary Internet sites at: www.galaxy-press.com, www.authorservicesinc.com and www.battlefieldearth.com.

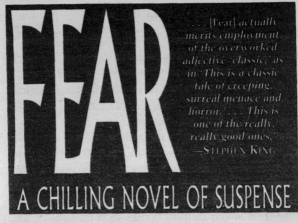

FEAR

> *...[Fear] actually merits employment of the overworked adjective 'classic' as in 'This is a classic tale of creeping, surreal menace and horror.'... This is one of the really, really good ones.'*
> —STEPHEN KING

A CHILLING NOVEL OF SUSPENSE

Professor James Lowry doesn't believe in spirits, or witches, or demons. Not until one gentle spring evening when his hat disappears, along with four hours of his life. Now the quiet university town of Atworthy is changing—just slightly at first, then faster and more frighteningly each time he tries to remember. Lowry is pursued by a dark, secret evil that is turning his whole world against him while it whispers a warning from the shadows:

If you find your hat you'll find your four hours. If you find your four hours then you will die. . . .

L. Ron Hubbard has carved out a masterful tale filled with biting twists and chilling turns that will make your heart beat faster as the tension mounts through each line of the story— while he takes a very ordinary man, in a very ordinary circumstance and descends him into a completely plausible and terrifyingly real hell.

Why is *Fear* so powerful? Because it really could happen.